Donated by
Kiwanis Club of Annapolis
Rachel Madden
June 5th 2013

J.Albert Adams
Academy Media Center

ALFRED KROPP

THE THIRTEENTH SKULL

Also by Rick Yancey

The Extraordinary Adventures of Alfred Kropp
Alfred Kropp: The Seal of Solomon

ALFRED KROPP

THE THIRTEENTH SKULL

BY RICK YANCEY

BLOOMSBURY

Published by Bloomsbury U.S.A. Children's Books
175 Fifth Avenue, New York, New York 10010
Distributed to the trade by Macmillan

Library of Congress Cataloging-in-Publication Data
Yancey, Richard.
Alfred Kropp : the thirteenth skull / Rick Yancey.—1st U.S. ed.
p.   cm.
Summary: Teen misfit Alfred Kropp, the last descendant of Sir Lancelot, is once
again in danger as he tries to uncover who is behind a top secret project called
SOFIA, while eluding a new enemy who seems determined to kill him.
ISBN-13: 978-1-59990-114-5 • ISBN-10: 1-59990-114-5
[1. Adventure and adventurers—Fiction. 2. Antiquities—Fiction. 3. Knights and
knighthood—Fiction. 4. Orphans—Fiction. 5. Conduct of life—Fiction.] I. Title.
PZ7.Y19197Alk 2008   [Fic]—dc22   2007050832

First U.S. Edition 2008
Typeset by Westchester Book Composition
Printed in the U.S.A. by Quebecor World Fairfield
1 3 5 7 9 10 8 6 4 2

All papers used by Bloomsbury U.S.A. are natural, recyclable products
made from wood grown in well-managed forests. The manufacturing processes
conform to the environmental regulations of the country of origin.

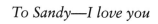

To Sandy—I love you

Countdown to
Final Extraction Interface

(in days, hours, minutes, seconds):

13:20:48:29

BEGIN TRANSMISSION.

Integrated Security
Interface System
[ISIS]

User Warning: Use of this interface is restricted to Company personnel with security clearances of A-17 or above.

Any unauthorized access of this system will result in immediate termination and forfeiture of all rights and privileges granted to personnel under Section 1.256 of the OIPEP Charter.

For security protocols related to use of ISIS, see Section 4 of the Charter.

User Login:
DIRSMITH

Password:
●●●●●●●

Welcome DIRSMITH!

Please Choose a Task:

Authorized Interfaces:

SES
Dossiers
SATCOM System
Current Operations
Archived Operations
Company Directory
Medcon Protocols
Locator Services
Special Weapons & Tactics Division

ISIS
Secure Special
Subject Dossier-System
[SSS D-SYS]

ENTER DOSSIER NUMBER OR CODE NAME:
05-5867564

[click HERE for Search Function]

DOSSIER # 05-5867564
SUBJECT: ALFRED KROPP
CODE NAME: little big lance
KNOWN ALIASES: NONE
COUNTRY OF ORIGIN: U.S.
CURRENT RESIDENCE: KNOXVILLE, TENNESSEE

Vitae: Subject is orphaned son of deceased special subject Bernard Samson, code named *Lionheart* (cf. Dossier #05-5847631). Reputedly the last remaining descendant of Lancelot Du Loc, subject materially involved as unrecruited third party in Sub.Sub.Sec.Op. Sword of Kings (cf. Main File 05-3128-01, Op SOK).

Subject is currently ward of special subject Samuel St. John, code named *Fallen Father* (cf. Dossier #80-4891207), and formerly the Company's operative under Section 9 of the Charter.

Subject Kropp is in possession of the Great Seal of Solomon (cf. Main File 06-5464-01) and has rejected all Company overtures for its return. Since the Company possesses the Lesser Seal, no operation (Sec., Sub-Sec. or Sub-Sub-Sec.) is currently being contemplated for its recovery BY ORDER OF THE DIRECTOR (cf. DIRORD #06-90876)...

Subject has NO SECURITY CLEARANCE

DEO WARNING: The following material in this Dossier is restricted to DIRECTOR'S EYES ONLY (DEO), with exception granted to the Company Operative Nine [see S. 2345 (d) and S. 9 (f) of the Charter].

ENTER DIRECTOR ACCESS CODE (DAC)
OR OVERRIDING SEC. NINE PASSWORD (ORSECNINE)

●●●●●●●

ITEM OF SPECIAL INTEREST

At some point during Op. Sword of Kings, Subject Kropp became endowed with special ability to heal, cure, and perhaps resurrect through application of his own hemoglobin.

Subject's blood showed promising results as an active agent in containment and control of intrusion agents during operation referenced in Main File 06-5464-01.

All efforts to replicate this active agent through synthetic or biotechnical means have failed.

KNOXVILLE, TENNESSEE

I parked the Koenigsegg CCR sports car, with its bicompression centrifugal supercharging system and twin parallel mounted Rotrex compressors in the garage beneath Samson Towers, in the space marked RESERVED. Beneath the word was the very dire warning that all violators would be towed at their own expense.

After taking the private elevator from the garage to the main floor, I walked through the huge atrium, past the waterfall gurgling and splashing in the center. The guards behind the metal scanner and X-ray machine waved me through with a smile, and the guy at the security desk gave me a respectful nod, and I thought of my uncle Farrell, who'd had the same job before my life got really weird.

I took the express elevator to the penthouse suite, twisting the Great Seal of Solomon on my finger, a nervous habit I couldn't seem to break. I was thinking about putting it on a chain to wear around my neck or maybe stashing it in the hidden compartment beneath my father's desk, where I'd found Excalibur about a thousand years ago.

Samuel came out of my father's old office wearing a worried expression. "Oh, there you are," he said. "I was getting concerned."

He followed me into the inner office and closed the door behind us.

I told him about the meeting with Abigail Smith in the old church.

"She's the new director of OIPEP," I said. "She didn't seem too thrilled about it."

"This is very grave news, Alfred," Samuel said. "As the director, Dr. Smith will be under great pressure to obtain the Seal from you. And the Company, as you know, can be ruthless."

"Sometimes good people have to do bad things," I said.

He nodded.

"Well, I'm still not sure I buy that argument, Samuel." I sank into the fat leather chair behind my father's desk.

Samuel sat across from me, clearly worried. "Perhaps I should not have left the Company."

"But if you stayed I wouldn't have a legal guardian. Well, I guess I would, but it might be Horace Tuttle, and I really don't like Horace Tuttle."

"I will do all within my power to guard you, Alfred." Samuel got very serious, which was a lot more serious than most people get. "I will never abandon or betray you, though hell itself contend against me."

"Don't say that." I laughed. "We've been down that road before."

He nodded, and a dark look passed over his features.

My face grew hot. I shouldn't have said that. It didn't come out right and now it was too late to take it back.

"Anyway, I told you to forget about it," I added quickly. "I know why you thought you couldn't come with me to face Paimon. That wasn't you at the Devil's Door."

"Oh, that is the terrible thing, Alfred, the thing I must live with until I live no more: it *was* me, and I have wasted many hours trying to convince myself otherwise. Too often we blame the temptation itself for our succumbing to it."

I winced. "Please, don't talk about temptation."

I got up and went to the window, turning my back to him. I stared down at the street thirty-three stories below.

A delivery truck was parked in the loading zone in front of Samson Towers. A guy dressed in a brown uniform was unloading boxes from the back onto a dolly. The day was sunny but very cold, and the man's breath exploded in curling white plumes over his head while he worked.

Nearly two months had passed since my final showdown with the demon king named Paimon, but the memory of what it offered me was still glittering and sharp.

A little house on a shady street. A kind older man and his pretty wife. And me. I went to school and hung with my friends. And that's about all I did. No adventures. No saving the world from total annihilation. Just a normal life.

Nearly every morning since that day I woke with a little stab of regret for turning down the demon king's offer.

A black SUV pulled up behind the delivery truck as the guy in the brown jacket and slacks wheeled the dolly toward the front doors, disappearing from view. A man in a dark suit emerged from the SUV, talking on a cell phone. One of the guards came out, pointed at the SUV and made a little waving motion with his hand, while the guy on the cell phone tried to juggle his phone conversation with the one happening with the guard.

Behind me, Samuel said, "Whatever the future holds, I will never forget this second chance you've given me, Alfred."

Before I could say anything, a car sped around the corner, screeched onto Gay Street on two wheels, and then accelerated until it rammed into the rear of the SUV. The sound of the impact carried through the frigid air up to the penthouse. The man in the dark business suit fell forward, colliding with the guard as he stumbled backward.

Samuel's faint reflection appeared behind me at the window. "What happened?" he asked.

The car's hood had crumpled completely against the SUV's bumper, shattering the windshield and deploying the air bag. I couldn't see the driver.

"That guy just rammed into—"

A fireball leaped into the sky, and instinctively we jerked back from the window. The guy in the black suit and the guard faded out of sight toward the front of the building.

A second later they were back, joined by two other guards from the Towers and a few other people who tried to approach the burning car, but I didn't think there was any way somebody could have survived that.

A voice spoke behind us. "Hey, what's up?"

We both whirled around. Samuel reached inside his jacket for his gun.

It was the delivery man. He was holding a large tube wrapped in brown paper. It looked like the kind of packaging posters come in.

"I got a package for a mister"—the delivery guy consulted his clipboard—"Alfred Kropp."

"I'll take it," Samuel said. He took a step toward the delivery man.

"All right," the man said pleasantly. The package turned

end over end as it fell to the floor, like it was falling in slow motion, the clipboard falling with it.

The man in brown was holding a sawed-off shotgun. He pointed it at Samuel's chest and pulled the trigger.

I screamed, but my scream was buried under the roar of the blast.

Samuel fell forward, both hands clutching his chest.

The singing of sirens was floating up from the street below, but my mind barely registered them. I rushed the shooter.

The barrel of the gun swung toward my face. My foot caught on Samuel's writhing body and I fell forward. Instinctively my left hand shot out and I shoved the barrel upward just as the guy pulled the trigger, sending the blast into the ceiling. I swung blindly with my right fist, landing a lucky punch square into the guy's Adam's apple. He countered with an elbow to my cheek.

I rolled to my right as he scrambled toward the doorway. I grabbed him by the collar and yanked him back. He kicked me in the groin with the end of his steel-toed boot. I curled up on my side, both legs jerking from the explosive pain of the blow and watched helplessly as he lunged through the open doorway into the reception area outside.

I crawled toward Samuel.

"Alfred," he gasped. "Don't let him escape . . ."

"No," I said. "I've got to get you an ambulance—"

He shook his head. "No! Must . . . find out . . . who sent him . . ."

He pulled out his 9mm semiautomatic and slid it across the floor. I picked it up.

Our eyes met.

"Go."

I went.

The door to the stairs was clicking shut when I came into the hallway. I kicked it open. I had taken two steps toward the railing when something hard smashed into my lower back—I guess the heel of his boot—and that flung me toward the steps that led down to the next floor. The classic hide-behind-the-stairway-door trick. I should have seen it coming.

My gun skittered and flipped and bounced down the stairs until it reached the little landing and came to a rest.

Then Delivery Dude was on me.

I saw a flash of metal. The blade in his hand was at least a foot long, tapered, thin. It sliced along my forearm as he swung it toward my gut. I smacked his wrist with the back of my left hand while I brought my right fist down on the side of his head. He stumbled back a couple of steps.

First I had to neutralize the knife: one of my long-term goals was never to be stabbed to death again. So I grabbed his wrist and slammed his forearm down as hard as I could against the metal railing. The knife flew from his fingers and dropped down the shaft of the stairwell.

The next step was to neutralize *him*. Unfortunately, he had the same idea, only he executed it just a split second sooner. He threw his shoulder into my chest and drove me backward. My foot slipped off the top step and I dropped about a foot . . . a good thing, too, because he chose your classic head-butt-to-the-face move and my face wasn't there to butt.

As his head snapped forward, I wrapped my arm around his neck, sidestepped to the right, and flung him down the stairs to the first landing. It was a pretty good maneuver, since it gave me a few extra seconds to recover. It was also a pretty bad maneuver, because I had hurled him to the exact spot as Samuel's gun.

Fight or flight? If the other guy has a gun and you don't, nine times out of ten, I'd suggest flight.

This must have been the tenth, because I didn't fly.

I jumped.

He broke my fall, but it was too late. He already had scooped up the 9mm. When I landed on top of him, his chest slammed into the concrete, and the breath went out of him with a loud *whumph*! I lay on his back and wrapped both arms around his sides. He came back at me with a reverse head butt, this one landing true, against my nose. I heard a popping sound and blood began to pour.

It achieved the desired effect: my grip on him loosened and he tore free, bringing up the gun as he slid on his back down the stairs toward the next landing.

The muzzle flashed and my left shoulder jerked backward with the punch of the bullet.

I stumbled upward to the top landing, bleeding from my shoulder, my nose and cheek, my forearm; I was throwing off blood everywhere. The steps were slick with my blood. I slipped and tumbled to the same landing I had just vacated.

When I raised my head, he was standing over me, the end of the gun about two inches from my face. He was bleeding pretty badly too, but he seemed pleased with himself.

He sneered one word before he pulled the trigger. *"Pitiful!"*

"No," I said. *"Empty."*

I hoped I had counted right. I was pretty sure I had, but even simple things like counting can get complicated when someone is firing bullets at your head.

Snap. Then rapidly as he yanked the trigger over and over: *Snap, snap, snap . . . snap snap snap snap!*

I jumped up and landed a haymaker to the side of his head. Then another to the other side of his head. Then a gut punch, as hard as I could throw it. He doubled over and my fists kept flying wherever I could land them: head, shoulders, arms, chest. He dropped the gun. It hit the edge of the landing and spun into the open space of the stairwell, disappearing from view.

He fell into me and we grappled like two exhausted prize fighters in the tenth round. He slowly drove me backward until I felt the metal bar of the handrail pressing against my lower back. I didn't need to look to know I was a foot away from taking a thirty-story tumble down the center stairwell.

He freed his right hand, which he used to force my head back, his fingers slick with somebody's blood, mine or his, or maybe both. I grabbed his wrist, yanked his arm down, and pivoted to my left, spinning him around as I went. The momentum carried him over the handrail—and pulled me with him.

Then everything froze. He dangled there with me holding his wrist as I leaned over the railing, my face about a foot from his. There was no fear in his eyes. There was no emotion at all, not even disappointment.

My grip slipped: too much blood.

"I don't want to drop you," I gasped.

"You should," he gasped back.

He kicked hard with his legs and yanked free.

I watched him fall. About a couple stories down, the brown jacket tore away and the top of a parachute appeared, one of those small chutes you see stunt skydivers wear.

That was enough for me. I raced back up to the hallway and hit the button on the express elevator. There was no time to check on Samuel, not if I had any chance of catching this guy.

The elevator door slid open. "Sorry, Sam," I muttered, and stepped inside.

I dialed 911 on my cell phone.

"Nine one one, what is your emergency?"

"There's been a shooting at Samson Towers. Penthouse suite," I said. "You gotta send an ambulance down here right away."

"Someone's been shot?"

"You bet someone's been shot, otherwise why would I be calling you guys?" I shouted. I watched the floor numbers ticking down: *25, 24, 23* . . . They seemed to be moving in slow-motion.

I heard the dispatcher say something to someone else like, "Another one from Samson Towers! Yeah, that's what he says."

"Hello?" I shouted into the phone, watching the floors slide by: *15, 14, 13* . . . "You gotta send an ambulance! Samson Towers!"

"Sir, someone's already called for an ambulance at that location."

"That's probably for the dude in the explosion. This is someone else."

"Another explosion?"

"No, a shooting."

"A shooting! How many people?"

"One! Just one!" *5, 4, 3* . . . "Penthouse suite. He's in the inner office, farthest one back through the main doors."

The door slid open. I stopped a couple steps past the door to the stairs. He'd fooled me once with the hiding-behind-the-stairway-door trick. Maybe he thought I would think he wouldn't try it again, but if it were me I wouldn't race onto a street swarming with cops.

I kicked open the door and stepped inside. I found the discarded chute and harness, his jacket and, lying on the bottom step, the empty 9mm, but no Delivery Dude. I scooped up the gun and dropped it into my pocket. At some point, Samuel would want it back.

The lobby was swarming with people. I saw the red flash of emergency vehicle lights on the street outside and the red hulk of the fire engine beside the smoldering wreckage of the car.

I pushed my way through the crowd and spun through the revolving doors into the freezing air outside. The brown delivery truck was pulling away from the curb as a cop trotted beside it, shouting for the driver to stop. I stood there for a second, unsure what to do. Then the driver pulled into the center of the street and floored the gas.

The entire block had been roped off, but I didn't think Delivery Dude was going to let that plastic yellow tape concern him. His front bumper clipped the back of a cop car as he roared forward, sending the car spinning into the curb.

I didn't spend much time mulling over the options. My car was in the parking garage two stories below the pavement. I ran to the nearest police car and flung open the passenger door. A young cop sat behind the wheel, writing on a clipboard. I dropped into the seat beside him and shouted, "Follow that truck!"

He hesitated for a half second before answering, and then he said, "No way, kid."

I leaned over and pressed the muzzle of the empty 9mm against his temple.

"*Follow that truck.*"

"Okay!"

"I'll take that," I said, and pulled the gun from his holster.

"The guy in that truck tried to kill me and it's important

I know who—and why," I shouted as we lurched from the curb. "Hit the siren!"

He did, and soon we were clocking eighty up Gay Street. The truck had a four-block jump on us though and I couldn't see it anywhere.

"It's gone!" he yelled over the wail of the siren. He looked only a couple years older than me and scared out of his mind. Maybe this was his first high-speed chase.

"He turned somewhere," I yelled back. "Slow down a little. You check left and I'll check right."

He glanced in the rearview mirror. I twisted in the seat and looked behind us. Two cops were giving *us* chase as cars swung into the curb to get out of their way.

"Don't stop!" I yelled at the young cop. "If you stop I'll shoot you!"

Of course there was no way that would happen, but he didn't know that. For all he knew, I was out of my mind. I wondered what he thought when he looked up and saw me sitting beside him, my face and clothes covered in blood and bruises.

"There, there, there!" I yelled, pointing down a narrow side street. "Turn, turn!"

He yanked the wheel hard to the right. The back wheels locked and the car slung around. The two cars behind us slammed on their brakes and barely missed us as we accelerated through the turn. The truck made another hard right and I didn't have to tell the young cop this time; he matched the truck's arc, getting us so close the bumpers almost touched.

I rolled down my window.

"Keep us as close as you can!" I shouted over the sirens, the radio chatter and the icy wind blowing in my face. "I'm going for the tires!"

"That only works in the movies!" he shouted back.

I heaved myself through the open window, grabbed hold of the mounting bracket for the lights with my left hand, and opened fire. The truck had led us into a narrow cobblestone alley barely wider than the width of the truck. The brick walls of the buildings beside me passed in a red and black blur, about two inches from my cheek. I was concentrating on my shots, so I didn't see the big metal bins used for construction debris up ahead.

But Delivery Dude did.

The brake lights flashed. The significance of that was lost on me as I frantically yanked on the trigger, coming nowhere near to hitting a tire—maybe it does only work in the movies. An instant later the cop hit his brakes too and we went into a skid.

We hit the truck, the force hurling me from the car. I landed on a plastic mountain of garbage sacks stacked against the side of the building.

Delivery Dude threw the truck into reverse and pushed the cop car straight back as its wheels howled in protest. I scrambled to my feet and ran to the passenger door of the truck. I jumped onto the running board and grabbed the metal bar that held the side mirror. At that moment, the truck leaped forward.

Its nose swung hard to the left to get around the construction bin. I had to press my body against the door to avoid hitting the bins and, as I did, the window shattered. I could see the gun in his hand in the side mirror. Well, of course he would have a gun inside the cab—I know I would have. I ducked down as he kept firing out the busted window, and my feet kept slipping off the step while I hung on to the mirror for dear life.

We flew through an intersection at the end of the alley and

the truck went airborne about two feet. The force of our landing broke my grip and I swung crazily back and forth holding on with just my right hand, my cheek and shoulder ramming into the door as he slung the truck hard to the left in an attempt to dislodge me.

He floored the gas. My fingers had gone numb from the cold—I wouldn't be able to hold on much longer. If I let go now, I might be sucked under the carriage and the back wheels would finish me. If I tried to climb into the cab through the broken window, he'd blow my brains out. And if I tried to jump, I'd hit the pavement at sixty or seventy miles per hour.

The mirror above my hand shattered as he fired at the only part of my body visible to him.

That helped me decide. I grabbed the door handle with my left hand and let go with my right. My body swung around, and I dangled like this for a few seconds before I managed to gain a foothold again and get both hands around the door handle.

I saw them coming up fast behind us: three cop cars, lights flashing, sirens blaring. Looking ahead, I saw three more cop cars parked bumper to bumper, spanning both lanes, about four blocks away. They had him trapped.

Brakes, Delivery Dude, I thought. *Now would be a good time for the brakes . . .*

I thought they had him and the cops probably thought they had him.

They didn't have him.

He hit the gas and, as he picked up speed, barreling straight for the barricade, the cops opened fire.

Maybe they saw me hanging there by the door handle. I doubted it, though. They were more concerned with the two-thousand-pound truck coming straight at them.

Then he swerved, slamming on the brakes as he swung the nose of the truck hard to the left. The rear wheels locked and the truck went into a slide: I guessed the idea was to crush me against the cop cars.

Nowhere to go now but up.

I swung my right foot onto the window ledge, using it as a stepping stool to heave myself onto the roof. At that second, as I threw my body across the top of the truck, Delivery Dude hit the barricade of police cars.

The impact hurled me across the span of the roof and off the opposite side, right over the driver's window. I tumbled into empty space.

Lucky for me, one of the cop cars chasing us had rushed forward to box in the truck. I belly flopped onto the car's hood, my forward motion hurling me straight at the windshield.

I flipped off the hood at the instant the front bumper struck the side of the truck. I landed on my butt, sending a searing knifelike pain up my spine.

I looked up to see Delivery Dude looking right at me, wearing this strange, enigmatic smile. He was holding something in his hand as the cops swarmed the truck, guns drawn, all of them shouting for him to come out with his hands up.

Delivery Dude was holding a small black device in the middle of which, blinking red, was a button and, over which, his thumb hovered. And he was smiling at me.

He gave me a little nod as if to say, *Touché, Kropp.*

I screamed for them to get down, but nobody heard me. I took cover behind the cop car as his thumb came down.

The truck exploded in a blossom of boiling red fire. The shock wave knocked me backward and the heat from the blast sucked the last molecule of oxygen from my lungs.

13:19:21:48

They took me to the emergency room first. Multiple lacerations and contusions. A broken nose. Twenty-five stitches on my forearm where he sliced me with the dagger. Bullet removed from my shoulder. And an X-ray of my butt to see if my coccyx was cracked.

After the doctors were done with my body, a couple of cops came by and took it to the police station. I asked for my phone call. I called the attorney for my father's estate, Alphonso Needlemier. He told me not to talk to anybody until he got there.

I was alone in one of the interrogation rooms. There was a mirror along one wall. It had to be one of those two-way setups.

I wondered who Delivery Dude was, who had sent him, and why. I had my suspicions. At the hospital, I took the Ring of Solomon from my finger and slipped it into my pocket.

At least thirty minutes passed. Nothing happened. No one

came in. The big clock hanging on the wall behind me clicked. My nose itched under the bandages. My butt was sore and I couldn't find a comfortable sitting position. I had a very bad feeling about it—not about my butt, but the situation in general. Where were the cops? Why had they dumped me in this room? Where was Mr. Needlemier? Who was Delivery Dude, why was he after me, was Sam okay, and why had they arrested me? I was the victim here.

Finally the door opened and two people came in, a man and a woman. He was older, with a huge bald head and a fat red nose; he might look like Santa Claus if he grew a beard. She was young-looking, with dark hair and even darker eyes.

She introduced herself as Detective Meredith Black. His name came out as a grunt, but it sounded like Kennard.

"Why did you arrest me?" I asked.

"How about reckless endangerment, kidnapping, willful destruction of property, assault and battery, and attempted murder?" rumbled the big-bellied Kennard in a voice about as far from Santa Claus's as you could get.

"That's a lot," I said.

"You a smart guy?" he barked at me.

"Not by any standard I can think of," I said.

"Let's see how smart you are after twenty years at Brushy Mountain," Kennard said.

"Here's what we know, Alfred," Meredith Black said, placing a hand on Kennard's hairy forearm. "A car collides with an SUV in front of Samson Towers and blows up. A minute later, a John Doe is shot at point-blank range in the penthouse suite of the building. Ten minutes after that, a high-speed chase that results in the deaths of five Knoxville police officers and an unidentified suspect who appears to have committed suicide by means of an improvised explosive device."

"How is Sam?" I asked. "The John Doe. They wouldn't tell me at the hospital."

She ignored me. "And now we have you. And you seem to be the common denominator in all of this, Alfred."

She pulled a small tape recorder from her purse and set it on the table between us.

"We'd like to hear what you have to say."

"I'm supposed to wait for Mr. Needlemier."

"Who's Needlemier?" Kennard asked.

"My attorney. Well, actually he's my dad's attorney. Or he used to be."

"Your dad fired him?"

"My dad died."

"Bernard Samson," Meredith Black said. It wasn't a question.

"That's right. That's why I was in that office when the car blew up. I guess that was all a setup so the phony delivery dude could get upstairs without running his package through security."

"What package?" Meredith Black asked.

"The package containing the shotgun. I guess you found the shotgun. He said he had a package and Samuel said 'I'll take it,' and he said something like, 'Okay,' and then he shot him."

"Who is Samuel?" Meredith asked.

"The John Doe. He's alive, isn't he?"

"So Samuel shot the delivery dude?" Kennard asked.

"No, the delivery dude shot Samuel."

"Why?"

"I don't know. Then he tried to shoot me."

"Samuel?"

"The delivery dude! Samuel's my guardian; why would he want to shoot me?"

"Why did the delivery dude want to shoot you?" Kennard asked.

"I don't know. He didn't say, but I didn't ask either. He ran. I ran after him. He did this to my arm and this to my nose and then he parachuted down the stairwell."

Kennard gave a belly laugh. Meredith shot him a look and said, "We found the chute." She turned back to me. "So you followed him outside, hijacked a police car, and forced the officer to give chase."

I nodded. "That's right."

"Why?"

"I wanted to know the same thing you guys do: why?"

"You don't know why someone would want to kill you?"

"No," I lied. I had been working on the list before they came in. There was Mike Arnold, the rogue OIPEP agent who had sworn to kill me. There was the remnant of the private army of Mogart, the black knight exiled from the Order of the Sacred Sword, who might want a little payback for my killing their leader. And, finally, OIPEP itself, which wanted the ring in my pocket. I wasn't sure OIPEP should be on the list, mostly because I liked and trusted Abigail Smith, the director, but like Samuel said, the Company could be ruthless.

"You never saw this delivery dude before?" Kennard asked.

I shook my head. "Never."

"Okay, Alfred," Meredith Black said softly. "So far you haven't told us anything we couldn't figure out for ourselves."

"You're a step ahead of me, then," I said.

Kennard came over the table toward me, biceps bulging in

his tight white dress shirt. His breath smelled bad, like stale coffee and cigarettes.

"Look, punk, five brothers of mine died today because of you—cops who had wives, families . . . and they ain't goin' home to see them tonight because some oversize kid wanted to act out a scene from *Grand Theft Auto*!"

Meredith grabbed his shoulder and eased him back into his chair. "Louis, come on. He's just a kid . . ."

"I didn't know he rigged the truck to explode," I cried. The remark about the dead policemen had hurt. "I swear I didn't! And I don't know who he was or who sent him to kill me or even why they sent him to kill me! I'm trying to stay out of crap like this."

I stopped myself. Kennard was sitting back in his chair trying to catch his breath. Meredith was staring at me. I glanced down at the tape recorder.

"You're trying to stay out?" she asked quietly.

"You bet. Yes." *Don't say any more. Wait for Mr. Needlemier.*

"Stay out of what?"

"Stuff."

"Stuff like—what?"

"Like what happened this morning. I've got enough blood—" I was going to say *on my hands*, but in a situation like this, you don't want to use phrases like *I've got enough blood on my hands.*

"I could relieve you of some, if you want," Kennard growled.

I took a very deep breath. "I really don't think I should say anything else until Mr. Needlemier gets here."

"We know who you are," Kennard said. "We ran you through Interpol. Didja think we wouldn't think to do that?

"No, because I don't even know what Interpol is."

"A year ago. Stonehenge and several thousand pounds of explosives. Ten Most Wanted list. Ring a bell?"

"That was all a mistake," I said. "A big misunderstanding."

"Uh-huh," he sneered.

"They took me off the list, didn't they?"

"Alfred," Detective Black said. "We want to help you, but we can't help you if you keep refusing to help us. You know more about what happened this morning than you're letting on. We already have you on the kidnapping and carjacking. The truth can only help you now. Tell us."

I chewed on my bottom lip. I really didn't know what the right thing to do was at that moment. How much should I tell them? Should I tell them anything at all? And even if I did tell them just a little of it, would they believe me?

"I think he was an assassin," I said slowly.

Kennard laughed. "You think?"

Meredith leaned forward. Her breath smelled as good as Kennard's did bad. Like cotton candy. "Who was an assassin?"

"Delivery Dude."

"Do you have any idea why someone would want to kill you?"

Should I tell them? And if I did tell them, what was going to happen to me? I couldn't prove anything and they probably wouldn't even believe me. But they were cops, even this nasty Kennard dude, and Meredith Black had a kind face and she gave off the attitude like she liked me and wanted to help me. And I had a feeling the only way to get out of this mess was to rely on the one thing you're supposed to rely on when things get really messed up: the truth.

So I said, "OIPEP."

"Oypep?"

"What's an OIPEP?" Kennard wondered aloud.

"The Office of Interdimensional Paradoxes and Extraordinary Phenomenon," I said. "OIPEP."

"Oh, sure," Kennard said. "I should have figured that." He turned to Meredith. "Give me five minutes alone with him. Five minutes, all I need."

"I had a meeting this morning with the director," I said. "And she asked for the—for something I have and I refused to give it back and I think she ordered . . ." I swallowed hard. I always liked Abigail Smith. I always thought she was one of the good guys. "I think the Company might have done all this to get it back."

"The Company?"

"OIPEP."

"Oy . . . pep?" Kennard asked.

"What do you have, Alfred?" she asked.

I looked away. I wanted to talk to Samuel. I *needed* to talk to Samuel. He was OIPEP's former Operative Nine, its top agent. He would be able to tell me if it had been a Company operation.

But I didn't have Samuel. And I didn't have Mr. Needlemier. I didn't have anybody.

"I'll tell you," I said to Meredith Black. "But he's got to leave first."

"I ain't goin' nowhere," he said.

"Then you better just take me to my cell," I said.

That produced a fierce whispering argument between them, an argument Detective Kennard lost, I guessed, because he pushed out of his chair so fast it fell over with a loud clang. He pointed a fat finger at my bandaged nose.

"This ain't done between us," he promised.

"You smell bad," I said.

He left. I looked at Meredith. I looked down at the tape recorder. The little spools were still turning. She pressed her finger on the off button. Her fingernails were painted a bright red, and I thought of Abigail Smith and her scarlet lipstick.

"All right, Alfred," she said softly.

13:17:35:51

We leaned across the table toward each other and we spoke barely above a whisper. I figured Detective Kennard had not gone far. I figured he was standing right behind the long mirror on the wall beside us.

"All right, Alfred," Meredith said.

"First I want to know if Sam's okay."

"Sam?"

"The John Doe shot in the penthouse suite. He's my guardian. Is he okay?"

"He's in intensive care at St. Mary's."

"Will he live?"

She slowly shook her head. She didn't know.

I stared at her for a few seconds. Then I said, "Do you know how my father died?"

"The newspaper said it was a plane crash."

"It was a beheading."

It spewed out of me then, an eruption of words that I

couldn't hold back even if I wanted to. I told her everything. Of Excalibur and the secret order of knights that protected it. Of Mogart, who was my father's heir until my father found out he had a son—me. Of Bennacio, my father's best friend and the last knight on earth, who died trying to win the Sword back from Mogart. Of the chase that ended in Merlin's Cave beneath the ruins of Camelot. Of my death and rebirth, and the death of Mogart.

"How did Mogart die?" she asked.

"He was beheaded," I answered.

"Him too?"

"By me."

"*You* beheaded him?"

"With Excalibur."

"King Arthur's sword."

"Actually, Michael's sword."

"Michael the secret agent of this OIPEP?"

"Michael the Archangel of heaven."

"Heaven."

"You know." I pointed toward the ceiling. "Heaven."

"Where is the Sword now?"

I pointed at the ceiling again.

"Right," she said slowly, making it two words: "Rye-ite."

"What's the matter?" I asked. "Don't you believe in heaven?"

"I just don't understand why this OIPEP might want to kill you if you don't have the Sword."

I almost said, "Because I have the Seal," but I wasn't sure I should tell her about the Great Seal of Solomon. She might frisk me and find it in my pocket. I bit my lip and looked away from her face.

"You know how this must sound," she said, not unkindly.

"I know," I admitted. "But it's the truth."

"The truth," she repeated.

I looked back into her eyes and said, "You say you want the truth, but you really don't because the truth is something that doesn't belong to your world. You know, the world of this table and these chairs and that clock on the wall. It doesn't fit, but that's where I am, in the place that doesn't fit and I don't think it's ever going to—fit I mean. If I could jump over this table back into your world right now, I'd do it. I'd do it in a heartbeat. But my world is holy swords and supersecret spy operations and angels who call me their 'beloved.' *That's* why somebody tried to kill me today. *That's* why those police officers are dead. I'm in big trouble and the guy who's supposed to protect me is in even bigger trouble and we need somebody to help us. Can you help us, Detective Black? Please, because we really need somebody to help us."

She didn't say anything at first. I couldn't put my finger on it, but there was something about her, not in her looks really, that reminded me of my mother.

"I'm going to do everything I can," she said.

13:15:18:09

An hour later, I was alone in a cramped holding cell when Mr. Needlemier finally showed up.

"Where have you been?" I asked.

He dropped his briefcase on the cot and mopped his bald head with a monogrammed handkerchief.

"I'm terribly sorry, Alfred. You didn't tell them anything, did you?"

"I told them everything."

He stared at me. He had just wiped his face, but it shone with moisture. "*Everything* everything?" he asked.

"Pretty much everything," I answered.

"Well, that explains it."

"Explains what?"

"They're taking you to St. Mary's Hospital."

"Why?"

"They suspect you may be psychotic."

"Crazy, you mean."

"Well, who could blame them?"

"St. Mary's. That's where they took Sam. Have you seen him?"

He nodded.

"How bad is it?" I asked.

"It's not good, Alfred. Not good."

"I want to see him."

"They're not going to let you see him."

"I'll need only about five minutes—"

"First they have to do the evaluation—"

"And then he'll be fine. Like it never happened—"

"And then you'll have a hearing before the judge."

He finally got my attention.

"What judge?"

"To make a determination."

"A determination about what?"

"Your . . . let's see, the best way to put this . . . your psychological . . . ah . . . readiness to stand trial."

"You mean if I'm too crazy to be found guilty."

He nodded. He seemed relieved that I got it. "Yes! Something along those lines."

"And what if the judge decides I'm crazy? I spend the rest of my life in an asylum?"

He didn't answer for a few minutes. "I told you not to say anything to them, Alfred."

"And if he decides I'm not crazy, there's a trial and I go to prison for twenty years."

"Only if the jury finds you guilty."

I thought about it. "So what's the strategy?"

"Strategy?"

"You do have a strategy for getting me out of this, right?"

"Well, the very first thing I'm going to do is find you a good attorney."

I stared at him. "I thought you were my attorney."

"Technically, I'm the attorney for your father's estate. And you wouldn't want me for an attorney, Alfred."

"Why? Do you suck?"

"Oh, no, I don't suck. I'm quite good at what I do, but unfortunately, I don't do criminal law."

He patted my knee.

"Don't pat my knee," I said.

He stopped patting my knee. "How are you feeling?" he asked.

"Like crap. My nose is broke. I've got fifty-nine million stitches in my arm and four thousand bruises all over my body and they think my butt might be cracked."

He frowned. "Aren't all butts?"

"I'm not kidding. I need you to call Abigail Smith for me. I used up my phone call on you."

"Who is Abigail Smith?"

"The director of OIPEP." I handed him her card.

"OIPEP," he murmured, staring at the card.

"You remember."

"Unfortunately, I do."

"Tell her I want a meeting. Today. Even if that means she meets me in the psycho ward."

"Do you think her agency had something to do with this?"

"Oh, you bet they're near the top of my list."

I pushed the ring into his pudgy hand.

"And I want you to keep this."

"This? Alfred, isn't this . . . ?"

"The Seal of Solomon. Put it somewhere safe and don't tell anyone where you've put it. Nobody, understand?"

"Even you?"

"Especially me."

He nodded. His fingers were shaking as he slipped the ring into his pocket.

"He tried to warn me," I said.

"Who?"

"Samuel. He said they could be ruthless."

"Apparently so."

"Unless it wasn't them. But if it wasn't them, who was it?"

"Alfred, if I may offer some advice. Perhaps, given what happened today, you should give Ms. Smith and her associates what they want."

"They had their chance," I said. "But I'll think about it."

"It might be the price you have to pay."

"The price for what?"

"For staying alive."

13:12:08:40

A cruiser took me to St. Mary's Hospital on Broadway, where I was escorted to the psych floor and put in a room with a door that locked from the outside. There wasn't even a handle on the inside part of the door.

There was no phone in the room, no TV, and everything was padded—the bed, the small dresser, even the corners of the windowsills. No sharp corners anywhere.

I sat in a chair and played with this little metal ring that hung from the side of the bed. Another ring was at the foot, and two more on the opposite side. I realized the rings were for the straps they used to tie you down.

A nurse's aide came in with a tray and hung by the door while I ate. I told her I'd rather eat alone—it kind of creeped me out, her standing there—but she said that was against the rules. She avoided making eye contact with me.

"When are they coming?" I asked.

"Who?"

"The experts who decide if I'm nuts or not."

"I don't know," she answered. "I just bring the food."

"Where's ICU?"

She didn't say anything for a second. "Second floor."

She knocked on the door. It was opened by a huge orderly with a smushed-in face, like a bulldog. They left me alone. I crawled into bed. I was very tired. She had brought me a pain pill with the food and, though I really thought I shouldn't, I took the pill.

I closed my eyes. I tried to sleep and couldn't. How was I getting out of a room with a door that had no handle, locked from the outside, and a huge orderly with a face like a bulldog posted in the hall?

I don't know how much time passed—they took my watch and there wasn't a clock in the room—when I heard the door lock snap open.

A man stepped into the room. He wasn't wearing a doctor's white lab coat. He was wearing a tailored suit. The suit was blue. The tie was red. The hair was long and dark and the eyes even darker. He was carrying a black cane with a gold handle, though he didn't walk with any limp that I could see.

I sat up and pulled the covers to my chin. You don't really appreciate the meaning of the world "vulnerable" until you're trapped in a room with a stranger and all you're wearing is a flimsy hospital gown.

He pulled the chair closer to the bed, a small, ironic smile playing on his full lips. They looked almost too fat for his thin face. He placed the cane's tip between his immaculately shined black shoes and rested both hands on the gold head.

Then he smiled. He had a great smile. The only person I knew who had a better one was Abigail Smith.

"Alfred Kropp, at last we meet."

He wasn't American. I'm no good with accents, but it sounded Spanish.

"Who are you?" I asked.

"I am your attending physician, Dr. R. U. Nutts. That is a joke, of course, but I note you are not laughing. You may call me Nueve."

"Noy-vey?"

"*Sí*. Nueve."

I said, "What do you want, Mr. Nueve?" I glanced toward the closed door. I might be able to get to it before he could stop me, bang on it, howl my lungs out, and hope the big orderly bulldog man opened it—but this Nueve got past him somehow, so there were no guarantees he would rush in to save me.

"Please, I shall call you Alfred and you shall call me Nueve. Just Nueve, *por favor*."

"Just Nueve," I echoed. He was resting his chin on his hands, sort of balancing his finely shaped head on the top of the black cane. "I got a D in Spanish last year, but I'm pretty sure *nueve* means *nine*."

He smiled, this time without showing his beautiful teeth.

"You're the Company's new Operative Nine, aren't you?" I asked. "The Superseding Protocol Agent, the one above all the rules."

"I am here on behalf of Director Smith," Nueve said. "She sends her apologies that she cannot personally answer your summons. She is en route to headquarters."

"She's out of the country?"

He nodded.

"But you're not. Why?"

He smiled.

"Maybe you're here to check on a special delivery," I said.

He laughed softly. "Do you really think the Company had anything to do with that?"

"Actually, I do."

"The work of rank amateurs. Complicated, risky, over-the-top theatrics. If you had been targeted by us, believe me, you would not now be enjoying these fine accommodations. You would be dead."

"I have the Seal," I said. "You're the only people who know I have it. You want it. Who else would come after me for it?"

"Why do you presume the Seal is their goal? Perhaps it is simpler than that—or more complex."

"All I know is twenty minutes after I told you people I was keeping the Seal some guy showed up and wasted my friend, stabbed me, and blew himself up."

He shrugged.

"So you're saying OIPEP had nothing to do with this?" I asked.

"I am here on the direction of Director Smith, who said you wanted to speak to us."

"And you, OIPEP's SPA, head honcho in the black ops department, just happened to be in town on the same day an assassin shows up to kill me."

"Call it serendipity."

"If you kill me, you'll never get your hands on it."

"I have no intention of killing you, Alfred. You are far too valuable to us alive. Perhaps as a gesture of goodwill, the Company could bring its resources to bear in finding those responsible for this most heinous and wicked attack."

"That would be really sweet of you guys. What about me?"

"You?"

"Extracting me. Isn't that what you call it? Extract me from this interface. Make these charges go away."

"That would prove a bit more complicated, I'm afraid."

"But you could."

He smiled, this time blessing me with an eyeful of his gorgeous orthodontics.

"And what in exchange for the benefits of such an extraction?"

He was talking about the Seal. I said, "It was never about killing me, was it?"

"I beg your pardon?"

"Mr. Delivery Dude. He wasn't supposed to kill me. The whole thing was a setup, to put me in a bind so I'd have to make a deal."

"Killing you seems more expeditious."

"But for all you knew I hid the Seal and told nobody where I hid it. If you killed me, you might never get it back. So you had to keep me alive but stick me in a trap only you could get me out of."

"You give me too much credit, Alfred. Even I would not anticipate your, shall we say, ruthless response to the attack this morning. Are you refusing to hand over the item?"

"If I hand it over now, there's no reason for you to let me live."

"As I've said, you're far more useful to us alive than dead."

"Why?"

He smiled. "The answer to that question, I would think, is obvious."

13:12:41:36

Before he left, Nueve asked if there was anything else he could do. I told him yes, there was, and he promised he would arrange it.

Then he studied my face for a long time without saying anything, until finally he said, "Does it not work on yourself?"

"What?" I asked, but I knew what.

"The healing power of your blood—you cannot use it to repair your own wounds?"

I shook my head. "No. It doesn't work on me."

"A gift, then—not a treasure," he whispered. "You carry a special burden, Alfred Kropp."

He paused at the door. "Allow me a few moments to make the arrangements, yes?"

He pressed a small object into my hand. It looked like a ballpoint pen.

"What's this?"

"Open it and see."

I pulled off the cap, exposing a tiny hole at the top of the cylinder.

"Press the button on the side."

I pressed and a hypodermic needle sprang from the hole.

"Only a single dose, but the poison metabolizes almost instantaneously, completely paralyzing the victim."

The needle glittered wickedly in the fluorescent lights. "For how long?" I asked.

"Depends on the subject. Up to five minutes. Press the button again."

I pressed, and the needle retracted.

"Why are you giving it to me?"

One of his eyebrows rose toward his dark, perfectly coiffed hair.

"You should refrain from asking questions to which you already know the answer, Alfred. It could create the impression that you are not as smart as you really are."

He tapped lightly on the door with the head of his walking stick. "Until our next meeting, Alfred Kropp."

"I'm really hoping there won't be one."

"The odds are against that."

Bulldog-Face Man opened the door. Nueve stepped quickly into the hall and the door swung closed behind him.

I sat on the bed and waited. I got tired waiting there, so I went to the window. The window faced south, and there was Broadway, a dark ribbon between the yellow streetlights. I looked down six stories to the parking lot. A long drop, but I had recently dropped a lot longer. The window didn't open, of course. I'd have to break the glass. And then the concrete below would break *me*. I guessed I could make a rope out of the bedsheets, but that would probably get me to only the fourth floor.

The door behind me opened and Bulldog-Face Man was standing there holding a bundle of clothes. He tossed them on the bed and stepped outside again without saying a word.

They were identical to his getup: white tube sox, white soft-soled shoes, white pants with a drawstring, a white short-sleeve shirt.

I dressed quickly and knocked softly on the door. He opened it, avoiding eye contact.

"Left down the hall, elevators on your right," he murmured. "Unit 214. You got ten minutes."

I started down the hall and he called softly, "*Other* left."

So I turned back and hurried the opposite way. Behind some of the locked doors came sounds: moans, screeches, strange whoops; and behind other doors just silence. Maybe those rooms were empty, but I doubted it, and somehow the silence was more disturbing than the muffled screams.

I took the elevator to the second floor. The hallway here was a lot more crowded than my floor, which had all the ambience of a haunted house. Nurses and orderlies were everywhere, and doctors with stethoscopes around their necks and white lab coats billowing around them as they hurried to the next life-threatening emergency. Nobody paid any attention to me. In a hospital, just like anywhere else, I guess, you see what you expect to see. I was just another orderly hurrying along like all the other, real orderlies.

I stepped into Samuel's room and eased the door shut behind me. There wasn't much light and I stood with my back against the door for a few seconds, waiting for my eyes to adjust. I heard the hiss of an oxygen feed and the soft, steady *beep-beep* of a heart monitor. To my right was a row of cabinets. To the left were the bed and the screens showing Samuel's heart rate, temperature, and blood pressure.

He looked very pale except for his eyelids, which were black as charcoal. If it weren't for the squiggly lines on the monitor and the beeps, I might have thought I was too late.

"Samuel?" I whispered. "Samuel, it's me, Alfred."

He was muttering something under his breath, the word a barely audible hiss. I leaned closer and thought I heard him say "Sofia." Sofia? Who was Sofia?

"It's okay," I said, patting his shoulder through the covers. "I'm getting you out of here."

"Sofia!"

"No," I said. "Alfred." Maybe Sofia was the name of his nurse.

I pulled open the drawers to the cabinet on the opposite wall until I found one containing an open box of scalpels, each one individually wrapped in paper. I tore off the paper, exposing the blade.

A gift then—not a treasure.

I went back to his side.

"I met your replacement," I told him. I laid the scalpel on the pillow beside his head and pulled back the covers. Practically his entire upper body was encased in white gauze.

"He's a little creepy, like you, only a different kind of creepy. More supersuave creepy than undertakerlike creepy."

I slowly peeled back the bandages. I didn't look at the wound. I looked at his homely, hound-dog face, the sunken cheeks, the prominent jaw, the deep lines across his forehead.

"He says OIPEP wasn't responsible. I don't know. It sure seems OIPEPish to me, but I wasn't an operative like you, so I don't know everything they're capable of."

I picked up the scalpel and held it for a long time, the diamond-edged blade hovering an inch above my left palm, already laced with scars. I had saved him once from the grip of demons in Chicago. And before that I had cut myself open to heal Agent Ashley in the Smokies. But having done it before didn't make it any easier now: it takes a special act of willpower to slice yourself open.

"The main thing is," I whispered, as much to me as to him. "The main thing is I'm in a real jam now and it's either the rest of my life in a funny farm or in a prison, and I don't like those choices. I've got to find a third way and you've got to help me find it."

I ran the blade along my palm and blood welled around the shiny metal.

"In the name of the Archangel Michael . . . the Prince of Light . . ."

I lowered my bleeding hand toward his stomach.

". . . in the name of Michael, who fell with me through fire . . ."

His hand shot upward and grabbed my wrist before I could touch him.

He spoke without opening his eyes.

"No . . ."

Then his eyes came open. The muscles of his neck bulged as he forced out the words.

"Not your will. Not . . . *your* . . . will!"

I tried to force my hand to his belly, but he was very strong. It was like some bizarre version of arm wrestling.

"What are you talking about?" I asked. "I can heal you."

"No," he gasped. "It is not . . . for you . . . to decide . . ."

He took a deep breath and I could hear something rattling in his chest.

"Well, it wasn't for that phony deliveryman to decide either," I snapped back. "Now stop being stupid and let me get this over with . . ."

His head came off the pillow and he spat out with such intensity I jerked backward, "Not your choice! Not my choice!"

I tried to pry his long fingers away from my wrist, but weak as he was he was still too strong for me. His head fell back onto the pillow and he closed his eyes, pulling hard for air.

"I will not let you, Alfred," he whispered.

"Maybe it isn't my decision, you ever think of that?" I asked. "Maybe all this happened so I could be here to save you. I didn't ask for this, you know that."

I yanked my hand away and held my clinched fist against my chest. The blood seeped between my fingers, staining the white shirt red.

"What's it for, anyway, if I can't use it?" I demanded, but he didn't answer. I wondered if he had passed out. "Huh? Why did this happen to me if I'm not supposed to save people with it?"

Someone stepped into the room. Maybe they heard me in the hallway; I was talking pretty loud. It was an orderly, who grabbed me by the shoulders and turned me away from Sam's bed.

"You're not supposed to be in here."

"You don't get it," I said, ripping away from his grasp and stumbling back toward Samuel's bed. "I can save him. I can save everyone."

The orderly grabbed me again and pulled me toward the open door and into the hallway. Droplets of my blood fell to the floor, like I was marking a trail back to Sam. I kept shouting at the orderly to let me go, that I could save him; I could save them all. I had saved them before, saved the whole world—twice—and I could empty out this hospital, every hospital and hospice and cancer ward, and no one would ever need to be sick or hurt again.

"What else is it for?" I hollered as he gave up trying to reason with me and forced me facefirst toward the floor. "What is it for?"

A hand pushed my head straight down, and I turned my broken nose to one side and pressed my right cheek against the cold white tile. My throbbing left hand was inches from my nose and I could see my blood, shining in the light.

12:08:38:02

It took four guys to drag me back to my room. They tied me down to the bed with canvas straps while I screamed and cursed and generally flipped out exactly like you would expect a psycho to do. Then they gave me an armful of sedatives to knock me out.

The next morning a psychiatrist came and interviewed me. Or tried to. I refused to answer any of her questions unless they untied me. She gave up after an hour. An aide came in with a tray and I thought they would untie me so I could eat. Instead, she tried to feed me like I was a baby. I refused. She left. I yelled for her to come back and untie me. "You forgot to untie me!" I yelled. She didn't come back.

The hours spun out. I don't know what time it was when Mr. Needlemier came in, but the sun had set and the room was dark. He turned on a light and sat by the bed and looked at me with a sad expression, or as sad an expression as his round little baby face could make.

"Here's what I don't understand," I said. "Some guy blows away Samuel, cuts me up, breaks my nose, wrecks half the downtown, and incinerates five cops, and *I'm* the one roped to a bed."

He didn't say anything. He sat in the chair with his briefcase in his lap, holding the handle with both pudgy hands like a kid sitting on the bus with his lunch box on the way to school.

"All I did was tell the truth," I said.

"What is the truth?" Mr. Needlemier asked.

"The thing that's supposed to set you free."

He cleared his throat and looked away.

"How is Samuel?" I asked.

"Better. They moved him out of ICU. The doctors are optimistic."

He wouldn't look at me. He was staring at the floor.

"Untie me," I said.

"I—I can't do that, Alfred."

"I'm not crazy," I said. "They tied me down so I wouldn't hurt anybody—or myself, I guess. But what's really crazy is I wasn't trying to hurt anybody. I was trying to save them."

"I don't think they interpreted it that way."

"What have the police found out about the delivery man?"

He shook his head. "I don't know."

"You know who might be behind this? Mike Arnold."

"That awful secret agent?"

"He's not a secret agent anymore. He disappeared after Abigail Smith arrested his buddy the director."

"And you think he might be seeking revenge."

"The last time he saw me he said, 'One of these days I'm gonna kill you, swear to God,' or something like that."

"I spoke with that detective, Ms. Black, and she's agreed to post an officer outside your door."

"Because whoever did this will try again."

He didn't say anything.

"Is that why you came, to tell me that?" I asked.

"No, Alfred," he said. He sighed. "No."

He opened his briefcase and took out a charred photograph, its edges black and crumbly.

"I found this after the . . . well, this morning."

He held it toward me.

"I can't move my arm, Mr. Needlemier," I said.

"Oh! Of course, sorry."

He got up and held the picture in front of my face so I could see it. Something had distorted the image, turning it a sickly, mustard yellow, but I could make out the face of my mother. She was young in the picture. She was smiling. That's how I recognized her. Her teeth. Some big brown blob floated just under her chin.

"What's she holding?" I asked.

"I think it's a child."

"It's me," I said. "She must have sent it to Mr. Samson."

He didn't take the photo away. He stood by the bed and held it in front of my nose until I told him to get it the hell away from me. He set it on the stand beside the bed.

"Why is it all burned up like that?"

He blinked several times and his mouth came open a little. "Oh. I'm sorry, Alfred, I assumed they had already told you."

"Told me what?"

"Alfred, last night Bernard's house burned to the ground. A total loss." He pulled out his monogrammed handkerchief and blew his nose. "They haven't made a determination yet, but they suspect that it was arson. And that isn't all. Your father's grave . . . it's been desecrated."

"What do you mean, desecrated?"

"They mutilated his corpse . . . left his body by the grave site . . . but took his head, Alfred. They took his head!"

He began to cry. Watching a grown man cry is never easy, but Mr. Needlemier's baby face made it seem more natural somehow.

"You know," I said. "I'm just guessing, but I think somebody's trying to send me a message."

11:05:29:08

Meredith Black stepped into the room, closed the door, and without saying a word unsnapped the buckles holding my wrists and ankles. I sat up as she sat down.

"I don't have anything to say to you," I told her.

"That's fine," she said. "I have something to say to you. Last fall two of my colleagues responded to a homicide in the Halls area just off Broadway. A security guard had been stabbed to death in his living room. There was an eyewitness: the victim's fifteen-year-old nephew, who told them a very odd story about a man named Arthur Myers and a company called Tintagel International and a very valuable sword, which also turned out to be the murder weapon. The victim's name was Farrell Kropp, and he worked for Samson Industries. For Bernard Samson."

She paused for a breath. I was rubbing my aching wrists and avoiding her eyes.

"It was an odd case. The manner of death, for example.

Not too many people in Knoxville—or anywhere else, for that manner—meet their Maker by means of an antique broadsword. The witness's story was odd, too. Secret chambers, saber-wielding monks, a sword that seemed to have a mind of its own. The two homicide detectives who responded to the call that night remember the case very well. They distinctly remember filing the report. Only now there is no report. There's no record anywhere of a murder happening that night. Bernard Samson showed up at that apartment and after that the report vanished. And do you know what happened next? Both those detectives abruptly quit their jobs—one was about six months short of full retirement—and moved to the Caribbean. To an island that is owned by . . . wanna guess? Samson Industries."

"I don't know anything about that," I said.

She acted like she didn't hear me. "Four months after the murder, the witness—you—vanished into thin air. As did the former head of security for Samson Industries, a man by the name of Benjamin Bedivere."

"I'm really tired," I said. "It's hard to sleep when you're tied down, so maybe we could pick this up after I've had a nice little nap."

"A few days later, a supervisor with the border patrol files a report that two fugitives in a stolen Jaguar try to run the Canadian border."

"That Jag wasn't stolen," I said. "Bennacio gave the guy a check for it."

"The supervisor's report, like the homicide report, later disappears as if it never existed. Three weeks pass, and the FBI issues an alert, adding this same kid to its Ten Most Wanted list for involvement in a plot to blow up Stonehenge. In another month, he will be removed from that list, with no explanation offered by the FBI."

"Because I didn't try to blow up anything."

"Now, the company called Tintagel International has not vanished, but there is no one—nor has there ever been anyone—named Arthur Myers affiliated with it. The actual CEO of that company is a man named Jourdain Garmot, and he's quite alive and well. The name itself struck me as a little odd, so I looked it up. Tintagel is the supposed location of Camelot, King Arthur's castle."

"Okay," I said. "What's the point? What do you want from me?"

She leaned forward. "You remember the SUV in front of the Towers that morning? The driver fled immediately afterward, but one of the guards got the tag number. It was a rental, charged to a corporate account."

"Let me guess. Tintagel International."

"Actually, a company whose major stockholder is a subsidiary to a franchisee of Tintagel International."

"What's that mean exactly?"

"It means someone is trying very hard to hide their tracks, Alfred."

"Does it also mean you believe me now and I can go?"

"It means there's one homicide detective who is very confused and the more she looks into this bizarre case, the more confused she gets. This Mogart you told me about, he's Arthur Myers, isn't he?"

"Yes."

"And this man you were traveling with to Canada, he was . . ."

"Bennacio, the Last Knight of the Sacred Order. I guess his alias was Benjamin Bedivere."

"And he died . . . ?"

"At Stonehenge. I got the Sword and that's when OIPEP

set up the whole deal with the FBI to try to catch me and get the Sword from me. I guess they also bought off your detective friends, or maybe Mr. Samson . . . my dad . . . did."

"Well," she said. "Here's the thing, Alfred. I'm not saying that I believe everything you've told me. All I'm saying is there's some very weird coincidences and connections going on, and it's driving me crazy. Why would someone connected to Tintagel International stage an elaborate assassination attempt on a fifteen-year-old kid?"

"Because Tintagel International is just a front."

"A front? A front for what?"

"For the AODs."

"What's an AOD?"

"Agent of darkness. That was just my name for them. It wasn't like their official title or anything. Basically, they were the private army Mogart raised after Mr. Samson kicked him out of the Sacred Order."

"Mogart was a knight?"

"Sort of a black knight. He left the Order and then decided to steal the Sword."

"Why did he leave?"

"Because Mr. Samson found out Mogart had a son."

"Ah," she said. "Ah."

"So Mogart raised this private army, some of them I guess still being around wanting a little payback for what I did."

"What would be the point now, though? You said the Sword was back in heaven."

"Well," I said, trying to think it through. "I guess because they're bad guys."

She laughed for some reason. "Well, that's what I hope to find out."

She stood up.

"It makes sense," I said. "They almost had it in their hands, the most powerful weapon on earth, and they didn't get it, all because of me. So they tried to kill me and then torched my father's house."

"If that's true," she said, "you'll never be safe, Alfred." Then she shocked me by kissing my cheek. "But it can't be true, can it?" she asked.

She left. I lay there for a minute, trying to wrestle to the ground at least one coherent thought. So it wasn't OIPEP and it wasn't Mike Arnold, the two likeliest suspects. It was Mogart's former henchmen. But other than revenge, what was the big deal about killing me? It wouldn't bring their boss back and it sure wouldn't bring the Sword back. Then I told myself maybe it was a good thing, my inability to understand evil minds.

Meredith had forgotten—or did she forget?—to strap me back to the bed. I swung my feet to the floor and pushed myself forward, and I nearly crashed into the chair; I guessed I was still pretty dopey. I found my balance and walked toward the window, trying to think it through.

It was like a vendetta or one of those Greek tragedies I'd studied in school. The first killing launches the next and it isn't over until *everybody* is dead. Mogart killed Uncle Farrell, my father, and Lord Bennacio. I killed Mogart and not a small number of his henchmen. Now it was my turn.

I stood at the window and stared at the parking lot six stories below. No, I thought, it went back a lot farther than my uncle dying in our apartment. That was just the most recent chapter in a story that went back a thousand years, to Arthur and his knights and the Sword of Righteousness. Arthur was killed by his own nephew or son (in some stories, Bennacio told me, Mordred was *both* his nephew and son) and that led to the Sword being passed down until it ended up beneath my father's desk, where I found it.

Meredith Black was right about one thing, I thought. They weren't going to stop. I'd gone toe-to-toe with these guys, and Bennacio had warned me how soulless and mean they were. They weren't going to stop until I was dead, and it didn't matter how long I holed up in a hospital. Sooner or later, I was dead.

And maybe that's where it would stop, I thought. Maybe that's where it *should*. You would think Michael taking the Sword back to heaven would put an end to it, but maybe it wasn't about the Sword but about the people whose lives it touched. And since the Sword was gone finally and couldn't touch any more lives, maybe mine was the last.

It seemed the longer I hung around, the more people died—those cops were just the latest victims in my wake. As long as Alfred Kropp walked the earth, people were going to find themselves six feet under it.

Maybe that's it, I thought. Not prison or the asylum—maybe the third way was what Mike Arnold called an "extreme extraction."

The problem was I didn't want to die. You don't normally consider something like that a problem—Delivery Dude sure didn't consider it one—but my choices had gotten very narrow very quickly and none of them were very pleasant. In fact, they were unacceptable. So that meant there had to be a fourth way and, if there wasn't a fourth way, I'd have to make one up.

So I did. It took a while, but I did.

08:16:26:46

The sixth floor of St. Mary's Hospital had a common room where the nonviolent patients could gather for a game of checkers or cards, with donated furniture and dusty potted plants in the corners, overstuffed sofas and lounge chairs and rockers. The windows faced north, offering a dramatic view of Sharp's Ridge about ten miles away.

Nueve was waiting for me by the windows, sitting in one of the rockers that had been painted the classic orange of the University of Tennessee. The color contrasted nicely with his dark suit. I pulled a rocking chair close to his and sat down.

"Senor Kropp," he murmured. "You look much better than the last time I saw you."

Like most winter days in East Tennessee, the light was weak and watery, eking through the dense cloud cover that got trapped between the Cumberland Plateau and the Smokey Mountains, but Nueve was wearing dark glasses. He might as well have worn a sign around his neck that said SECRET AGENT.

"The Seal," I said, getting right to business. "I have it. You want it."

"Ah. And your price?"

I took a deep breath. "Twenty-five million dollars."

He didn't say anything at first, but I could almost feel those dark eyes of his, staring at me behind the dark glasses.

"I must say, that is unexpected."

"It's not for me. It's for Samuel. I want him taken care of."

"I see. Well, twenty-five million would do that—and quite nicely!"

"See, here's the thing, Nueve. There's no other way out of this mess. It's me they want. Take me out of the equation and everything's equal again."

"Equal?"

"Back to normal. Back the way it was. So the first thing to take care of is Samuel. He left the Company for me and I don't think you'd consider hiring him back, so I want to make sure he's taken care of, plus a little extra for his trouble."

"It's a generous severance, Alfred. But I cannot see how that balances this particular scale."

"That's the second part," I said.

"I thought there might be one."

"I want you to extract somebody from the civilian interface."

"And that somebody would be . . . ?"

"Me."

05:06:01:41

After breakfast, two doctors came in, escorted by the police-man Detective Black had stationed outside my door. At least, the cop *thought* they were doctors. One carried a stainless-steel valise. The other walked with a cane.

"More tests, huh?" I asked.

"More tests," the one with the cane said.

The cop left. Nueve leaned his cane against the bed rail and sat in the chair while his buddy got to work. He gently peeled off the bandage over my nose and leaned over me, examining the damage. His breath smelled like cinnamon.

"How bad is it?"

He sniffed. "Seen worse. We'll make it work."

He dug into the valise. I glanced at Nueve, who was smiling without showing his teeth.

"We're stopping by Samuel's room before we leave," I told him.

"Unnecessary. It increases the risk."

"I don't care. I want to say goodbye. I owe him that."

He shrugged. Cinnamon-Breath was leaning over me again, applying latex prosthetics piece by piece, using a small brush and a foul-smelling adhesive.

"What did you find out about Jourdain Garmot?" I asked Nueve.

"Age: twenty-two. Citizenry: French. Marital status: single. Occupation: president and chief executive officer of Tintagel International, a consulting firm based in England that specializes in the research and development of security-related systems and software."

"What's that mean?"

"It means its business is war."

"War?"

"Fighting them, winning them."

"And it's big."

"There is no bigger business than war, Alfred."

"Hold still," Cinnamon-Breath scolded me. "Look up at the ceiling and don't move. I have to do your eyes."

"The lavender goes better with the outfit," Nueve said to him.

Cinnamon-Breath rolled his eyes. "Do I tell you how to kill people?"

Nueve shrugged. I said to Cinnamon-Breath, "He shrugs a lot."

"He's European," he said. "They're world-weary. Close your eyes."

"Tintagel's board of directors voted him to the presidency after the untimely demise of our friend Monsieur Mogart," Nueve said. "Prior to that he was a university student in Prague."

"Why would a superrich, multinational corporation

put a twenty-two-year-old college student in charge?" I asked.

"Watch him," the makeup man said. "He's going to shrug."

Nueve was holding himself very still in his chair.

"He fought it back," Cinnamon-Breath said. He reached into the valise again and removed a gray wig.

"I don't know why I have to be so old," I said.

"Who do you see the most in hospitals? Huh? What's the demographic?"

He shoved the wig over my head and began tucking my own hair up into it. He gave a soft whistle and said, "Hey, love your hairstyle and I'm really digging the gray—very post-mod radical chic—but we really should shave it off."

"You're not cutting my hair," I told him.

"Maybe I should just wrap some gauze around it. Like you have a head injury. We're gonna be too lumpy this way."

"Where is Jourdain Garmot now?" I asked Nueve.

"Pennsylvania."

"Pennsylvania?"

"He flew into Harrisburg two nights ago, where he rented a car and drove to a tiny hamlet called Suedberg."

Something clicked when he said the name, but I couldn't pin down why Suedberg sounded familiar to me.

"What's a Frenchman who runs a company in England doing in a tiny hamlet in Pennsylvania?" I wondered aloud.

"Here it comes," Cinnamon-Breath said. Then Nueve shrugged. "Maybe it's more a tic than a gesture."

"More of a mannerism," Nueve said.

"You mean affectation."

Nueve shrugged.

Cinnamon-Breath gave the wig one last violent tug, then

fluffed the tight gray curls with his fingertips. He tsk-tsked at the effect.

"Think I should have gone with a darker shade. All this hair underneath is making it bulge. And the color—you look like a human Q-tip. Oh well. All done but the lips."

"Don't do the lips," I said.

"I gotta do the lips. I don't do the lips, people are going to notice the hair. And we don't want them noticing the hair."

"Why would an old lady be wearing lipstick in a hospital?" I asked.

"She's *leaving* the hospital, Kropp. A *Southern* hospital. Jeez! Now make like you're going to kiss me."

"Make like I'm going to what?"

"Kiss me! Give me a smooch."

"Perhaps you should purse your lips, Alfred, as if you're going to whistle a happy tune," Nueve suggested.

I pursed my lips and avoided Cinnamon-Breath's eyes as he applied the lipstick.

"Now *that* completes the picture!" he said.

"Too red," Nueve said.

Cinnamon-Breath ignored him. He held a hand mirror in front of my face.

"Soooo? What do you think?"

"I think I look like my grandmother."

"Grandmother! Perfect! Now out of bed, quick; let's get you dressed."

He pulled a flowery purple dress from the valise and laid it on the foot of the bed.

"Can't we just throw a blanket over me?" I asked.

"We could," Nueve said. "But the transition to the car could prove difficult."

I sighed. The makeup guy turned his back, Nueve closed his eyes, leaning his head against the wall, and I slipped the dress over my wig-covered head. I asked Cinnamon-Breath to zip me up and he laughed for some reason.

"You're beautiful," he said. "Grandma Kropp. Oh wait. I nearly forgot."

He pulled a pair of white orthopedic sneakers from the bag.

"Oh, no," Nueve said. "All wrong. It should be heels."

"She has bunions—that's the idea," Cinnamon-Breath said. "And if for any reason he has to run, you wanna see him try it in pumps? Oh, did I say one more thing? I have one more one-more-thing."

He pulled a shawl from the valise and wrapped it around my shoulders. Then he stepped back and admired his handiwork.

"See why the lavender was all wrong?" he asked Nueve. "The rose goes much better with the shawl. How's he look?"

"Like an octogenarian on steroids," said Nueve.

"How do we get past the cop?" I asked.

"Uh-oh," Cinnamon-Breath said, winking at Nueve. "I guess we should have thought of that!"

He picked up his valise and knocked twice on the door. It swung open and he stepped out of the room. After the door closed, Nueve turned to me.

"Do you still have the little gift I gave you?"

I retrieved the poisoned pen from under the pillow and slipped it into the side of my orthopedic shoe.

"Why do I need it?" I asked, following him to the door.

He smiled without showing his teeth. "No, the question is why do you persist with stupid questions?"

"A teacher told me once there's no such thing as a stupid question."

"Your teacher is an idiot."

He knocked on the door.

There was no policeman sitting outside. Bought off? Dragged into the stairwell and hit on the head by Cinnamon-Breath? I didn't know and I didn't dwell on it. I told myself all this clandestine crap would soon be a part of my past.

A wheelchair sat against the wall. I plopped down; Nueve tucked his cane under his arm and wheeled me to the elevator.

"Samuel's room," I said as Nueve reached to press the button for the first floor.

"You insist?"

"I do."

They had moved him to a private room. Nueve left me sitting in the hall and went inside. I could hear the rise and fall of their voices as they argued. Occasionally a word or two made it through the thick door. A couple of times I thought I heard the name "Sofia," but it also could have been "sofa," only it was hard to imagine why they would be arguing about a piece of furniture. Samuel had said the "Sofia" in ICU, and I wondered again if she was his nurse. But why would they be arguing about a nurse? Maybe Sofia was someone from Samuel's past that Nueve was trying to use against him: *Watch yourself or we're going after Sofia.* I tried to imagine Samuel having a girlfriend, and failed.

Then Nueve came out and wheeled me inside the room. Samuel was sitting next to the window, a book open in his lap.

He took in the getup. "You look ridiculous."

"It's a disguise, Samuel."

"The shoes are all wrong," he said to Nueve. "You should have gone with pumps."

"I tried," Nueve said. "I was overruled."

He took a long white envelope from the outer pocket of his doctor's coat and laid it on top of Samuel's book.

"What's this?" Samuel asked.

"Your severance pay, courtesy of Senor Kropp."

Samuel peered at the piece of paper.

"I thought you might prefer it in a Swiss account," Nueve said.

"Twenty-five million . . ." Samuel said softly. He looked up at me.

"Well," I said. "I don't really know how old you are, but I wanted you to have at least a million dollars for every year until you, um, died."

"Alfred Kropp," Nueve said. "Boy adventurer, actuary."

Samuel shoved the paper toward me. "I don't want it."

"Of course!" Nueve murmured.

"I will not take it, Alfred."

"Why not?"

He tore the certificate in half, then in quarters, and let the pieces flutter to the floor around his bare feet.

"You are letting your fear get the best of you," Samuel told me.

"Well," Nueve said. "You have made your noble gesture, Senor Kropp, and the driver is waiting."

"Hiding solves nothing, Alfred," Samuel said. "You have not thought this through." He turned to Nueve. "Leave us."

"I will not," Nueve said.

"There is something I must discuss with him and I will not discuss it with you here."

Nueve lost his ironical grin. "I give you five minutes." He turned to me. "Five minutes, Alfred Kropp, or you may consider our contract null and void."

He left, popping the butt of his cane angrily against the linoleum. Samuel gestured for me to come closer. He tugged on the flowery sleeve of my dress, and I went to one knee beside the chair so he could look me straight in the eye.

"Alfred," he said softly. "Do you know why I refused your touch in ICU?"

"No. It was stupid."

"There is a reason you have been given this power, Alfred. Do you believe that?"

I thought about it. "Well, it seems pretty accidental to me the way it happened."

He placed his huge hand on my shoulder and squeezed. "You are the beloved of the Archangel Michael, Alfred Kropp. You have been chosen by the Prince of Light himself. Turn your back on that choice and you turn your back on heaven."

I remembered my fall from the demon's back, the feeling of warmth and light and someone's arms around me as he fell with me from fire into fire, from darkness into darkness, and the voice whispering, "Beloved."

I cleared my throat. "If that's true—and I'm not saying it is—but if it is, then why didn't you let me heal you? See, even you don't really believe it."

"I would not let you touch me for the very reason that I *do* believe it."

"You may not be the Op Nine anymore," I said. "But you still talk in riddles."

He shook his head. It hit me again how truly homely he was, with the droopy hound-dog face and black rings under his eyes, with the sallow skin and huge ears.

"These men who tried to kill you will not abandon their mission simply because the object goes into hiding. Eventually, no matter how cleverly OIPEP hides you, you will be found. Better to turn and face the danger head-on, now, at a time and place of your choosing, not theirs. In a few weeks, I can help you . . ."

I shoved his hand off my shoulder and stood up, backing

away as I talked. Now I didn't feel so much like crying as punching him in his sad hound-dog face.

"It isn't my fault this time," I said. "All I want is a normal life. Why can't I have that? Why can everybody else have that but I can't? You *chose* to be an Operative Nine . . ."

"Yes, and I also chose to be your guardian, and now you would deny me that."

"That's it? *That's* why you're pissed? Okay, then, come with me. They'll let you. They'll do anything for the Seal—"

"I am still your guardian, Alfred, whether I go with you or not. And as your guardian, I must do what I feel is best for you. These people trying to hurt you—whoever they are—will continue to hunt you, though the Company hides you in the remotest corner of the globe. Do you understand? *They will not stop hunting you until you are dead.*"

I turned my back on him and went to the door.

"Alfred!" he called after me. "You should not trust this Nueve."

"What makes you think I trust him?"

"He is the Operative Nine. For him, the Company's interest trumps all others."

"I'm giving him the Seal, Samuel. He's getting what the Company wants."

"The Company's wants are many."

"What's that mean? What are you talking about?"

He looked away from me. "The promises of an Operative Nine are written in water, Alfred."

"Okay . . ." I waited for him to explain what the heck he was getting at.

"He may have . . . other interests that conflict with yours. With ours."

"I'll be careful."

I hung by the door, waiting for something but not sure what. Then it occurred to me it might not be a "what," but a "who."

"Who is Sofia?" I asked. He looked startled, as if I had shouted an obscenity. "You said her name in ICU and I heard you say it again when you were talking to Nueve. Who is Sofia, Samuel?"

He didn't say anything at first. Then he said, "A ghost from the past, Alfred. That's all. A ghost from the past."

"Another riddle," I said. "I should have figured."

He nodded. "Yes. You should have."

"Goodbye, Samuel," I said.

"For now," he said.

No, I thought. *Forever.*

05:04:49:10

In the hallway, Nueve said, "Your mascara's running."

He handed me his handkerchief. I dabbed my eyes.

"How do I look?" I asked.

"Like an eighty-year-old raccoon."

I settled into the wheelchair as he pushed me to the elevators. Nueve instructed me to tuck my chin toward my chest. "It will help hide your face," he said.

"Who is Sofia?" I asked as we waited for the elevator.

"Ah. Finally, a question to which you truly do not know the answer, yes? Or did Samuel tell you?"

"He said she was a ghost from his past."

"She is many things. A ghost from the past, a promise for the future."

"Huh?"

"Sofia is the Judeo-Christian goddess of wisdom, Senor Kropp." His voice had a playful tone. "Have you ever been to the Sistine Chapel?"

"I've been meaning to get there."

"She is there, under the left arm of God as he reaches with his right to touch Adam. A beautiful woman who represents truth and knowledge and all that is beneficent and worth-while. She is the source, the font of all righteousness. I am surprised you've never heard of her."

"Why?"

"Because according to some accounts, Sofia is the Lady of the Lake who brings Michael's Sword to Arthur."

So that was it. Samuel must have brought up the same point to Nueve that he argued with me: I was Michael's beloved and by running away I was turning my back on heaven. I wondered why he and Nueve had picked that moment to have an argument about religion. Sam used to be a priest, but I doubted Nueve even believed in heaven. He didn't strike me as the religious type. He struck me as someone who really didn't believe in anything at all, except power. Samuel had called being an Operative Nine a burden, but I didn't think Nueve looked at it that way. I had the impression he *liked* being the Operative Nine. He liked it a lot.

The elevator doors slid open. Nueve swiveled the chair around and pulled me backward into the elevator.

A voice called from the hallway outside, "Hey, hold the door!" Nueve stopped the doors from closing with the end of his cane. Two orderlies stepped inside, both a bit out of breath.

"Thanks, man," one of them said.

They stood on either side of us. Nueve was standing directly behind my chair. The elevator began to descend. The four of us stared straight ahead, like everybody does in elevators.

Then Nueve leaned forward and whispered calmly in my ear, "I shall take the one on the left."

"Take what?" I asked, because I had no idea what he meant.

His black cane whistled over my head and slammed with a sickening crunch against the orderly's Adam's apple. The blow dropped him.

The one to my right was already on me. I saw a flash of fluorescent light play across the blade in his hand as he brought a black dagger toward my stomach.

Nueve was too quick for him. He caught his wrist and twisted it upward while the cane swooshed again over my head, landing against the side of my attacker's jaw.

As he went down, a gun went off; the report was very loud in the small space. The bullet caught Nueve in the left shoulder. He barely winced. A six-inch tapered blade sprang from the end of his cane.

"Duck," he hissed.

I ducked, covering my head with my hands, like a passenger going down in an airplane. I heard the cane whistle through the air and then a wet, gurgling noise and the sound of the gun clattering to the floor. An instant later the man to my right went "Huh!" as if somebody had just told him a shocking piece of news. His body thudded to the floor as the elevator jerked to a stop: Nueve must have hit the emergency button.

I sat up. The guy on my left was lying in a pool of blood, clutching his gashed throat. The one on the other side wasn't moving either, so I guessed Nueve had done the Company's standard extreme extraction number on him too.

I looked at Nueve. Besides the saucer-sized bloodstain on the shoulder of his lab coat, you couldn't tell he'd just been in a close-quarters fight to the death. He wasn't even breathing hard. In fact, he was smiling.

"Uninjured, yes? Good! Up, now, Kropp. I need the chair."

I stood up. My legs didn't feel too steady, even with the help of the orthopedic shoes. Nueve locked the wheels on the chair and climbed onto the seat. I looked down at the dead men.

"How did you know?" I gasped.

"The shoes," he said.

I looked at their shoes. They were the same white soft-sole numbers all orderlies wore.

"What about them?" I asked.

"They're brand-new. Both pairs. One is understandable, but both?"

"Still, it could have been a coincidence."

He shook his head. "No such thing in my experience. Yours?"

He popped open the access door in the ceiling with the butt end of his cane.

"I guess we're not riding this to the bottom," I said.

"Catch," he said. He dropped the cane and I caught it before it hit the floor. There was a recessed slot in one end where the bayonet nested.

"I wouldn't hold that too close to your face, Alfred," he said. He heaved himself through the hole and disappeared into the darkness of the shaft. Then I heard him say, "Cane." I handed it up to him.

"They must have been watching the room," I called up to him. "I told you this was a lame idea. What are you doing up there?"

"Waiting for you."

I took a deep breath before stepping onto the wheelchair seat. I hated heights, hated the dark, hated close spaces. On the other hand, I liked staying alive. Nueve reached down, slid his hands under my arms, and pulled me the rest of the way.

The elevator had come to a stop just past the second floor. Nueve hit some hidden button in the handle of his cane and the blade sprang out. He slipped the blade between the doors and then twisted it, forcing the doors open a couple of inches.

He put a hand on either door and slowly forced them open. He laid the cane lengthwise in the track between the doors to keep them open.

At that moment, the elevator motor revved, the big cable behind me began to move, and the whole thing started down.

"We're moving!" I shouted unnecessarily.

He pushed himself through the opening, yanked the cane from the track, and held one end toward me as I began to accelerate away from him.

"Jump!" he called down.

I jumped, my right hand closing around the end of the cane with half an inch to spare. I looked down between my dangling feet at the roof of the elevator as it shot downward.

"Pull me up!" I yelled over the noise.

"Can't! Climb," he grunted back.

After a couple of hard pulls and kicks against the wall, I managed to grab the cane with my left hand and began to pull myself up. Nueve was having trouble keeping the cane still as my weight shifted back and forth.

"Faster please," he said.

"I'm going as fast as I can!"

"Not fast enough, I think."

I was about to ask why not when I heard the elevator motor revving below me. I didn't have to look to know it was coming back up.

"Hand!" he yelled, letting go with his right and stretching it toward me. I let go of the cane with my left and reached toward his wriggling fingers. Not close enough. My fingertips brushed against his.

"Five seconds!" he yelled over the noise. "Pull!"

I pressed the pads of my feet against the concrete wall and pushed as hard as I could while yanking downward on the cane. The force of it nearly pulled Nueve into the shaft with me. His thin fingers entwined with mine and he heaved himself backward through the doors, pulling me up with him. The hurtling car caught the tip of my foot as I flew through the doors, ripping the shoe off my foot.

The doors closed, and we lay side by side on the cold floor, gulping air while a small crowd gathered to gawk at the old lady and the bloody doctor sprawled in front of the elevator, hugging each other.

A nurse finally said, "Can I help you, Doctor?"

Nueve scrambled to his feet and then pulled me up to mine. He scooped up his cane and gave the nurse an icily professional smile. Not a doctor's smile—an Operative Nine smile.

"Elevator trouble," he said. I started for the stairs. We were on the second floor, only one flight away from freedom. He grabbed my arm.

"No, Alfred—Freda—*Alfreda,* your room is this way."

He pulled me across the hall to the nearest room. An old man lay in the bed under an oxygen tent.

"Harriet?" he called hoarsely to me. "Harriet—I knew you'd come!"

Nueve ignored him. He strode across the room to the window and pulled aside the curtains. He looked out, nodded, took one step back, and then slammed the gold head of his cane into the center of the glass. The window shattered on impact. Nueve cleared the remaining shards from the frame, then motioned to me.

"Quickly," he hissed.

"We'll break our legs," I said, and then I saw we were directly above the overhang for the emergency room entrance on the first floor. Only a half-story fall, but still far enough to snap an ankle if you hit it wrong.

Behind us, the old man called, "Harriet! Harriet, don't leave me!"

Nueve's eyebrow went up. "Well, Harriet?" he asked.

Police sirens wailed in the distance. Somebody must have found the two dead guys in the elevator.

"Jump *down*, not *out*," Nueve cautioned me.

I put one foot on the sill. The old man got mad.

"Always running out on me, Harriet!"

At that moment the door flew open and three men rushed into the room. They wore black jumpsuits and black bandannas across their faces. Nueve smiled and nodded, as though he had expected them: *Ah, of course, the ninjas have arrived!* The blade leaped from the end of his cane.

"Go, Alfred," he said softly.

He shoved me through the window. I tumbled into empty space as the old man screamed after me, "Good riddance to you, then, you old witch!"

I hit the roof of the overhang feetfirst, bending my knees at the last second, so I managed to hit without breaking or twisting anything I really might need in the near future. I rolled a couple of times, coming to a stop at the edge, lay on my stomach for a second, then flipped over in time to see one of the ninjas coming through the window.

He landed about three feet away and pulled a tapered dagger from some hidden pocket in his black jumper. I recognized that dagger: thin, black-bladed, with a dragon's head on the hilt, its mouth open in a silent roar. The signature weapon of Mogart's private army, the agents of darkness who had chased me from Knoxville to Canada, from Canada to France, from France to England.

"Okay," I said to him. "You got me. I give up."

I raised my hands in the air. He came toward me slowly, the dagger pointed at my gut.

"Just make it quick, okay?" I asked.

He lunged forward with a hoarse yell. I had two seconds before he was on me. I used those two seconds to rip the shawl off my shoulders. I dropped the shawl over his head, twisted the two ends to wrap it tight, and then slung him forward with a shot-putter-like motion. He sailed over the edge of the overhang.

I turned back toward the building—where the heck was Nueve?—and saw another dagger-wielding AOD coming toward me. I got lucky with the first one but, based on the past, my good luck wasn't going to hold.

At that moment sirens screamed to life directly beneath us: an ambulance was leaving on a call. Maybe my luck hadn't completely run out. I sprinted to one side of the overhang. I had a fifty-fifty chance this was the correct side. The AOD's fingers tugged on the back of my dress as I threw myself over the side.

I had guessed right: the ambulance burst into the open the moment we went down, and we tumbled head over heels onto its roof.

The ambulance whipped hard to the right coming out of the parking lot, slinging us against the opposite edge. Then it began to accelerate toward the entrance ramp to I-40.

He rushed me. I scooted backward until my butt smacked against the red spinning lights mounted near the front of the ambulance.

We hit the on-ramp clocking sixty at least, and then he was on me. I drove my shoulder into his stomach, knocking the breath out of him. My momentum carried us toward the rear of the ambulance, where he finally went down, his head falling back over the edge. I landed on top of him and caught his wrist just as he brought the dagger around to the side of my neck.

The tip nicked my skin as he tried to force the blade forward. I could feel the blood trickle down my neck and soak into the collar of my dress.

Nueve's present . . . which shoe was it in? The one on my foot or the one lying on top of the hospital elevator? Had all my luck run out or was there still a drop or two left?

I clawed at my shoe as the wind tugged at my wig, pushing it forward until I was looking at him through a curtain of gray curls.

The fingertips of my right hand brushed against the hard casing of the poisoned pen. An inch . . . a half inch . . . but in a situation like that a half inch might as well be a mile.

He was too strong, too determined, too *focused*. Even if I managed to grab the pen, by the time I got the cap off— assuming I could—the dagger would be slicing my carotid artery and I would be one dead old lady.

So I spit right in his eyes. His grip loosened for an instant, and I gained the half inch I needed. I flicked the cap off the pen, pressed the button, and slammed the needle into his neck.

His eyes flew open and then froze that way. His body went stiff as a board beneath me. The dagger fell from his hand.

I picked it up and scooted toward the front of the ambulance. It was slowing down. I glanced over my shoulder and saw we were in the emergency lane, coming up on the scene of a pileup that blocked all three westbound lanes.

The ambulance screeched to a stop. I slid off the back before the paramedics could exit the cab. I sauntered over to the guardrail, just another old lady out for a stroll on the interstate with her six-inch dragon-headed dagger. Unfortunately, a cop was standing about twenty feet away. I looked at him and he looked at me, and so I gave him a little nod like, *Hey, sonny, don't mind me. I'm just your average old lady out for a stroll on the interstate with my six-inch dragon-headed dagger.* Then I threw one leg over the concrete railing and steeled myself for the thirty-foot plunge to the embankment below.

The cop shouted something and started to run toward me, his hand resting on the butt of his revolver. Like he would actually shoot an old lady, dagger-wielding or not.

Still, on the off chance that he might actually shoot a dagger-wielding old lady, I froze on the barrier.

I shouldn't have.

A black Lincoln Town Car pulled up behind the ambulance and two men in dark suits jumped out. One had a semiautomatic pointed at my head. The other man was focused on the cop.

"That's all right, Officer," he said in a gentle Southern drawl. "We'll take it from here." He looked at me and smiled. "Hello, Alfred."

The cop didn't lower his gun. He didn't know who to aim at now—me or the dark-suited guy.

Dark Suit pulled an ID from the breast pocket of his jacket and held it up.

"Vosch," he said to the cop. "FBI." He smiled a second time at me. "Step down, Alfred. You made a good run, but it's over."

"I gotta call this in," the cop said. He still hadn't lowered his weapon.

The man who called himself Vosch nodded, still smiling,

while his buddy ripped the dagger from my hand, pulled me from the barrier, and handcuffed me.

"Look . . ." I said to the cop.

"Shut up, Alfred," Vosch said pleasantly. Then he said to the cop, "Terrorism, murder, conspiracy to commit murder, and interstate flight."

The suit with the gun—now he had the muzzle jammed into my rib cage—dragged me toward the car as I shouted at the bewildered young cop, "These guys aren't FBI! Check out their wheels—since when do FBI agents drive Town Cars?"

I was slung into the backseat. Vosch's partner slid in beside me and slammed the door. The driver, a big guy with slits for eyes and a crooked nose, glanced at me in the rearview mirror.

"*Bonjour, Monsieur Kropp,*" he murmured.

I could see Vosch talking to the cop, who had put away his gun, which I interpreted as a sign that he was buying Vosch's story. Vosch was showing him some papers, probably a phony warrant for my arrest.

"At least tell me why you guys want to kill me so bad," I said.

They laughed.

Vosch walked back to the car and got in beside the driver. We roared straight back a few yards, spun around and then proceeded the wrong way to the next exit. I could see cars jamming all three lanes; the interstate was backed up for miles.

We exited onto Kingston Pike and headed east, toward downtown. I waited for the killing blow. It was the perfect time: I was handcuffed and helpless, trapped behind dark-tinted glass. They had been trying awfully hard to kill me and this was the perfect opportunity.

The blow didn't come. As we waited at an intersection for

the light to change, I said, "Something's happened. Where are you taking me?"

Nobody answered. Vosch hit the speed dial on his cell phone. After a few seconds, he said, "He is acquired. Alive, *oui*. We will be there in ten minutes." He had lost his Southern accent. Now he sounded French. He closed the phone and slipped it into his breast pocket.

"Whatever you guys want—whatever it is you're after—I don't have it," I blurted out. "I don't have anything!"

"Be quiet," Vosch said.

"Just promise me you won't hurt anyone. Take me, but don't kill anybody else because of me, okay?"

The guy beside me leaned forward and whispered something to Vosch in French. Vosch nodded, whispered something back. The guy beside me pulled a truncheon from his coat pocket and slammed it against my head.

05:04:10:51

I woke to the sound of a train rumbling nearby. For a few precious seconds, before the memory of what happened in the car came crowding back, I was ten years old again, lying in my bed in Ohio. My mom was in the next room watching TV, and I was drifting off to sleep, listening to the trains pass on the tracks about a half mile from our house. I'll never say I had a perfect childhood, but there were moments in it that *were* perfect, and that was one of them.

I heard chairs scraping across a wooden floor. Whispers. A stifled laugh.

Then someone said, "He's awake."

Someone else said, "Open your eyes, Alfred Kropp."

I did, but only because I knew I'd have to eventually.

Propped up in a straight-backed wooden chair with my hands still cuffed behind my back, I was sitting in the middle of a huge room, the ceiling at least two stories above my head, the walls lost in murky shadow. Detecting the distinct odor of coffee, I wondered if they had taken me to the old JFG warehouse at the edge of the Old City.

"Behold, the last in the line of Lancelot!"

The speaker was leaning against the edge of a table a couple of feet in front of me. Dark hair. Dark eyes. Slender. I'd never seen him before, but his face looked vaguely familiar. Like Vosch and his buddies, he spoke with a faint French accent.

"It seems fitting somehow," he went on. "That you would meet your fate dressed like an old woman!"

"That wasn't my idea," I gasped. I had a horrible headache from the knock in the car.

"I am not surprised," he said. "That would be like drawing water from a dry well."

I wasn't sure what he meant by that but figured he was calling me stupid. I squinted up at his face, at the aristocratic nose and sharp chin. Why did he look so familiar? I dropped my bucket into the well, trying to figure it out.

"If you have any lingering hopes of rescue, I would suggest you abandon them now," he said. "We've taken extraordinary measures to ensure you were not followed."

We. The shadow of a man hovered near one of the tall, narrow windows. Vosch? Where were the driver and the guy who bopped me on the head? I held my breath and listened. Someone coughed directly behind me and I thought I heard shoes shuffle on the hardwood to my left. At least four, counting the guy in front of me.

"Do you know who I am?" he asked.

"I could take a stab at it," I said.

"Stab."

Age: twenty-two. Citizenry: French. Marital status: single. Occupation: president and chief executive officer of Tintagel International . . .

"You're Jourdain Garmot."

He laughed softly like I had said something funny.

"I said it was a stab," I said.

"I didn't ask if you knew my name; I asked if you knew who I *am*."

"You're the boss at Tintagel International," I said. "And you've been trying very hard to kill me."

He nodded slowly. "Which has proved more difficult than I anticipated."

"You had your chance in the Town Car."

"I've decided to let you live a little while longer."

"Not that I'm ungrateful or anything, but why?"

He smiled. There was something familiar about that smile, though I couldn't put a finger on it. And his name. Garmot. Why did that seem familiar too? *Gar-mot. GAR-mot. Gar-MOT.* What was it?

"A selfish desire on my part," he answered. "I wanted to meet you—and naturally I wanted you to meet me."

He walked around to the other side of the table and sat down.

"And that brings us back to my original question, Alfred Kropp. Do you know who I am?"

Garmot. G-A-R-M-O-T.

"I told you what I know," I said.

His dark eyes glittered in the weak light streaming through the high windows. He nodded to someone behind me and Vosch appeared carrying a black case about the size of a bowling bag. He set it on the table between me and Garmot and melted back into the shadows.

"What's in that bag?" I asked.

Garmot didn't answer. Instead he asked very slowly and deliberately, "Who . . . am . . . I?"

Garmot. Gar-mo. Gar-gar-mot-mot. Mot-mot-gar-gar.
Sweat trickled down the back of my neck.

He stood up and now in his right hand he held a black sword. I had seen a sword just like it before. In fact, I *owned* one just like it. Tightly cuffed, my hands twisted uselessly behind my back as he came toward me, and all I could think was *How did he get my sword?*

"Perhaps some context would help," he said.

"That'd be great," I gasped. "Anything helpful would help."

"For we are not so different, you and I. We are both—how shall I say it?—reluctant players in a game not of our choosing. A mere two years ago we were living quite normal lives. You here in America and I in France. Both normal students in normal towns going about our normal lives. Until our normal lives were ripped away, yes?"

He leaned against the table, dropping the sword point between his spread legs and spinning it. Light raced up and down its length and sparked off the dragon's head embossed on the hilt.

Garmot. Gar-Gar. Gra-Gra. Mot-Mot. Mar-Mar. Mart? Marty . . . Marty-Gra . . . ?

"Like you, I resisted," he said. "I refused to play. I wanted a normal life. And until someone very close to me was murdered, I thought—I had every reason to believe—I would have that life. As did you, I am sure."

"I still want that," I said. "That's all I want."

"Irrelevant," Jourdain Garmot said. "We have no choice now but to see the game to its bitter end. Bitter for you, of course, since you will not survive this day. But bitter for me, as well, for killing you will not mend my broken heart or return my beloved friend to me."

He leaned the sword against the table and picked up the black satchel.

"You have lost many close to you," he said. "Your father. Your uncle. The knight called Bennacio. But none so close as he who was lost to me. He was my mentor, my constant companion, my best friend. When news came of his death, I wept like a young child. He was all I had in the world, and though he was taken from me, I keep him with me, always. Would you like to meet him, the one who was so cruelly stolen from me?"

I wasn't looking at him. I was looking at the hilt of the black sword. It wasn't my sword; my sword didn't have the dragon emblem, but it was a knight's sword. All the Knights of the Sacred Order carried the black sword.

Dragon. Garmot.

He unsnapped the first clasp.

"I cannot bear for us to be parted, you see . . ."

My thoughts started to spin in a panicky whirl.

Gar-Ger, Gera-gar, Gra-mot, Gram-ot, Gra-gri-mot-mot-ger-grot, gram-to, mar-gro, mar-gor, mar-got, mog-art . . .

Mogart . . . !

"It's a . . ." I whispered. "It's a—I don't know what it's called, but I think it's like ana-something—*Garmot* for *Mogart* . . ."

"The word you are looking for is 'anagram,'" Jordain said.

He flipped open the second clasp. "And as you say in America . . . *speak of the devil.*"

Then Jourdain Garmot reached into the bag and pulled out a human head. It was the head of the man I killed in Merlin's Cave. It was Mogart's head.

"Say hello to my father, Alfred Kropp."

05:03:48:21

"I didn't have a choice," I choked out. My stomach rolled and I looked away from Mogart's mummified head. The skin had turned a deli mustard yellowish brown, tightening against the shape of the skull beneath. The lips had pulled back, revealing the teeth and giving the illusion of a snarl. The eyes had long since rotted away, leaving two empty black-filled holes. "He was going to kill me—he *did* kill me . . ."

He ignored me. " 'The last knight.' I understand the one called Bennacio tried to take that title for himself, but in reality my father was the last knight—the last to fall as a result of your treachery."

"*My* treachery? I don't think you know the whole story. Nothing against your dad, but he turned on the other knights—"

"Enough."

"He betrayed them—"

"I said *enough*!"

He dropped the head back into the satchel, thank God, and slung it onto the table. He pressed the tip of the black sword against my throat. *That's it,* I thought. *I'm dead.* If you're nutty enough to carry around your father's mummified head, there's not much that will keep you from chopping off the head of the guy who killed him.

"The knights are no more, thanks to you," he cried. "The Sword has departed, thanks to you! My father is dead, again thanks to you! His blood and the blood of all the knights cry to heaven for justice!"

His cheeks were flushed and he was breathing so heavily I could see his nostrils flaring. He nodded to someone behind me.

It was Vosch. He yanked me up and kicked away the chair.

I had a pretty good idea what was going to happen next, and my mouth went dry.

"The knights are departed, their time on earth brought to an end by you, Alfred Kropp," Jourdain said. "And so, like the knights of old, after I assumed my father's place, I embarked upon a—what is the word?—a quest. A quest, yes! To finish what was begun. To complete the circle. The last knightly quest . . . for the Thirteenth Skull."

Two men appeared on either side of me, the guy who clubbed me in the car and the big driver. Each grabbed an arm while Vosch stayed behind me, hands on my shoulders.

"Jordain, listen to me," I said. "I don't know about any Thirteenth Skull. I don't know about any skulls, period. All I know is all this crap has to stop somewhere and maybe we could agree it stops now, with me and you."

Jordain nodded to Vosch, who forced me down to my knees.

"It won't work, Jordain—why do you think your goons couldn't kill me before? He won't let it happen . . ."

He was standing over me, the black sword shining in his hand, as I knelt at his feet.

"Who? Who will not let it happen?" he asked. He seemed genuinely puzzled that anyone would care.

I almost didn't answer. Did I believe it myself? Did I really believe it the way Bennacio and Samuel believed it?

"Michael," I whispered. "The Archangel."

He stared down at my upturned face without expression.

"I'm—um—I'm his beloved."

They burst out laughing, even Mr. Flat-Face, who didn't strike me as someone with a finely developed sense of humor. Except Jourdain. Jourdain wasn't laughing.

"Yes, the Angel," he whispered. "It is almost time for Michael's return—and the return of the gift. She has promised me and I believe her. The gift shall be given again to the true heir of Camelot, but not before the Thirteenth Skull is borne home." He nodded to Vosch, who shoved his knee into the middle of my back, forcing me down. My right cheek smacked against the hardwood.

"I don't understand!" I hollered. Maybe if I kept him talking I could postpone the inevitable. "Who promised you what? What gift? What true heir of Camelot?"

"*Au revoir*, Alfred Kropp," Jordain Garmot said. He raised the black sword over his head, gripping the dragon-headed hilt with both hands.

"Saint Michael," I whispered. "Save me."

As if in answer, every window in the storehouse exploded inward and wide shafts of bright white light shot into the room.

05:03:42:19

It happened very fast.

Black canisters sailed through the broken windows, vomiting thick white smoke as they fell. My captors screamed at one another in French, except for the word "Kropp," which I guess is "Kropp" in any language.

In seconds the room was filled with a thick, choking fog; it felt like someone was pressing hot matches against my eyes. I couldn't see anything but could hear the sharp *pop-pop* of small-arms fire and the bumping and cursing that always came with people stumbling around in the fog. Someone yanked me to my feet and I instinctively flung my head back to butt him. He blocked my head with one hand and slapped a hood over my face with the other, I guess to protect my eyes from the tear gas.

"I am trying to help you, Miss Alfreda," a voice purred in my ear.

Nueve.

He whipped me around, only I couldn't see him through the hood. I heard a loud *snap!* and the handcuffs fell off my wrists and clattered to the floor. Then he lifted me right off my feet and slung me over his shoulder. The hood fell off my head.

He sprinted to the wall, grabbed a thick black cord hanging there, and pulled it through a harness he wore around his waist. He gave the cord three sharp tugs. The rope pulled taut and we began to rise toward the broken-out window.

I heard Jourdain screech in a voice filled with rage, *"Alfred Kropp!"* before we were pulled through the window and then straight up. An Apache helicopter was at the other end of the black cord, and soon we were six stories high, swooping over the rooftops of the Old City. Since I was slung facedown over Nueve's shoulder, I had a real bird's eye view of downtown Knoxville.

I shouted, "Why don't they pull us up?"

"Too dangerous!" he shouted back.

Too *dangerous*?

We soared over downtown, past the First Tennessee Bank building and then Samson Towers, where this whole mess started, a dark monolith of glass and glittering steel; then we were over the river and the boats bobbed four hundred feet below my swaying head, anchored in the murky water. And there was the UT Medical Center and the Army Reserve base on Alcoa Highway, which we seemed to be following as it snaked through the foothills. We were heading toward the airport.

I guessed it was finally safe to pull us up, because the helicopter paused over the highway and we began to rise toward the open hold. I heard sirens below and, peering around Nueve's torso, saw the spinning red lights of two motorcycle cops as they barreled around a hairpin curve, coming from the city. I slapped him between the shoulder blades and screamed over the roar of the helicopter: *"Cops!"*

Nueve spun us around so he could get a look. One of the bikes raced ahead, passing directly below us before disappearing around the next curve. The rider had something long and black, bigger than a rifle or a shotgun, hanging over his shoulder.

"Hey!" I shouted, hoping Nueve would hear me over the roar, but at the same time wondering what it would matter. "I think he's got a rocket launcher!"

Nueve raised his arm and gave some kind of signal to the pilot. We stopped rising and the chopper took off again, banking to the right, taking us away from the road and over an open field.

The maneuver flung us backward and then into a spin, like a dead yo-yo at the end of its string, and as I spun back in the direction of the highway I saw it: the contrail of a surface-to-air missile rocketing toward the chopper.

My scream was buried in the *wuff-wuff-wuff* of the blades' draft. A second later the chopper erupted into a fireball. For an instant, before gravity took hold, we hung in midair, and then we fell.

Fast.

It hadn't been that long since the last time I fell to earth, except that fall began thirty thousand feet up, not a hundred, and that time I fell with an angel holding me, not an OIPEP agent who didn't even have the good sense to bring a parachute to an aerial-rescue mission.

I didn't look down. I just closed my eyes and waited for the end.

Then I hit water.

The chopper had carried us over a dairy farm, and the explosion had hurled us directly above a pond. I hit the muddy water facefirst, swallowing maybe a gallon of it. I broke the surface choking and spitting and coughing, opening my eyes to find myself face-to-face with a milk cow. The cow looked at me, I looked at the cow, and the cow cried chicken first: it bellowed a warning call to its buddies and whirled away, mud and cow crap flying from its hooves as it took off across the pasture. A big glob of the stinking goop landed smack in my eye.

Nueve appeared in the shallows beside me.

"Those weren't cops," I gasped. I had a very weird taste in my mouth, and I wondered if I'd discovered the flavor of cow poop.

"Who weren't cops?" a deep voice intoned.

We looked up. Two people on horseback towered over us, an old man and a kid about my age.

"This is a national emergency," Nueve said to the old man.

The old man glanced toward the burning wreckage of the downed chopper. "Sure looks like some kind of emergency."

"We need to commandeer your horses," Nueve went on. He grabbed my arm and pulled me out of the muddy shallows where I stood, shivering, in my summery frock.

"You need to *what* our horses?"

"Commandeer. Take them," Nueve said pleasantly. In the distance, over the crackle and pop of the smoldering chopper, you could hear the sirens of the phony cops' bikes, and the sound was getting louder.

The kid barked a laugh. "You and what army, Tinker Bell?"

Nueve answered with a sarcastic echo of the kid's laugh, then pulled a weapon from his jumper. It was shaped like a gun, but it looked more like a blaster from *Star Wars* or those shiny metallic pistols from *Men in Black*. He pointed it at the kid's head.

"I wouldn't do that if I was you," the old man said, matching Nueve's calm, pleasant tone. A revolver had appeared in his hand, and the revolver was pointed at Nueve's head.

Some of the color returned to the kid's face. I was still a little tense myself, and my mind barely registered the fact that the world had gone very quiet—no more sirens, just the sound of the burning chopper and cows lowing in the distance.

The kid's eyes grew wide as it dawned on him. "Hey, Granddaddy, that ain't no girl—that's some ol' boy in a dress!"

He started to laugh and as he laughed a jagged hole appeared in his jeans, just above his left kneecap. He screamed and fell out of the saddle, clutching his leg and writhing in agony in the poopy mud.

"Sonny!" the old guy cried.

Nueve leaped forward and hurled the grandfather from his saddle. The old man's gun went off as he went down, but the muzzle was pointed toward the sky.

"I told you it was an emergency!" Nueve hissed at him. He swung into the saddle with the grace of an accomplished horseman.

"Come, Kropp!" he cried.

A bullet flung up a clod of mud an inch from my left foot. I felt another rip through the hem of my dress. I heaved myself onto the other horse with a lot less alacrity than Nueve.

"I don't know how to ride!" I shouted.

"An excellent time to learn!" Nueve shouted back and flung the reins into my lap.

And then he was gone at full gallop, riding toward a dense stand of trees fifty or so yards from the pond.

I scooped up the reins and gave one quick snap against the horse's neck while popping his sides with my heels, like I'd seen in a dozen movies. It worked. The horse bolted forward, nearly hurling me over its bouncing rump. I clung hard to the reins, yelling at the top of my lungs, not trying to steer or guide it, just employing the Kropp method of dealing with disaster: hang on for dear life and pray you don't get killed.

I was almost to the trees when I heard the motorcycles. I risked a glance over my shoulder: two of them, coming up fast on big Harleys, wearing the standard-issue black jack boots and tinted visors. Only these weren't cops; they were agents of darkness, and that meant one thing: they wouldn't stop until they were dead—or I was.

I wasn't sure how much horsepower a Harley had, but I figured it was more than what I had. Nueve had disappeared into the trees, leaving me totally defenseless, and what kind of rescue mission was that? A trail snaked through the winter-bare trees, and I hit it at full gallop as bullets hit the trunks on either side, peppering me with five-inch splinters and chunks of wooden shrapnel.

The trail widened and suddenly Nueve was riding beside me. I guessed he had pulled off to wait.

"We'll never outrun them!" I shouted over the thundering of the hooves and the roar of the killers' bikes.

"I'm drawing one off!" he cried. "Here!"

He tossed the shiny weapon he had pointed at the farmer into my lap. "Wait till I'm clear," he called. "The rounds are heat seeking!"

And then he was gone, whipping the horse off the trail and into the trees, riding with his cheek practically laid on the horse's neck to avoid being knocked off by low-hanging branches.

A bullet whizzed by my ear. I twisted around and pulled the trigger without bothering to aim. The gun kicked in my hand and I saw a tiny contrail stream from the muzzle toward the rider no more than twenty feet back.

There was a soft *whumph!* on impact. The bullet tore through the bike's gas tank. The rider was close enough for me to see my reflection in his visor as the Harley exploded into a fireball, hurling his body forward, a fiery human projectile that came straight at me.

I goaded the horse's flanks and snapped the reins against its neck, and he answered with a burst of speed. The burning rider missed hitting my horse's rump by a foot.

Nueve and the other rider were nowhere in sight, but I didn't pull up and I didn't slow down. The trees were thinning out and I could see open pastureland ahead. Now what? Just keep riding or stay in the trees?

With ten yards between me and the naked sky, I yanked the reins hard to the right, and my horse lunged off the trail. He must not have liked dodging trees at full gallop any more than I did, because all at once we were back on the trail—or it may have been a different trail; I was very disoriented by that point.

Same trail or different trail wasn't the thing that mattered though. The thing that mattered was the dude on the Harley coming straight at me at fifty miles per hour.

I raised my weapon. Even without the heat-seeking rounds, I don't think I could have missed, we were that close.

My finger tightened on the trigger as he spun the bike around, waving an arm over his head frantically before yanking back on the throttle and spraying me with dirt and slimy dead leaves from his back wheels. I noticed then he wasn't wearing a helmet and the back of his head looked awfully familiar, but it was already too late: I'd pulled the trigger.

Spitting smoke, the round took off toward the back of Nueve's head.

The Spaniard had guts, I'll give him that. He waited until the mini bomb was almost on him, then dove off the bike into the trees. He didn't fool the missile though. It veered away from the bike and toward him, hitting the tree trunk he dived behind and exploding on impact. The tree jerked, swayed, then tumbled down across the trail, the sound of its branches cracking and splitting very loud in the cold air.

I dismounted by the fallen tree and walked unsteadily to where Nueve lay curled in a ball. When I bent over to check his pulse, his hand shot up and grabbed me by the throat.

"I told you to be careful, Kropp. You could have killed me!"

I lost it. It really was too much, after all I'd been through that week, to have this jerk scold me like I was some little kid. I hadn't asked for any of it—in fact, I had wanted the exact opposite, and here he was acting like *I* had dragged *him* into this crap.

I grabbed his wrist and tore his hand away, and then I hit him as hard as I could in the jaw. He fell back onto his butt with a startled expression.

"Maybe that's my problem," I snarled at him. "Maybe that's why I can't extract myself from you nutcases—I keep killing the wrong people! You knew who Jourdain Garmot was the whole time, didn't you? You knew he was Mogart's son, didn't you?"

"Does that matter?" he asked, rubbing his jaw, but somehow smiling his annoying ironic smile.

"You're damn right it matters! You knew who he was and where he was, and you could have stopped him!"

I pulled my fist back to pop him again. He scooted backward and rose to his full height.

"I am authorized to kill you if I have to," he said.

"Really? Well, that's where I'm one up on you. I don't need anyone's authorization!" I raised the handheld rocket launcher and took dead aim at his little Spanish smile.

"Do that and you will never reach the airport alive," he said.

"How did you find me at the warehouse?" I asked.

"We followed Vosch, of course."

"Jourdain said they weren't followed."

Nueve shrugged.

"What is the Thirteenth Skull?"

He stared at me, stone-faced.

"Jourdain needs it so Michael will return the gift. The gift is the Sword, isn't it? Jourdain's after Excalibur and he needs the Thirteenth Skull to get it."

He didn't say anything. He just shrugged.

"Don't shrug," I said. "Don't ever shrug again in front of me, understand?"

"It is only a shrug."

"Don't change the subject either."

"I didn't. You changed the subject."

"Stop it. It doesn't matter who changed the subject."

"Then why tell me not to?"

"Yes or no, you knew the whole time Jourdain was behind all this."

"Why does it matter?"

"Because you could have stopped him!"

"Have we not done that? Are you not still alive? Have I not saved your miserable *las nalgas* more times than either of us can recall?"

"So why didn't you stop him?"

"Do you still understand so little about the Company,

Alfred Kropp? We are not a private security company. We are interested in only one thing as it relates to you and that one thing is not your personal welfare. And if you fail to deliver that one thing, we shall leave you to your fate at the hands of Mogart's son."

He brushed past me and righted the motorcycle. "Now come, you ungrateful little drag queen; they are waiting for us at the airport. I've had my fill of this godforsaken town and more than my fill of *you*."

I climbed onto the seat behind him.

"Give back my weapon," he said.

"I think I'll just keep it, thanks."

He started to say something, seemed to think better of it, and then opened up the bike full throttle. I clung to his waist, closed my eyes, and hung on for dear life.

05:02:34:26

Nueve took us straight to the airport. I didn't know if any back roads existed, but I wish they did: Alcoa Highway is one of the busiest streets in Knoxville, and at every stoplight more than a few drivers stared at the big kid dressed like an old lady on the back of a mud-spattered police motorcycle. And I worried we might run into a real cop. What clever cover story could Nueve invent to explain *this*?

I closed my eyes, pressed my cheek against Nueve's back, and tried to organize my thoughts. That was an exercise I struggled with even in the best of circumstances, but I gave it a try anyway.

Mogart had a son. A son who, like me, had no idea what kind of business his father was wrapped up in until he was dead. Then somebody brings him his father's head and tells him a kid named Alfred Kropp chopped it off with the sword of the Archangel Michael. So Jourdain comes to Knoxville looking for a little payback . . . or something else called the

Thirteenth Skull, because somebody promised if he got it he'd get Excalibur back . . . Or did killing me have anything to do with the Skull and Excalibur at all? But if killing me didn't have anything to do with it, why tell me about the Skull in the first place?

What did he say? *She has promised me and I believe her. The gift shall be given again to the true heir of Camelot, but not before the Thirteenth Skull is borne home.*

The gift of Saint Michael must be Excalibur, and he must have been referring to himself as the true heir of Camelot, but who was this *she* he was talking about? The Lady of the Lake?

According to some accounts, Sofia is the Lady of the Lake who brings Michael's Sword to Arthur.

Sofia. Sam had said her name in his sleep and later argued with Nueve about her. Did *Sam* know Jourdain was after me? Did he know the whole time and, if he did, why didn't he tell me?

At the airport, Nueve drove to a hangar set off by itself in the corner of the airfield and surrounded by a ten-foot-tall chain-link fence topped with razor wire. A couple of big guys dressed in blue jumpers with 9mm Glocks strapped to their waists patrolled the compound. They met us at the padlocked gate, and one hit the button on his radio.

"Alice is up from the hole," he said. "Repeat, Alice is up."

He unlocked the gate and Nueve rolled the bike into the compound. I walked beside it with rubbery legs and an aching butt from the horse ride. I wondered who "Alice" was, me or Nueve. I was pretty sure who though.

Nueve walked rapidly toward the hangar. I lagged behind. I was tired.

"Come, Alfred Kropp," Nueve said without looking back. "Journey's end."

"She's here," the guard huffed at Nueve. "And she's not happy."

The pedestrian door to the hangar was padlocked and the guard fumbled with the keys.

"Who's here?" I asked.

He popped the padlock and pulled open the door for Nueve. He gave me a look as I followed Nueve inside.

"What?" I asked.

"Thought you'd be prettier."

A black Learjet sat facing the hangar doors. Guys in gray coveralls were messing all around it, getting it ready for take-off, I guessed. *Just a couple more flights,* I told myself. *Three tops, and then I'll never fly again.*

A woman approached us, the click of her cherry-red high heels on the polished concrete echoing in the vast space. She was wearing a pin-striped business suit and her blond hair was piled on top of her head.

It was Abigail Smith, the director of OIPEP, and the owner of the most magnificent orthodontics I had ever seen.

"Alfred dear, so good to see you again, alive if not particularly well." She was beaming. She kissed me on the cheek. She turned to Nueve and the beaming went away. "Another botch, Nueve."

"Would not a botch be defined as Kropp's demise?"

"We've been busy enough with the hospital attack and the incident on the interstate. Now Medcon has a downed Company chopper to deal with." Medcon was OIPEP-speak for "Media Control," the part of the Company that invented cover stories for its operations.

"Unavoidable," Nueve said archly.

"I don't want to interrupt," I interrupted. "But do you think maybe I could change my clothes before we leave?"

Like the sun bursting through the clouds, Abby's brilliant smile returned. "Of course, Alfred. This way."

She put her arm around my shoulder and we walked toward the back of the hangar. A wooden staircase led up to an office suite with a large window that overlooked the bay.

"I understand you've had quite the time of it since I saw you last," she said.

"That's putting it mildly," I said.

"You've made a wise decision, Alfred. At least in regards to the Seal—but I wonder about the wisdom of your asking price."

"I made a mistake," I said.

She turned to me at the top of the stairs.

"Before I sent him back to the Holy Vessel," I went on, "the demon king showed me this vision . . . He offered me what I'm asking for now, only I told him no, because the price was too high."

"What was the price?"

"His freedom."

She gave me a long, quizzical look. "That's it, isn't it, Alfred? Freedom."

I nodded.

"Nueve won't play straight with me, Abby, but you always have. If I give you guys the Seal, you'll keep your promises, won't you?"

She smiled, and this time her smile was of the sad variety, and then she put a hand on my cheek.

"As long as I am director," she said, which was as iron-clad a promise as I was probably going to get.

She opened the door and I saw Mr. Needlemier's bald head rushing toward me, his stubby arms flung wide. He bumped Abby out of the way and buried his chubby baby face into my chest.

"It's okay, Mr. Needlemier," I said. "I'm fine."

"Thank God!" he cried. "When they lost contact with the helicopter I feared the very worst!"

Nueve stepped into the room, his dark eyes lighting up at the sight of Mr. Needlemier.

"Ah, the lawyer. Excellent!" He turned to Abby. "The plane is ready, Director. We can affect the exchange."

"In a moment," Abby Smith said. She was still aggravated with him. "Alfred is changing first and meeting his extraction coordinator."

"My what?"

"This way, Alfred."

"I'll wait right here," Mr. Needlemier whispered.

Abby led me into another room. A girl with skin the color of copper, blond hair, and huge blue eyes was sitting on the sofa. She stood up when she saw me.

"Ashley?"

"Hi, Alfred," she said, and then she hugged me. I smelled lilacs. I looked down and there were those enormous blue eyes looking up at me.

"They told me you'd changed," she said.

"The dress wasn't my idea," I said.

"I don't mean the dress."

She stepped back—the hug had lasted about four seconds too long.

"I thought you quit," I said.

"They made an offer I couldn't refuse." She glanced toward Abby.

"Ashley agreed to return to the Company on the condition we assign her as your extraction coordinator."

"Oh," I said. "What's that mean?"

"It means Ashley is in charge of coordinating your extraction from our interface."

I looked at Ashley. "I hate OIPEP," I said.

She laughed. "Why don't you change, Alfred? I'll meet you outside."

She left, a bouncing swirl of golden-haired blondness.

"Bathroom over there, clothes in the closet beside it," Abby said. She looked at her watch. "We need to leave in the next fifteen minutes to stay within security parameters."

She patted my arm and started to go.

"Abby, wait," I called after her. "About Samuel."

"Samuel?"

"You know, Op Nine . . . Samuel. Is he okay?"

"Yes, Alfred. We've moved him to a safe location."

"Well, if I've learned anything from the past, there's no such thing."

Abby laughed.

"I wasn't making a joke," I said. "So he's not here."

"There's no reason for him to be, is there?"

I thought about it. "No, I guess not. It's just, we kind of had an argument the last time I saw him. Can you let him know I'm okay—that everything's going to be okay now?"

"Of course, Alfred."

"Who is Sofia?"

She looked at me for a second without saying anything, reminding me of Nueve's stone-faced stare at the dairy farm.

"Sofia?"

"He said she was a ghost from his past."

She slowly shook her head. "I'm sorry, Alfred, I don't know any person named Sofia."

"Nueve said she was the goddess of wisdom."

Abby gave a weird little laugh. "Did he?"

"What's the Thirteenth Skull?"

"The . . . what?"

"Thirteenth Skull. Jourdain is looking for it."

"Is he? How . . . extraordinary."

"So you know about it?"

She nodded.

"You're about to tell me it's classified, aren't you? You've got that 'it's classified' look."

"I was about to tell you Jourdain is chasing a chimera if he is searching for it. The Thirteenth Skull is a myth."

"What's the myth?"

She shook her head. "What does any of it matter now, Alfred? In a few days, none of this"—she waved to indicate the world according to OIPEP—"will be your concern. You're free now."

She turned on her cherry-red heels and hurried from the room. I took a quick shower to wash off the mud and cow poo, found a toothbrush by the sink, and scrubbed my teeth, then yanked on a regulation black OIPEP jumper I found hanging in the closet. Using the mirror in the bathroom, I combed my hair with my fingers, thinking I probably wouldn't be combing my hair if Ashley wasn't my extraction coordinator. She had quit OIPEP after encountering sixteen million demonic fiends in the Sahara, which totally freaked her out, and I never thought I would see her again. Just my luck when I did I was wearing a dress. But I'd also lost a lot of weight and grown another inch and my hair had those funky, cool gray streaks in it and I was thinking that's what happens when you go through a big change, the old you lingers in your mind's eye, like a ghost limb of an amputee.

They were waiting for me in the outer room, Ashley, Abby, Nueve, and Mr. Needlemier. I slid into the empty seat next to Ashley and said, "I'm a guy again."

"Smooth," Nueve murmured.

He turned to Mr. Needlemier. "In ten minutes we depart for happier climes. The Company has agreed to extract Senor Kropp in exchange for the item stolen from Company possession."

Mr. Needlemier nodded nervously. I thought of bobbleheads.

"So," Nueve said, "do you have the item?"

Mr. Needlemier looked at me. I nodded. He unlocked his briefcase and pulled out the Great Seal of Solomon. I took a deep breath. Now OIPEP would have both the Great Seal and the Holy Vessel with all those demons locked up inside it, able to free them and do whatever the hell they wanted with them. I looked at Abby. If she wasn't the director now, I thought, I wouldn't do it. I didn't trust OIPEP that much—never had—but I trusted her. Abby would keep the Seals safe. She'd make sure nobody ever released the Outcasts of Heaven again.

Nueve reached over and practically snatched the ring from Mr. Needlemier's quivering fist. His dark eyes shone as he held it up. The Seal glittered under the fluorescent lights.

"Good," Abby said crisply. She was all business now. "We're at the edge of the security envelope." She stood up, Ashley stood up, and then Nueve stood up. Mr. Needlemier and I didn't stand up.

"Alfred," Abby said.

"Alfred," Ashley said.

"Alfred," Nueve said.

"May I have a few moments alone with Alfred?" Mr. Needlemier asked.

Nueve was immediately suspicious. "For what purpose?"

"For the purpose of saying goodbye."

Abby looked at her watch. "Five minutes."

On their way out, I heard Nueve say to Abby, "Sentimentalist!"

The door closed. Mr. Needlemier glanced through the window to make sure they weren't trying to eavesdrop. I could have pointed out they probably had the room bugged. He scooted his chair close to mine.

"Alfred, are you sure about this?"

I nodded. "It's messed up, Mr. Needlemier."

"I can't argue with that. You may call me cynical, Alfred, but money does have a way of fixing things. You understand you are walking away from close to half a billion dollars?"

"Ever since this thing started," I said, feeling like I was going to cry. "Ever since I stole the Sword, people have been dying. A lot of people, most of them bad, I guess, but a lot of them good, including my uncle and my dad. It's like a wheel, Mr. Needlemier, a big wheel of death that just keeps turning and I'm like the axle. A wheel can't turn without its axle."

He was nodding like he was following me, but I didn't think he was. I went on. "Samuel won't take OIPEP's money, so I want you to make sure he has some of mine. The rest I want you to give away. Orphanages and places like that, although the only places I can think of like that are orphanages. You know what I mean; you're the lawyer—check into it. I can't help the dead, but I can the living."

"Yes, well, Alfred . . . about that . . ."

"About what part of that?"

"The money. There's been a development."

"I hate it when you say that. What development?"

"All the money has been frozen."

"Why?"

"By order of the court. You see, that's what I wanted to talk to you about privately. There's been a challenge to your father's will."

I was about to ask *who* when it hit me *who*.

"Jourdain Garmot," I said.

"Why, yes. How did you know?"

"His dad used to be Mr. Samson's heir. Mr. Samson had picked Mogart to take charge of Excalibur if something happened to him. Then he found out about me and cut Mogart out, which led Mogart to use me to steal the Sword and everything else."

Mr. Needlemier was nodding. "Exactly. Now we can fight this, Alfred. Bernard's will bequeathing everything to you postdates the will naming Mogart as the heir."

"So Jourdain won't get the money."

"Not without committing a very serious crime," Mr. Needlemier answered.

"I don't think that would bother him," I said. "You know what he does, Mr. Needlemier? He carries his father's head around in a black leather satchel."

"Dear God!"

"And that might not be the only one. I think he took my father's head too. He's totally whacked. He took his head and blew up his house and now I guess he's after all the money. I think he wants to wipe everything to do with me off the face of the planet."

I stood up.

"And the Skull. He wants that too, but I'm not sure what wiping me out has to do with that."

"The Skull?"

"The Thirteenth Skull. Have you ever heard of it?"

He said, "Why in the world would I?"

"You worked for the head man, the captain of the Order of the Sacred Sword. Maybe it came up."

He just stared at me with a blank expression. I was getting that look a lot lately.

"It must have something to do with the knights," I went on. "How else would Jourdain know about it?"

"I don't know anything about any skulls, Alfred."

I nodded. "I didn't think so. Well, it's like Abby said, it doesn't really matter now. Like Sofia."

He was totally lost by this point. "Sofia? Who is Sofia?"

"A ghost from the past." I took a deep breath. "This is it," I said.

And he said, voice shaking, "Yes. It."

I headed for the door.

"Oh! Alfred, I nearly forgot. There is one more thing."

I turned and saw him standing there holding a black rapier.

"What should I do with this?"

It was Bennacio's sword, the sword of the last knight to walk the earth. At a château in France, I had laid my hands on that same sword and sworn a vow to heaven. If I turned my back on it now, was I turning my back on something else, something that called me *beloved*?

"This isn't running," I choked out. "I'm not trying to save myself. That's not what this is."

"Alfred, I don't understand. Are you saying you don't want it?" He was talking about the sword.

"It's over for them, Mr. Needlemier. The time for the knights is gone and even if it wasn't, all the knights are." I swallowed hard. Talk about ghosts from the past! But weren't all ghosts from the past? "You should melt it down or smash it and scatter its pieces into the sea."

He nodded, but then he said, "All the same, I think I shall put it somewhere safe. You might need it one day."

Fat chance of that. Mr. Needlemier didn't know it, but in a few hours Alfred Kropp would be dead.

05:01:54:11

Fifteen minutes later I was a couple thousand feet above Knoxville and climbing, looking out the window at the winter-brown landscape, the broad ribbon of the Tennessee River curving through the foothills, knowing I would never see it again.

Beside me, Ashley asked, "What are you thinking, Alfred?"

I cleared my throat. "I was wondering why you decided to come back to OIPEP."

I looked at her. She was very pretty in a kind of all-American way, with the blond hair and blue eyes, a nicely proportioned nose and very white teeth.

She looked away. "They asked me to," she said.

"And you said yes, just like that?"

"They said they needed an extraction coordinator."

"That's a plush job or something?"

She laughed. I thought of bubble gum. "I said no," she said. "And then they said it was for you."

"You came back for me?"

She laid her fingertips on my forearm. "After they told me what happened with the Seals. What you did to get them back. I didn't see how I could say no. I know how hard it is . . . to leave."

"Was it? Is it? Did you just pick up where you left off before you got into OIPEP?"

"I tried. It's hard, Alfred. After seeing what you see there . . . knowing what you know . . . to just go back into the civilian interface as if nothing had happened, when *everything* had happened. You still feel . . . I don't know how to say it . . . even though you're back, you're still on the outside looking in. Wherever you are, you look at people and think about all the things they don't know and what it would be like if they *did* know all the things they *can't* know. All the things they don't *want* to know."

"I know exactly what you mean," I said. "The same thing happened to me."

Five thousand feet below, the interstate snaked through the monochromatic hills, the same road that took Bennacio and me north in our quest for the Holy Sword.

Ashley said, "There's a saying they teach new recruits: *the Company is forever.* It doesn't mean OIPEP will last forever—nothing does. It means what happens to you inside the Company lasts forever. It does things to you that can't be undone."

"Doom," I said softly.

"What?"

"Doom. You know, fate. Destiny. The thing-that-can't-be-undone. And it doesn't matter whether you think it's right or wrong, fair or unfair. You don't have a choice. Well, I don't buy it. I won't buy it. I still have a choice."

I turned from the window to look at her and saw her look-ing back at me with a funny expression, almost as if she felt sorry for me.

"Where are we going exactly?" I asked.

"Camp Echo. It's a Company facility in Canada."

"Do you know where I'll eventually end up?"

She shook her head.

"What's that mean?" I asked. "You don't know or you know and can't tell me?"

"I don't know. We've got it narrowed down to a couple possibilities."

"Do I get any say in it?" She nodded. "Good. I don't want to end up someplace like Paraguay herding goats."

She laughed and shook her head again. When Ashley moved her head, her blond hair moved with it but a millisec-ond later, a swirling effect like a long blond cape: move-swirl, move-swirl.

"Paraguay was just a random country," I said. "The truth is I'm not even sure they herd goats in Paraguay. I'm not telling you guys how to do this. You're the coordinator and everything, but if it's up to me I'd rather stay in America because the idea is to blend in, right?"

Abby and Nueve were sitting in front of us, near the cock-pit, and their heads were almost touching as they talked. I couldn't hear what they were saying, but the rise and fall of their voices indicated a fierce argument was going on.

"That's the idea," Ashley said.

"How far does it go? I mean, I'm guessing this is a kind of ramped-up version of the Witness Protection Program, and I know OIPEP has all kinds of supersecret, James Bond–type technologies . . . What I'm getting at is, do you erase my memories? I mean, can you, like, wipe my slate clean?"

"Nobody can take away your memories, Alfred. Not even OIPEP."

I thought about that. "That's too bad." I looked out the window again. We had climbed into some clouds and the earth was hidden from view. "That's too bad."

She reached under her seat and pulled out a laptop. As it booted up, she said, "A Level Alpha Extraction is all about permanence. An LAE is forever, Alfred. When you leave here, you won't be *you* anymore. You'll have a new name, a new past, even a new face. This procedure is sometimes called the 'Phoenix Protocol,' because the old you is burned away, metaphorically speaking, and a new you rises in its place. I hope you've got a good memory, because there's an awful lot you've got to memorize. We're going to literally make you into another person, and that means reprogramming you to recognize yourself as someone totally new and different."

"A new *face*?"

She nodded. "You wouldn't believe what our plastic surgeons can do."

"What if I like my face?"

"An LAE is an all-or-nothing protocol, Alfred. Giving you a new identity would be a waste of time without giving you a fresh appearance to go with it. We may also alter your height."

"My height?"

"You're much taller than average. It's a quality that makes you stick out, and the last thing you want as an extractee is to stick out. We may need to remove a vertebra or two."

"Oh my God!"

"Don't panic. That's still under discussion."

"You're going to carve up my face and rip out a chunk of my backbone, and you don't want me to *panic*?"

She clicked on an icon labeled "LAE_SUB_KROPP."

"Check this out," she said quickly. "It's pretty neat."

The program launched into a slide show of computer-generated photographs of someone who seemed vaguely familiar: full-on shots of his face, profile shots, fading into full-body pictures of an average-looking teenager, leaning toward the thin side, with short blond hair and blue eyes.

"Who is it?" I asked, though deep down I knew who it was: "SUB_KROPP."

"It's you—or one possibility of you."

"I have brown eyes."

"We have a technique to change eye color. I used to have brown eyes too."

I looked into her sparkling blue ones. "You were extracted?"

"Kind of. When I joined the Company . . . well, it was sort of what we're going to do with you, only in reverse. Everyone who joins the Field Ops division is extracted from their former interface."

She looked away. There was something she wasn't telling me.

"So that's why all you female OIPEPs look alike with the blond hair and blue eyes. Did they change your face too?"

"They changed everything," she said softly.

Tears welled in her eyes. I couldn't change that, so I decided to change the subject.

"There's some things I like about it," I said, meaning the picture. "Like the nose. Can I see the nose again? Yeah, I never was too happy with my nose. I'm not sure about the blond though. I know you'll have to get rid of the gray—hard to blend in as a sixteen-year-old with gray hair—but maybe just darken it. Not red. I'd look like a clown and I hate clowns. Though that dude from *CSI: Miami* is pretty cool.

Face looks kind of thin, though, like are you going to chisel my cheekbones or something? I guess you can't make me too good-looking—good-looking people stand out more than average-looking ones. Not that I turn many heads now, and I guess you wouldn't want to go too homely either."

"Oh, they'll give you input on that. Up to a point." The tears were gone, and that made me feel good.

"One thing I was wondering . . . I don't know really how to put it, but once I'm like totally extracted and inserted into this new life, would there be or is there ever a circumstance where I'd see anybody from the, um, don't know what to call it, the 'old' interface? For example, does the extraction coordinator do checkups or follow-ups or anything along those lines?"

She was smiling. "Are you asking if you'll ever see me again?"

I started to say something and then decided that would be a very bad idea, to even try to talk. So I just nodded.

Her smile went away. "Do you know what's happening back in Knoxville? They're cutting the headstone. Alfred Kropp is dead now, and the only place I can visit him is his grave."

CAMP ECHO

SOMEWHERE IN THE CANADIAN ROCKIES

04:23:36:47

We touched down at a private airstrip nestled in a narrow valley between the snow-crowned peaks of the Canadian Rockies. Ashley pulled two parkas from the overhead compartment and tossed one into my lap.

"Doesn't OIPEP have any bases in the Caribbean?" I asked her.

I pulled the hood of the parka over my head as we descended the stairs to the tarmac. About a hundred feet away sat a helicopter, engine throbbing, blades slowly turning. The only building I saw was a one-room log cabin, smoke rising and curling from the chimney before being ripped away by the frigid wind. Two men wearing helmets and OIPEP jumpsuits emerged from the building as we walked toward the helicopter, Nueve and Abby Smith in front, me and Ashley taking up the rear.

The two guys from the cabin conferred with Abby before we piled into the chopper. They sat up front, one riding shotgun beside the pilot. We took our seats behind them and, with no warning at all, the engine roared, we shot straight up and then banked sharply to the left, the face of a mountain coming straight at us. We cleared it with maybe ten feet to spare.

It was a cloudless day. For as far as I could see were row after row of mountains, the snow on their peaks glistening in the bright sunlight. I saw ravines and deep river gorges lost in mountain shadow and once, in the distance, a solitary bird soaring, its dark body sharply outlined against the white backdrop of snow.

Thirty minutes later we descended into a wide cleft between two ranges. I could see a lake below, maybe three and a half football fields' long and two wide, and a cluster of cabins the color of Lincoln Logs, connected by trails to a three-story château on the shores of the lake. The land behind the château was heavily wooded and dropped steeply toward a ravine.

Ashley touched my shoulder. "Company Base Echo!"

The chopper landed and we dove into the cold, hands on our heads to keep the hoods from flying off as we ran to the edge of the helipad. The two guys from the airstrip didn't get out. When we were clear, the helicopter took off and swooped out of the valley, disappearing behind the jagged peaks. Then it got very quiet, so quiet you could hear our breath as it condensed and boiled out of our mouths and noses.

We hiked up a trail toward the château. I don't know what it was, but suddenly I was very tired, the most tired I'd been in a long time, and I wasn't sure I could make it. The trail wound through a dense stand of pine trees, the ground hard and frozen and covered with a thin sheen of ice. I kept slipping. Once I just stopped and leaned against a tree, trying to catch my breath. It felt like my heart was traveling up my esophagus on its way to my mouth.

"We're almost there," Ashley assured me.

"The Caribbean," I gasped. "Or some remote island in the South Pacific. Where's *that* Company base?"

"Come on," she said, smiling. "Lean on me."

"I'll knock you over."

"I'm stronger than I look."

So that's how I made it up the last fifty feet of the trail, my left arm around Ashley's shoulders, until we reached the steps to the front porch and I could use the railing. Abby's fingers raced over the keypad by the front door, a green light flashed twice, and then we were inside, standing in a huge entryway, the ceiling soaring three stories over our heads. A fire roared on the opposite wall of the great room. A long table sat in front of the fireplace, its top crowded with steaming platters and bowls.

"Food," I said. "Thank God."

Abby, Ashley, and I sat down to eat, but Nueve said he had pressing business and disappeared up the staircase. Abby and Ashley exchanged a look, and then Abby dropped her napkin into her plate.

"Excuse me for a moment," she said quietly, and raced up the stairs after Nueve.

I turned to Ashley. "What's going on? I heard them fighting on the plane."

"They don't like each other," she said.

"Why?"

"I'm not sure, but the rumor is he wasn't her choice for the new Operative Nine."

"I read that section," I said. "It says the director gets to appoint the Op Nine."

"The board kind of forced Nueve on her."

"The board?"

She nodded. "It's a lot like a board of directors for a civilian company. The board chose Abby to be the new director after Merryweather was arrested."

"So what does she have against Nueve?"

"I don't think she trusts him."

We could hear their voices above us, rising and falling like waves smashing against a seawall, though I couldn't make out the words.

"I agree with Abby," I said. "There's something kind of slimy about Nueve."

"Oh, I don't think he's slimy," Ashley protested. "He just has a tough exterior."

"Right," I said. "Like an oyster. And inside: slime."

"It isn't easy being an Operative Nine," she said.

"It isn't easy being a lot of things."

After we finished eating, Ashley led me back outside. I felt stronger after my meal and didn't have to stop or lean on her on our way to one of the one-room cabins. A small plaque was mounted over the keypad by the door: 13

"Oh, good," I said. "Cabin thirteen."

"You're superstitious?" Ashley asked as she punched in the code.

"The number keeps cropping up."

" 'Cropping'? Is that some kind of pun?" She was smiling.

"In reference to a skull," I said.

"What skull?"

"That's what I'd like to know."

It was a cozy little cabin. There was a fireplace, a couple of rustic rocking chairs, a bed with a small writing table beside it, and a bathroom in the back. I opened a slatted door by the bathroom and saw thirteen identical OIPEP jumpsuits hanging there. There was that number again. I wondered if somebody cosmically connected was trying to tell me something.

"What now?" I asked Ashley.

"Try to rest. We're getting started first thing in the morning."

"No TV?"

She smiled. "The reception here isn't very good."

"There's always satellite," I said.

She left. I heard something go *snick* when the door closed. I tried the handle.

I was in lockdown.

04:04:25:31

That night I dreamed I was flying. Maybe it was the eagle I saw the day before, soaring high and alone over the mountains, but I was flying, arms outstretched, a thousand feet high, and below me I could see mountains and rivers, vast plains and open, empty desert. And cities, from sprawling metropolises to mud hut villages, until I soared past a rocky coastline and then I was over the open ocean, heading west toward the setting sun, cut in half by the horizon. I was alone, and for once it felt good to be alone, above a tranquil sea that had no boundary, the sparkling ribbon of reflected light from the dying sun the path that guided me.

I dove down like a seabird going in for the kill, my arms against my sides, and the wind drove my hair straight back away from my face. I wasn't afraid. I felt alone, but in this aloneness there was a sense of complete freedom.

I woke up kind of dissatisfied with the fact that eventually you have to wake up from dreams. Someone was knocking on the cabin door.

"Alfred," I heard Ashley call. "Alfred, it's time."

I washed up, pulled a fresh jumpsuit from its wooden hanger, slipped on my hiking boots and parka, and then followed Ashley up the trail to the main cabin.

Breakfast was already laid out, and we ate alone by the crackling fire.

"Where is everybody?" I asked. The place felt deserted and had an almost haunted-house feel to it. I thought it would be crawling with Company operatives, doctors and researchers and the support staff, like cooks and maids and maybe even a bodyguard or two. But the only people I had seen since arriving in Canada were the two guys from the airstrip, Abby, Ashley, and Nueve.

"They're in the conference room upstairs," Ashley said. I guessed she was talking about Nueve and Abby. "Meeting with the board."

"The board is here?"

"By video phone."

"Oh. Why are they meeting with the board?"

Before she could answer, a door slammed upstairs and Abby Smith came rushing down, Nueve hot on her heels.

"I don't care," Abby was saying. "It wasn't the bargain we made, Nueve."

"A bargain impossible to keep, Director," Nueve said. "As the board pointed out to you."

Abby whirled on him. "This is entirely your doing."

He had stopped three steps above her, and his back stiffened when she snapped at him.

"I am the Operative Nine. All Items of Special Interest fall under my jurisdiction."

"He's not an 'Item,' Nueve. He's a human being."

Ashley stood up. "What going on?" she called across the room.

They turned and stared at us. I don't think they knew we were there.

"Ah, Alfred," Abby Smith said with forced pleasantness. "How did you sleep, dear?"

"I had a great dream," I said. I looked at Nueve, then back at her. "And now I'm kinda sorry I woke up."

Nueve said to Abby, "Tell him."

She came over to me and put both hands on my shoulders. "Alfred, I'm afraid there's been a minor modification to the extraction protocol."

I shrugged her hands away. "Cut the Company double-talk and tell me what's going on. Are you going to extract me or not?"

"The short answer is yes," Nueve said from the stairs.

"I'll handle this," Abby snapped at him. She looked up at the ceiling. I looked up too, wondering what was the matter with the ceiling . . . and then I heard it, the low growl of heli-copters in the distance.

Nueve fairly bounded toward the front door.

"They're here," he said. He flung open the door and then flung himself outside, slamming the door shut behind him.

"Who's here?" I asked Abby.

She sighed. "My guess is Dr. Mingus."

"Mingus?" I asked.

"Mingus!" Ashley gasped.

"And a security detail," Abby added. "Nueve is quite thorough."

"Who's Dr. Mingus?" I asked Abby.

"The head of GD," Ashley answered when Abby hesi-tated. "Why is *he* here?" she asked her.

"I know what 'GD' usually stands for," I said. "But what does it stand for in OIPEP-speak?"

"Nueve ordered it," Abby said. Her face was very pale. "Before the conference call, obviously. He must have already known the board's decision." She gave my arm a quick squeeze. "He's here to conduct the standard preextraction evaluation, Alfred. It's part of the protocol and perfectly SOP."

Ashley choked out a laugh. "SOP—right!" She turned to me. "Alfred, 'GD' stands for Genetic Development."

04:03:43:05

Abby led us to a conference room on the second floor. We sat at a long table, Ashley right beside me and Abby Smith across the table with a laptop in front of her. She pressed a button and a screen slowly lowered from the ceiling. She tapped another button and the lights in the room dimmed.

"What's going on?" Ashley demanded. "Alfred has a right to know."

"A minor shift in the extraction protocol." Abby hit a key on the laptop and a picture faded in on the big screen. It was an aerial shot of a tropical island on a sunny day. Palm trees, waves breaking on a sparkling white beach, a few buildings with whitewashed walls and straw roofs. It looked like something from a travel-agency poster.

"What is that?" I asked.

"That is Camp Omega-I, an uncharted island in the South Pacific," Abby answered. "And our most secure base, other than headquarters. Besides the personnel permanently assigned to COI, only myself and the Operative Nine—and now, Ashley, of course—are even aware of its existence."

"Well," I said. "It's not the Caribbean, but it's more like it."

Beside me, Ashley breathed, "Oh, no."

"Why 'Oh, no?' " I asked. When Ashley didn't answer, I said to Abby, "I don't get it. What's this COI have to do with me?"

Abby refused to look at me. She was staring at the picture of the island. "It's your new home, Alfred."

She hit a button, and the picture changed to a closer shot. I saw a cabana and some clothes drying on a line. The water was emerald blue. *Paradise,* I thought. And for some reason a shiver went down my spine.

"It looks pretty nice," I said slowly.

"Alfred, you don't understand," Ashley said. "They're not going to give you a new identity. There isn't going to be a reinsertion into the civilian interface. They're going to drop you there and keep you there. *Forever.*"

"For now," Abby said.

"I still don't get it," I said. "Why are you dropping me on an unchartered island?"

Abby said, "I was informed of the modification just this morning, Alfred. The board's decision is final, I'm afraid. It believes that, given the peculiar circumstances involved here, a standard extraction is out of the question."

"How come?"

Abby glanced at Ashley. I went on. "And if you say 'that's classified,' I'm coming over this table at you."

"Because of his blood, isn't it?" Ashley asked. "Because of what it can do."

A voice spoke up behind me. "We cannot risk losing the carrier of the most important active agent in Company possession."

Nueve. He was standing just inside the door, leaning on his black cane. Smiling. Eyes glittering. For some reason I thought of pirates.

"In short, you are simply too important, Alfred," he said, patting my shoulder as he walked around the table to slide in next to Abby. "A vital concern for people your age, as I understand. More vital than small pores. Even if the Phoenix Protocol succeeds, there is still a chance, however small, that something, oh, shall we say *irreversible,* could happen to you."

"If you're worried about Jourdain and his boys, you could just kill him," I said. "Extract him extremely or whatever you call it."

"It is not merely that," Nueve said with a shrug. "Of course, we could execute an extreme extraction order upon Monsieur Garmot, but that doesn't preclude the possibility of your demise by other, more mundane, means. An accident, for example. Jaywalking across a busy street and *squish!* no more Alfred Kropp. We cannot risk that."

Abby had hit another button and a slide show began to run of Camp Omega-I. Pleasant walkways that weaved among the tropical foliage. An Olympic-size swimming pool at the base of a hundred-foot waterfall. Tennis courts. A movie theater. A shining glass structure that sat high on a promontory overlooking the empty sea—my new house? Club OIPEP.

"Isn't it beautiful?" Nueve asked with no hint of irony. "All the amenities. The finest chefs. A staff that would be the envy of the world's greatest vacation resorts, if the world knew of it. There's even a masseuse!"

"Omega," I said. "Isn't that like the last letter of the Greek alphabet?"

Nueve nodded. "Not just like it, Alfred. It *is* the last letter of the Greek alphabet."

"End of the road," I said.

"You'll be safe there," Abby said. She started to say something else, and then stopped herself. "It's not what either of us wanted, but sometimes necessity trumps desire, Alfred. You of all people surely can understand that."

"What if we just go ahead with the original plan and I promise to be very careful—like never jaywalking and always riding the bus?"

Abby shook her head. "I'm sorry, Alfred. I tried. I fought to keep the original protocol but"—she glared in Nueve's direction—"I was overruled."

"And what Ashley said . . . about *forever*. I can't leave?"

Abby said, "We—*I*—may be able to arrange brief trips back . . ."

Nueve stifled a laugh.

"It's a prison," I said. "Maybe it doesn't have the bars and the cot and toilet in the corner, but it's still a prison. You're flying me to that island and dumping me there, and that's where I'm going to stay for the rest of my life."

A hand touched mine under the table. Ashley's. She slipped her fingers through mine and squeezed hard, and I felt tears come up in my eyes, like she was pumping them to the surface.

"Nothing is definite," Abby said.

"Everything is definite," Nueve said.

Abby ignored him. "I'm leaving tonight to make a personal appeal to the board."

"And what if the board still says no?" I asked.

"It will," Nueve said.

"How do you know?" I asked.

"He doesn't," Abby said. She looked at Nueve, who was smirking at her.

"I know all that needs to be known," he said. He lost all his smirkiness and leaned toward me, black eyes shining.

"Do you really think my interest in you terminated with obtaining the Seal, Alfred Kropp? Are you so naive or foolish that you can't see where the true value of extracting you lies? In your veins flows a power not seen in our world for over two thousand years. Why that power would be given to you, of all people, is for greater minds than mine to ponder. Nevertheless, because that power exists, we have an obligation to protect it and see that this Item of Interest more important than Solomon's trinket does not fall into the wrong hands or become lost through carelessness and neglect.

"*That* is the purpose of our Office. *That* is the reason we exist. *That* is the mission, and I am the Operative Nine. I *am* the mission, and the mission *will* be accomplished."

He shouted over my shoulder, "You may come in now!"

The door opened and a guy built like a tree trunk came into the room. He had a wide square head and a body to match. His eyes were narrow and his lips thin; you really had to look hard to see them. He gave a short, militarylike bow in Abby's general direction.

"Alfred," Nueve said. "May I introduce Dr. Mingus. He'll be examining you today."

03:17:15:23

After my examination by Dr. Mingus, a couple of guys from the security detail took me back to my cabin. They *had* to take me back, because I wasn't able to move under my own power. I noticed other dark suits outside the main house and along the trails, even a couple slipping in and out of the trees. All of them wore black and all wore the same dark Ray-Bans. The OIPEP Mafia.

It was around five o'clock and nearly dark. They dumped me on the bed and the lock went *snick*. I listened to the absolute silence—if you can listen to absolute silence.

Dr. Mingus had a funny accent, thick and slushy. Tiny beads of spit hung on his sliver-thin lower lip as he talked.

This will go easily enough, if you cooperate. We'll take some measurements, run a few nonintrusive tests, sample a bit of your blood . . .

Beneath the château, behind a sealed metal door, at the bottom of a flight of stairs was a medical complex. Operating rooms. Examination rooms. A room with a gleaming white CT scan machine. And other rooms I didn't get to look in, though I may have been inside them, because Dr. Mingus gave me a shot that put me under, I'm not sure for how long, but it seemed like a very long time. I don't know what he did to me while I was out. I just know when I came to he was just beaming, like a little kid who had found a special surprise under the Christmas tree, and I was feeling like a scooped-out pumpkin from a different, darker holiday.

In cabin thirteen, I buried my face in the pillow.

I am a genetic engineer, Alfred. Do you know what a genetic engineer does?

Needles extending from syringes the size of my wrist. Vials of dark, arterial blood—my blood—rows of them, each with a different colored label: *Spec Ops . . . GDT . . . Sofa . . .* That last one confused me, but it was about the tenth he drained out of me and my vision was pretty blurry by that point. Sofa? What the heck was Sofa?

This is very exciting. The most significant development in the field in my lifetime. In anyone's lifetime, Alfred! You are at the center of the most astounding breakthrough since Watson and Crick cracked the code!

Dr. Mingus injected me with something that made me feel very good, sleepy, and floaty. His wide face swam in and out of focus as he leaned over me. I was tied to a gurney and they were wheeling me toward the room with the big scanner.

This will not hurt, Alfred, but you must remain very still while we image your brain. Have you ever had a CT scan before? It's not painful.

As I lay inside the scanner I think I heard Nueve's voice and the name "Sofia," but I told myself I was dreaming or hallucinating, but it reminded me of Samuel. He was my guardian and he had sworn to protect me. Where was he? And who was going to protect me now?

After the scan, I looked up into Dr. Mingus's face and whispered, *Am I done?*

For today. Tomorrow we have a few more tests. I'm going to need some tissue samples. Tell me, Alfred, have you ever had an operation?

They were going to put me under, open me up, and take samples of all my major organs. Dr. Mingus was particularly interested in my heart . . . He was going to slice out a piece of my heart.

You are blessed, Alfred Kropp. Do you believe that?

As he slid a needle into my groin.

A gift to all mankind . . .

As he shined a blinding light into my eyes.

The power of life, yes?

Like some horrible Halloween mask, his face. Wide and flat and blank. He barely had any eyebrows and his eyes were black, death-dark eyes, like a shark's. The only expression I saw in them the whole time reminded me of a kid I knew in Ohio who enjoyed burning ants with a magnifying glass. The truly scary thing is there's a lot of Dr. Minguses running around in the world, but I had the Dr. Mingus-iest of them all. He didn't just like his work and he more than loved it. Like Nueve, he *was* his work.

The power of God himself . . .

The pillow on my bed smelled of lavender. Spit ran out my open mouth and I breathed that in, the smell of spit, the smell of lavender.

They brought me into the last room, the worst room, where a dentist's chair was anchored to the floor. The two goons dragged me across the tile floor and my toe scraped across the metal drain cover in the middle of the room. They threw me into the chair and tightened straps across my arms and over my ankles. Dr. Mingus swung the chair around and brought his face very close to mine. His breath smelled very sweet, as sweet as cotton candy, and my stomach rolled.

One last test for the day, Alfred, more for my own benefit than science's, for I am curious and I will confess a little skeptical. Like a Missourian, I wish to see it with my own eyes.

He stepped away and I saw Ashley standing between the two stone-faced goons. They were holding her arms out from her sides. I was still pretty dopey from the shot, and at first I thought I was hallucinating. What I was seeing couldn't be what I was *seeing*.

Dr. Mingus stepped between me and Ashley, but I could see her face over his shoulder—she was at least a head taller than him—and I could also see what he held in his right hand.

A scalpel.

I jerked in the chair. The straps yanked me back. Mingus's shoulder hunched and pivoted forward as he shoved the scalpel into the middle of Ashley's chest.

Then he pushed the blade straight down toward her belly button. Her knees buckled, but the two guys kept her on her feet.

Mingus stepped away. Ashley's chin dropped to her chest. A swirl of blond hair and the *drip-drip-drip* of her blood splattering on the cold tile, forming rivulets that ran toward the metal drain, and I remember thinking, *Oh, that's why there's a drain in the floor.*

Mingus turned to me.

Show me the gift.

Candy-breath, whispering.

Show me the power of God!

He cut a four-inch-long groove into my palm, threw off

the straps, and flung me out of the chair. The men holding Ashley stepped away, and she crumpled to the floor as if in slow motion, coming to rest on her side, curled up like I was curled up now on my little bed in my little cabin, breathing in lavender and the smell of my own spit.

I crawled to her.

Her eyes were open, but I saw no spark of life in them.

Then a voice I had heard before whispered inside my head, *Beloved!*

My vision clouded. I was seeing her through a white film, a mist of shadow and light.

My beloved . . .

Something familiar and warm had come to me—or was it always there? I had felt it first in Merlin's Cave, a being at once intimate and alien, so familiar but at the same time so terrifyingly *different*. The Sword of Kings, the gift passed down by heaven's hands, was *in* this world but not *of* this world, my father had told me, and so was this presence around me now, between me and Ashley, joining me to Ashley.

Lying beside her, I pressed my bleeding hand into the gaping wound in her chest, and with my other hand I smoothed the blond hair away from her face.

In the name of Saint Michael . . .

I couldn't feel the floor beneath me. I was floating in the white cloud. I was still in that room but also in a different place, a place where Mingus and the OIPEP Mafia couldn't go. A still place that didn't touch any other place on earth. A place with no center.

Prince of Light, hear my prayer.

Her eyelids fluttered, black butterflies, and her hands gripped my wrist. Our blood mixed. I could feel the beat of her heart.

She was going to live.

03:04:27:51

I dreamed I was sitting on a hilltop with an old man. We leaned against an ancient oak tree, watching workmen on the promontory below stack great white stones, one on top of the other, and when one stone slid into place more workmen filled the cracks with mortar.

I asked the old man what they were building.

"Camelot," he answered.

The castle was rising three hundred feet above an inlet filled with jagged rocks and razor-sharp outcroppings of stone. I could hear the crash of surf and, just beneath it, a high-pitched wail, like a swift current hidden beneath calm water.

"I've been here before," I told the old man.

He nodded. "So have I."

"Who's that crying?" I asked.

He smiled at me. "It is I."

Then he reached up and unzipped his face. The flaps of skin fell away. He pulled out his skull, white at first, like the stones of the castle beneath us; then it turned clear as glass. Only the eye sockets remained dark, filled with a shadow that no light could chase away.

"Touch."

I woke up soaked in sweat, still lying on top of the covers in my jumpsuit, my wounded hand throbbing beneath its bandage. Someone was in the room with me. I saw his hiking boots and, resting between them, the end of his black cane.

"Ashley," I whispered.

"Far from it," Nueve said.

"I know you're not Ashley, you jerk. Is Ashley alive?"

"Why wouldn't she be? She's been touched by an angel."

I lunged toward him. His cane swooshed through the air and I felt the tip of the knife poking into the soft flesh beneath my chin.

"Inadvisable, Alfred."

"You won't kill me. I'm a Special Item now."

"Dr. Mingus believes he may have more than enough material to accomplish our goal. Like most scientists, he possesses an optimism bordering on arrogance. One might say, however, that that is precisely what arrogance is: optimism taken to its extreme. What? You'd rather not discuss philosophy?"

"You tricked me."

"You asked to be extracted from the civilian interface and Camp Echo could not be farther from it."

"You know what I mean. You were never going to give me a new identity."

"My mission was twofold: the immediate concern of obtaining the Great Seal and the long-range one of protecting a Special Item of vital importance to international security."

"My blood."

He smiled. "You know what I am, Alfred."

"That's right. You're a jerk."

"I am the Superseding Protocol Agent."

I knew what he meant. What I wanted didn't matter. Even what his boss Abby Smith wanted didn't matter. Only the mission mattered. I wondered how that worked. Normally a boss can tell you what to do or not do, but a SPA didn't have to follow those rules. And if that was true, then what rules *did* he have to follow? I thought I knew the answer, and that made my heart speed up.

"Where is Abby?" I asked.

"As I told you in Knoxville, you should avoid asking questions to which you already know the answers. It creates the false impression of stupidity. Director Smith has returned to headquarters to plead your case personally before the board. The director suffers from a certain sentimentality coupled with a startling naïveté about the dynamics of our organization. The true power of OIPEP, Alfred, does not lie with the director. It lies with the board, and he who controls the board, controls the Company."

"What about Ashley?"

"What about her?"

"She's my extraction coordinator. You're not going to extract me now, so what's going to happen to her?"

"That, Alfred, you will never know."

I looked at him. He looked back. He had no expression except one of mild curiosity.

"You have had thoughts of escape," he whispered. "You may put away such fantasies. You will never leave Camp Echo."

It took a second for that to sink in. Even after my "examination" by Dr. Mingus the day before, I figured at some point they would take me to the island in Abby Smith's PowerPoint presentation. I assumed at some point they would be finished with me. My heart rate kicked up another notch.

"You're not dumping me on OIPEP Island?"

"You've taken your last dump. Tomorrow morning Dr. Mingus will perform one final procedure: a frontal lobotomy. Do you know what a lobotomy is?"

"I think it's where they cut off part of your brain."

"Precisely. The thinking part. The human part."

"You're gonna make me a vegetable."

"It's quite painless."

"Really? Is that how yours went?"

He smiled. He picked up a small black box sitting on the little table beside the bed. "Do you recall the good ship *Pandora*?"

"Yes." The *Pandora* was an OIPEP jetfoil where I had first met Samuel and Ashley, the boat that had taken us to Egypt after Mike Arnold stole the Seals of Solomon.

"It was on that ship that your dear friend, your surrogate father, Samuel St. John, the former Operative Nine, first extracted your wondrous hemoglobin—without your knowledge or consent, I might add."

"Right, to stick in the bullets to fight the demons. I already know that."

"Yes, but there is something you do not know. While you were under anesthetic, before you awoke in your cabin aboard that most excellent vessel, he also ordered the insertion of Special Device 1031."

He waited for me to ask what a Special Device 1031 was. I didn't.

"How does your head feel right now, Alfred? Does it

hurt? Have you been suffering from headaches since you returned to Knoxville?"

He didn't wait for me to answer. The black metal box turned over and over between his hands. I saw two buttons, one blue, one red, and some kind of numeric keypad beneath them.

"Do you remember, after we rescued you from the clutches of Jourdain Garmot, asking me how we found you, since he had assured you Vosch had not been followed?"

This time he did wait for an answer. The silence drew out. I couldn't tear my eyes away from the little black box.

"You put something inside my head."

"Not I. Samuel St. John did. Aboard the *Pandora*. I believe we covered this. Special Device 1031 is no bigger than the eraser of a pencil, Alfred. It has been implanted near the corpus callosum, the structure that connects the two hemispheres of your brain."

"It's a tracking device?"

"That's one of its functions, yes. It has another. Inside Special Device 1031 is a tiny pellet, no bigger than the lead of our metaphorical pencil."

He scooted forward in his chair and held the black box about a foot from my nose.

"The blue button arms the pellet. The red button begins the detonation sequence. Thirty seconds."

"And the keypad?"

"A failsafe. If the correct code is entered before the thirty seconds expire, your headache is nothing that two hundred milligrams of ibuprofen can't handle. If not . . ." Now whispering: "*Boom.*"

I watched as the pad of his index finger mashed down on the blue button. The red one lit up.

"You will cooperate, Alfred." His finger now hovered over the red button. The red light lit up the grooves of his fingerprint. "And abandon any foolish notion of escape."

He pressed the button. The number 30 popped up in the display window right above the keypad. It seemed to switch to 29—then 28—then 27—faster than a normal second lasted.

"It may seem cruel—even diabolical—but it's really quite humane. Your head will not literally explode, like you're imagining right now. It really takes very little explosive to kill a human being. The only outward sign usually noted is a distinct reddening of the eyes, as blood pours into the ocular cavities."

15 . . . 14 . . . 13 . . .

"The code," I whispered. "Punch in the code, Nueve. I know you won't do it."

He went on like he didn't hear me. "Although some test subjects did bleed profusely through the ears and nose . . ."

8 . . . 7 . . . 6 . . .

I lunged for the box—like that would do any good. He scooted back into the chair and his fingers flew over the keys. I couldn't see what numbers he punched, but the red light went out.

I fell back gasping. My imagination was working overtime; I thought I could really feel it in the middle of my brain, the tiny explosive pellet, red hot and pulsing.

I closed my eyes and tried to catch my breath. His voice had no playfulness when he spoke again. It was as hard and sharp as one of Dr. Mingus's diamond-bladed scalpels.

"There is no place on earth you can hide. Run from us, and we'll find you. Try to have it removed, you'll die. Defy us, and we'll literally blow your brains out. No heavenly being holds your fate in the palm of his hand, Alfred Kropp.

I do. I am your guardian now and, like the angels themselves, I am above the laws of men. Beyond remorse, beyond pity, beyond judgment, beyond all moral consideration. From this moment forward, if you wish to pray to anyone, I suggest you pray to me."

03:04:01:20

I lay on the bed for a few minutes after he left. I knew I wouldn't be alone for long.

It was probably a good idea bordering on a great one, while I still had a little privacy, to figure a way out of Camp Echo.

I gave myself a little pep talk.

"Okay, okay, the main thing is *don't panic*. This isn't so bad. You've been in worse situations. Fighting against a sword that can't be beaten. Battling sixteen million unkillable demons in the middle of the desert. Falling from thirty thousand feet without even a freakin' parachute. This is nothing. This is cake. Held hostage by ruthless secret agents. Separated from civilization by hundreds of miles of hostile, unfamiliar terrain. A tracking device implanted in your skull. And a bomb that literally blows your brains out with a touch of a button . . . Is that it? Is that the best they got?"

I sat on the edge for a minute or two, holding my head in

my hands, rocking back and forth, as if to restore equilibrium to my flip-flopping thoughts.

"What is the mission? What must be done? That's what Samuel would say. What's the thing-that-must-be-done? Samuel, where are you? You're going after the wrong guys. Jourdain just wanted to burn down my house, take all my money, and kill me—these Company guys *really* want to mess with me.

"Forget about him; forget about Samuel. Samuel isn't here. Abby isn't here. Ashley's here. What are they going to do to Ashley? Kill her. But why would they kill her? Because she knows. She knows the plan and she'll rat them out to Abby. But Ashley's not dead yet. If she was, Nueve would have told me. He'd *enjoy* telling me.

"So Ashley's alive. I can't escape without Ashley. But I can't escape anyway. He'll just track me down. Well, I'll have take that chance . . . Maybe if I get a head start on them . . . The transmitter is tiny, the size of an eraser; its range can't be that great. With a good head start maybe . . . maybe . . .

"So I've got to get Ashley. Then we've got to get out of this valley. Then we've got to get out of Canada. Then we've got to get . . ."

Where?

Where in the whole world could I hide from them? Where would be safe?

"I've got to find Sam. He put the thing in my head; he'll know how to get it out."

I pushed myself off the bed and swayed, holding my arms out from my sides like a tightrope walker for balance. Dr. Mingus must have drained half my blood the day before. What did OIPEP plan to do with my blood? They had taken it before to fight the demons, but they had the Seal now—why would they need my blood to fight demons they could control with Solomon's ring?

"Something else," I muttered, closing my eyes, but that made the dizziness worse, so I opened them again. "Not demons. Something really evil. Mingus is a genetic engineer. . . . Cloning! They're cloning Kropp to make a . . . make a what? A clone army? Army of the Kropp clones? Man, that's *sick*."

Sick . . . and senseless. The power of my blood didn't make me invincible. It wasn't like holy armor or anything.

Thinking of armor reminded me of the Knights of the Sacred Order. I never saw one of them in armor, but I did see a suit of it in a closet once, at a little Hansel and Gretel type house in Pennsylvania, where the mother of one of the knights lived. I wasted a few seconds trying to remember her name. I could see her face in my mind's eye, and the house set back in the woods. The house was close to a state park whose name I also couldn't remember near a little town not far from Harrisburg . . .

He flew into Harrisburg two nights ago, where he rented a car and drove to a tiny hamlet called Suedberg.

Jourdain Garmot went to Suedberg, where the knight named Windimar had lived. Why? What was he looking for?

The last knightly quest . . . for the Thirteenth Skull.

So the Skull must have been connected somehow to the Knights of the Sacred Order. Maybe it was something they kept hidden, like the Sword. Maybe destroying my father's house wasn't about revenge . . . maybe Jourdain was there looking for the Skull and then set the house on fire to destroy the evidence.

I was losing focus. Jourdain Garmot and the Thirteenth Skull didn't matter now. Medcon had planted the story of my death before I even came to Camp Echo, so Jourdain Garmot thought I was dead.

Maybe if I started moving something would come to me. The plan. The-thing-that-must-be-done. Take a step. Then the next step. Don't think about the 779th step. Just the first one.

I stumbled into the bathroom. That was like fifteen steps already.

Time for an inventory. Shower curtain and those little rings holding it to the rod. The rod? I gave it a shake. Aluminum, too flimsy. A bar of soap. A travel-sized plastic bottle of dandruff shampoo. Why had they given me dandruff shampoo? Was I flaky? I turned to the mirror and was shocked by my reflection. My face was no longer the familiar oval shape I'd had since childhood. I had lost nearly forty pounds since I stole Excalibur from beneath my father's desk. My face was thin and angular, which made my eyes seem very large on either side of my nose, now slightly crooked after being broken by Delivery Dude. I was so shocked by my appearance I forgot to hunt for dandruff. I looked like a vampire—only I was the opposite of a vampire: vampires drink other people's blood to give themselves life; I gave my blood to others to give *them* life.

I opened the medicine cabinet. No razors or other sharp objects, not even a pair of tweezers. A toothbrush, but it was plastic and the end was blunt—I'd have to sharpen it somehow and, even if I had a way to do it, I didn't have the time.

I decided to brush my teeth. God knew when I'd have another opportunity and, besides, brushing your teeth is one of those normal, mundane things that really center you.

A glob of toothpaste fell from my mouth onto the bandage around my hand and I rinsed it off without thinking.

I grabbed a towel and dabbed off the extra water, but the bandage still felt moist. I could feel my heartbeat in the palm.

Maybe I should take it off and wash the wound with some soap. The last thing I needed was an infection.

I'd unwrapped about half of it—Mingus had really wound me up with a lot—when I got an idea. It was a tiny germ of an idea, so I stood there at the sink, not moving, until the idea grew a little, then a little more, until it was not so little and germy anymore.

Grabbing the shampoo from the stall, I unscrewed the cap, emptied the contents into the sink, and then I rinsed it out a couple of times. I sidestepped to the toilet, but couldn't make myself go. That's what pressure does to you, like when you're at a ballpark or movie theater, trying to go while five guys stand in line behind you, waiting for you to *finish already*!

Water. Lots of water and hopefully enough time for it to work through my system. I ducked my head under the tap and drank until I lost count of the swallows. I wondered why I was bothering to count them. I left the empty shampoo bottle on the back of the toilet and went to the closet in the main room. I dressed in a fresh jumpsuit, and then took the empty wooden hanger and snapped it in two across my knee. I tossed the piece with the hook onto the closet floor, sat on the bed, and pulled the rest of the gauze from my hand. How much time until they came for me? Ten minutes? Five? Two? And how much wrap? Too short and I wouldn't be able to position it. Too long and I wouldn't be able to tighten it.

I tore off an arm's length of the gauze, using my teeth to get the tear started, twirled it until it was firm and ropelike, then tied the two ends together to make a loop. I dropped the loop over my head. Might be a little too big, but there was no time to mess with it. I pried the knot open just enough to slip the broken piece of wood through. After I tightened the knot around the wood, I yanked on the loop to test it.

I went back to the bathroom and grabbed the empty shampoo bottle. An imaginary clock ticked loudly inside my head as I tried to force myself to go. The shampoo bottle had a very small opening, maybe the size of a quarter, and I couldn't let loose full stream, but thank God my aim was true. I screwed the cap back on. It was one of those flip top numbers: you pressed down on one edge, exposing the little rectangular hole for the liquid to pass through. It wouldn't have the power or distribution of an aerosol and I'd have just one shot at it. Samuel had told me once that if something was necessary, it was possible. He'd better be right.

I heard the stomp of boots on the steps outside.

Time's up, Kropp. Step-by-step now. Step-by-step.

I ducked into the main room, grabbed my socks from the closet shelf, and plopped on the bed.

The electronic *tings* answered fingers punching keys on the pad by the door.

Step: Pull on right sock.

Step: Stuff bottle into sock.

The *pop!* of the lock snapping open.

Step: Left sock.

Doorknob turning.

Step: Jam hanger and rope into left sock.

The door flew open. A blast of freezing air rushed in.

I had jumped from the bed and was shaking my left leg to make the pants fall over the big bulge in my sock when the two goons from the day before—in my mind, I called them Thing 1 and Thing 2—filled the doorway.

"Up already?" Thing 1 rumbled.

"My first lobotomy," I said. "I'm pretty excited."

03:03:26:31

I stepped into a postcard-perfect landscape of snow-covered mountains and bright blue sky reflected in the glass-flat surface of the lake. The thin air cut into my lungs and halfway up the trail to the main cabin I was huffing like a marathon runner on the twenty-fifth mile.

Ten minutes later we were inside the château. There was the ubiquitous fire roaring. There was all the eerie silence and pooling shadows of a haunted house. Past the kitchen, where I mentioned breakfast and where Thing 2 reminded me it wasn't wise to eat before going under general anesthesia. Down a long, narrow hallway, where I stumbled once and Thing 1 caught me. Through the metal door and down the steps into the medical facility, where I looked down and saw the loop sticking out beside my boot. I was busted if they noticed. They didn't notice. "Dead man walking!" Thing 2 called, and Thing 1 laughed.

They shoved me into an empty examination room and

slammed the door. I heard the locking mechanism thump home.

A couple minutes later, the lock went *beep-beep* and Dr. Mingus came into the room. Thing 1 and Thing 2 took positions on either side of the door.

"There's something I have to tell you," I blurted out. I was sitting on the examination table with my hands behind my back.

He glanced at the Things, then turned back to me.

"About my blood powers," I went on. "Something even OIPEP doesn't know. Nobody knew about it except the knights, and they're all dead. You should know about it before you cut me open."

"Yes? I'm waiting."

"Not in front of them," I said, jerking my head toward the door.

His small eyes got even smaller.

"It's something you're really gonna want to know," I said.

He waved the Things outside. The door locked behind them. We were alone.

"There's a risk of explosion," I said.

"Explosion?"

"Exposing too much of my blood to the air can make it like—um, I don't know the scientific term for it—expand rapidly maybe . . . ?"

"The scientific term is *explode*."

I nodded. "Right. Like a bomb."

He laughed. He didn't have a nice laugh. It wasn't the scary-villain type *har-har-har*, guttural and harsh; more like the *hee-hee-hee* giggle of the mad-scientist-cackle variety. I know that's a stereotype, but there's a reason we have stereotypes.

"So how are we feeling this morning? Yesterday was a bit trying, yes?"

"I slept okay, except I had this weird dream about an old man pulling his own skull from his head and then I found out about Special Device 1031. I guess you wouldn't consider yanking that puppy out while you're in there."

"I won't."

"Too bad. Can we talk about the frontal lobotomy?"

"You don't like the idea?"

"I'd rather have a bottle in front of me."

Nothing. Not even one *hee*.

"That's an old joke," I said.

"I don't get it."

You will.

"How's the hand?" he asked.

"Hurts like heck."

He stepped between my dangling legs.

Step: Pop open the shampoo lid.

"Let's have a look."

"Okay, but I'm warning you, there's something nasty in it."

"I'm a doctor, Alfred. I'm used to nasty."

"You asked for it," I said. I brought the bottle around fast and blasted both his beady little eyes. Instinctively, he brought his hands to his face. He took a couple of stumbling steps backward. I jumped from the table, spun him around, pinned his arms to his sides, dropped the loop over his head, drove my knee into his lower back, and forced him to the floor. I lay spread-eagled on top of his squirming body and spun the wooden handle of my homemade garrote, each turn tightening the noose around his thick neck, until his cries for help were reduced to choking, barely audible sobs.

It happened very fast, no more than fifteen seconds from the time I squirted him with my pee to me whispering into his beet-red ear, "I've got a couple of questions. Here's the first: *do you want to live?*"

He managed to nod, the muscles of his clammy neck rolling beneath my knuckles.

"Good. Here's the next: where is she?"

"You'll never—*ack!*—you won't get past the guards—"

I twisted the broken hanger a half turn.

"Down the hall! Right, right, left, right, first door on left, bottom of stairs—room 202!"

"Okay. Right, left, right—"

"No! Right, *right,* left—"

"Right, left?"

"Right."

"Right, left, right . . . right?"

"No, no. Two rights—wrong! It's right, right, left, right!"

"The last right means you turn right, not 'you're correct' right, right?"

"Right, right! Right correct-right!"

I slid off him and pulled back on the garrote.

"On your feet," I said. "Slow. Good. Now walk slowly to the door."

"They're armed; you won't get past them," he gurgled as we shuffled toward the door.

"I'm not going past them," I said. "They're going past me."

03:03:02:16

So here's the setup: You're standing in the hallway outside the locked door of the examination room, just kickin' back with your partner, your OIPEP killer bro, and maybe you're talking about the kids or where you're going on the next vacation or the latest episode of *Law & Order* or maybe trashing *MI:3* (like you believe Tom Cruise could be a secret agent or any of that crap in the movie could happen, like Hollywood knows how it *really* works), and you hear the keypad on the wall go *beep-beep* and the gears of the locking mechanism rotate on their well-oiled axis. You step back, waiting for the boss to come out with the lobotomy patient, the tall kid with the gray-streaked hair and weird gray-flecked eyes, only the door doesn't open. The doc unlocked the door but didn't come out. How come?

You glance at your partner, who looks back at you like *Hey, don't look at me,* and you hang there for another couple of seconds, hand resting on the butt of your Glock 9mm, chewing on your bottom lip, trying to decide while you wait for the moment to make a decision for you. A minute. Two. Two and a half. Did Kropp jump him? you wonder. Did he change his mind about coming out for some reason? Why unlock the door if you're not coming out?

You nod to your partner. *We go.* He turns the knob. Pushes open the door.

A blur of white flying toward the far wall. It's Mingus, sitting on the rolling stool, sliding across the smooth floor, his white lab coat flapping as he spins.

And no sign of the kid.

You rush in, guns drawn, and what registers in your head when Mingus screams, "Behind the door, you idiots! He's *behind the door!*"?

You freeze halfway in, but it's already too late. The door slams and there's no kid. He's on the other side.

The side with the master control panel.

I smashed one end of the broken hanger into the keypad. On the other side of the door, I could hear them, shouting and cursing, banging on it as if to get me to answer the door. "Shoot the lock! Shoot the lock!" one of the Things was yelling.

I ran down the hall, reviewing the directions. "Right, right, left, right . . . R, R, L, R. Reggie, Reggie, listen, Reggie. Really, really, lame, really!"

A guard was stationed by room 202, his black jumper shimmering under the fluorescents. I hadn't planned for a guard and there was no time now to develop a plan, so I just went on instinct and my experience in dealing with seemingly hopeless situations: I rushed him.

He managed to free his weapon from the holster before I barreled into him, but there was no time to get off a shot. I grabbed the wrist of his gun hand and slammed my fist into his solar plexus, knocking the wind out of him. Then I spun him around, pushed his face against the wall, and twisted his arm behind his back, lifting it toward his shoulder blades until his fingers loosened and the gun fell to the floor.

I picked it up.

"The code," I said.

"Screw you," he gasped.

I let go and stood back, keeping the gun pointed at his head. He turned around and leaned against the wall, hands on his knees, trying to catch his breath.

"I'll shoot you," I said.

"Yeah, right."

I shot him in the foot.

He dropped. I stepped over him to the keypad by room 202.

"The code," I repeated. "Or I take out the knee."

Ashley was hiding behind the door. She came at me as I burst into the room, holding a metal stool that I guessed she intended to smash over my head. She froze when she recognized me.

"Alfred?"

"You bet," I said.

The stool fell to the floor and then the girl into my arms, burying her face between my shoulder and the base of my neck. A world of blond under my nose and its sweet atmosphere of lilacs. She touched my cheek.

"Are you okay?" I asked.

She nodded. Just outside the door I saw the legs of the guard as he started to crawl toward the stairs.

"Hold on," I said. I went into the hall, yanked him to his feet, and pressed the muzzle of the gun behind his ear.

"We're leaving," I told him. "You're our guide."

"I don't think I can walk," he said.

I squatted, pushed my left shoulder into his gut, and stood up. His head smacked me in the back when I swung around to motion Ashley out of the room.

We trotted down the hall, away from the stairs that led back to Mingus and the OIPEP twins, Ashley on my right side, her guard flopping over my left shoulder.

"Tell me there's a back door to this place," I said to him—or rather to his butt, which was two inches from my nose.

"There's a back door to this place."

I grabbed his dangling legs with both hands and swiveled hard. His head hit the wall with a satisfying smack.

"Hey!" he said, like he was shocked I whacked his face against the wall.

I did it again. *Whack!*

"Stop that!"

I started walking again. The hall ended. One corridor branched off to the right, another to the left.

"Which way?" I asked him.

"The right way."

I smacked him again—*whack!*—and he shouted, "No, the right *hallway*—literal right, literal right!"

We took the passage on our right. Ashley had said she was okay, but she was wincing with every step and breathing hard. My head hurt. Was my head pounding now from all the running and fighting—or was it broadcasting our position on the Kropp Channel?

"I've got a bomb in my head," I told her.

"I've got a bullet in my foot," the guard said.

I ignored him. "An SD 1031. It's also a tracking device."

"I didn't know," she said.

"Didn't know about the device or didn't know it was in my head?"

"Didn't know they implanted you."

"Well, probably best you knew, in case I go down with blood pouring from my orifices."

We came to some stairs.

"Up the stairs, first hall on the right, door at the end of the hall," the guard said.

"Where's that put us?" I gasped. He was gaining about a pound with every step I took.

"Back door."

When we reached the door, I dropped him, grabbed a fistful of his collar, and pulled him to his feet. I shoved him toward the keypad.

"If this is a trick, you die," I promised him.

He punched in the code, the little light flashed green, and the door swung open, revealing a white landscape shimmering like a Courier and Ives print.

Then Nueve stepped through the doorway, his gun pointed at Ashley's head.

"No, Alfred," Nueve said softly. "*She* dies."

03:02:55:21

"A most ingenious and impressive attempt," Nueve said. "But ultimately fruitless. Drop your weapon. You know I will not hesitate to kill her."

I did know that. And I also knew this was my last chance to escape. If I gave up now, I would spend the rest of my life at Camp Lobotomy, a locked-up lab rat at the mercy of this slick Spanish madman. That didn't really appeal to me, but neither did Nueve putting a bullet into Ashley's head. I didn't think Abby Smith knew what Nueve was up to, but that didn't matter. By the time she found out, it would be too late. I'd be a vegetable and Ashley would be dead.

When you get to that place where desperation meets despair, the best thing to do is zig when the baddies expect you to zag.

It went very fast but felt very slow.

I raised my gun.

And then I pulled the trigger.

And then the bullet smashed into Ashley.

That bought two seconds, because it was the last thing Nueve expected. I used those two seconds to leap over Mr. Bullet-Foot and hit Nueve full force, wrapping him in a bear hug and driving him to the ground.

I straddled his chest, put one foot on his gun hand, and pinned his left arm with my knee. I pushed the barrel of my gun against his finely developed cheekbone.

"The box," I said. "Where is it?"

"Left pocket," he said.

I pulled the gun from his hand, stuck it in my pocket, then switched my gun to the other hand so I could get into his left pocket. Once I had the box, I stood up and backed away, putting Mr. Bullet-Foot between me and Nueve.

Nueve sat up, holding his right wrist, red from the pressure of my boot. "Now what?" he asked. "You are surrounded by hundreds of miles of wilderness. How far do you think you can go? If we don't get you, the elements will."

I pulled Ashley to her feet. I whispered her name, but she didn't answer. Her eyes rolled in her head. I didn't think I had much time.

"Call me crazy," I said. "But I'm gonna risk the elements."

I brushed past him, holding Ashley against my side.

"Alfred," he called softly.

I turned.

"You should shoot me."

I turned away.

"You know what will happen if you don't kill me," he said. "I will not stop. You know I will not stop. You know there are no boundaries that *can* stop me. Dispatch me, and the director might be able to persuade the board to let you go."

He smiled. "It is the thing-that-must-be-done."

"I should shoot you," I said. "For all those reasons plus a couple more."

I kicked the door closed in his face.

03:02:52:28

We were standing at the back of the château, looking down a steep, densely wooded slope, the bottom of which was lost in the shadow of the mountain range directly in front of us. Ashley's breath exploded from her mouth, crystalline white puffs of air that barely escaped her pale lips before the wind whipped them away.

"Can you walk?" I asked.

She mumbled something against my chest. Her knees buckled. I held her up and glanced back at the château. Pushed against the wall were six large plastic garbage cans, their lids held down with bungee cords, I guessed to keep the bears from rifling through the trash.

I eased her to the ground. "Be right back," I said. I trotted over to the cans, freeing one lid and leaving the thick rubber cord threaded through the lid's handle. I placed the lid upside down at the top of the slope and then returned to her.

"What are you doing?" she asked as I scooped her up.

"Ever go sledding?" I asked.

"I'm from Southern California!" she gasped.

I plopped her into the center of the overturned lid and positioned myself behind her. She drew her legs up to her chest as I wrapped mine around her shivering body. We fit, but barely. At that moment, the door behind us flew open and a mass of black-clad agents swarmed out. No time to think about it now. No time to work up my courage or even consider the wisdom of what I was about to do. There was no clear path below and the odds were we'd hit a tree before we went twenty feet, but *if it's necessary then it's possible,* and our getting away from the Company's clutches was pretty darn necessary.

I grabbed the metal hooks on either end of the bungee cord and pushed off.

The fresh snowfall from the night before was a blessing—and a curse. It covered fallen branches and small bushes and the twisted upraised roots of the trees, but it also made us go faster. The lid was slightly concave, so by pulling on the cord and shifting my weight from one side to the other, I could kind of direct our descent as we flew down the mountain. We almost tipped straight over a couple of times, until I yelled at Ashley to lean back against me. I didn't dare look to see if they were coming after us; I didn't think they could without jumping on some lids themselves or fetching some skis.

They were shooting at us, though. The bullets tore into tree trunks and snapped off small branches as we rocketed past, flinging chunks of wood and toothpick-sized pieces of shrapnel on impact.

Maybe three hundred yards down, we went airborne, clearing a small ledge, smacking down so hard my jaws slammed together with enough force to bite my tongue in two if it had been between them. The trees thinned out and, looking over Ashley's shoulder, I could see the slope abruptly ended: we were heading straight for a deep gorge. If I didn't find a way to stop us, we were going straight over the edge of a cliff.

I flung my legs out and pulled back hard on the cord, like a rider trying to rein in a runaway horse. We went into a spin and the world whirled around us, trees, snow, rock, sky.

Instinctively, I shoved Ashley as hard as I could. She tumbled away and then I dove after her. The lid tumbled over the cliff, swallowed by the deep shadow of the crevasse.

I was sliding toward it on my back, frantically kicking my heels into the snow, trying to slow my descent. My flailing right hand touched Ashley's forearm and I grabbed her. Dumb idea: if I went over the edge, I'd take her down with me. I let go.

We came to a snow-crunching stop with five feet to spare, flat on our backs, staring up with open mouths at the cloudless, brilliant blue sky. After what seemed like a very long time, I looked at her, and saw the snow beneath her was red.

I didn't dare stand up. The ground was steep and slick with snow. So I scooted to her side like a marine in the barbed-wire portion of an obstacle course.

"Nothing personal—gotta do this, Ashley," I breathed in her ear as I unbuttoned her jumpsuit. I pulled back the material to reveal the wound: the bullet had torn into her left side, between a couple of ribs; I probably got one of her lungs. I tried not to look, but I did notice—I swear not on purpose—that her bra was pink.

Then I dug into the snow until I reached the hard, frozen ground beneath and slammed my wounded palm against it until the cut burst open and began to bleed.

I pressed my palm against the bullet hole and I also pressed my lips against her ear, which was bright red and very cold, whispering, "In the name of Michael, Prince of Light, I command you to be healed, Ashley. Be healed . . ."

My heart pumped blood down my arm, into my hand, through the jagged lips of my wound and entered her body. *A gift . . . not a treasure.*

Ashley's eyes came open and she said in a clear, strong voice, "I can't believe you shot me, you jerk."

"Well, it worked, didn't it?"

She didn't answer. She blew into her hands. Her fingers were bright red. No gloves, no parkas, and a night that promised temperatures well below freezing. My zagging might just kill us yet.

I started to unlace one of my boots.

"What are you doing?" she asked.

"I saw this on a show," I said. "You take a stick, make a bow from your shoelace, and use it to spin the wood until the friction makes a fire. We've got to make a fire, Ashley."

"Or we could just make a huge sign in the snow that says, 'Here we are!' " she said.

"Maybe you'd rather die of hypothermia," I said.

She stood up and walked deeper into the trees. I started after her and tripped on my loose shoelace, falling facefirst into the snow. When I looked up, I saw her kneeling, digging like a dog after a bone, snow flying everywhere.

I laced up my boot and went over to her.

"What are you doing?"

"Digging a snow cave. It would go faster if you helped."

I knelt beside her and together we hollowed out a space wide and deep enough for both of us to crawl inside. She ordered a halt every few minutes—not to rest, but to keep ourselves from sweating. You sweat in these temperatures and your sweat freezes and then you're an ice sculpture. Her every gesture and every word, even the word "faster" or "deeper," had an undercurrent of anger to it. I wondered why she was angry at me—or if she was just angry at the situation. Of course, I did put a bullet into her, but she was a former field operative and had to understand the zigzag theory. The important thing to understand about girls is *you can't understand them*. Girls are complicated. You can understand the complication, but not the girl.

02:17:16:44

The sky was darkening, the first stars were poking through the atmosphere, and the temperature had dropped at least ten degrees when Ashley lowered herself to the ground and leaned against a tree, gasping.

"Can't go on . . . Got to rest," she said.

That was fine with me. We'd been hiking along the ridge for hours, staying near the cover of the trees, stopping only to eat snow to keep us hydrated and to listen for any sound of pursuit. There was lots of snow but no pursuit, though once I thought I heard the sound of a helicopter to the south, where the compound was.

"Why did you shoot me?" she asked.

"If I tried to shoot Nueve, he'd shoot you. If I didn't shoot, we were both shot. He thought those were the only two options: shoot him—not shoot him. So instead I shot you. He thought I'd zig, so I zagged."

"You zagged?"

After half an hour, teeth chattering, muscles singing with fatigue, we crawled inside our makeshift cave—more a trench or shaft than a cave, barely wide enough for both of us. We lay on our sides facing each other, and Ashley of the blond hair and perfect skin and eyes the color of a winter sky wrapped her arms around me and pulled me close.

"We have to conserve our . . . our b-b-b-body heat . . ." she stammered.

So I folded her into my arms. Her face pressed against my neck; I could feel her warm breath on my cold skin.

"I didn't know," she said after a few minutes. "What Nueve was planning."

"I figured that," I said. "Hard to believe anyone would willingly let herself be sliced open like that. The big question is, did Abby Smith know?"

"No. In the conference room, after you left with Mingus, she gave Nueve a direct order you were to be given nonintrusive tests only until she got back from headquarters."

"So she's not in on the lobotomy."

"Lobotomy?"

"That's what I figured. Nueve's gone solo-loco and it's better to apologize later than ask for permission first. He had the fix in from the beginning."

Her arms tightened around me. "I'm cold. I'm s-s-s-o *cold.*"

I rubbed my hands up and down her back. "It's gonna be okay," I said. "I've been through worse than this and I'm not dead yet. I've got Nueve's box . . ."

"Not the only one," she said. "If he doesn't have a backup for it in camp, they'll chopper one in tomorrow."

"What's its range? Do you know?"

"N-n-not sure . . . maybe a mile, two . . . Doesn't matter . . . can't hike out—they'll find us eventually, if we don't die of exposure first."

"Well," I said, trying to think of a bright side. "I'd rather die that way than their way."

"I'd rather not die at all."

I felt something wet on my neck.

"Hey," I said. "Don't, Ashley. I'm working on it."

"What are you working on?"

"A plan to get us out of here."

"Oh. Okay. Thanks. I feel much better now."

We didn't say anything for a few minutes. Night had fallen and I couldn't see a thing, not even the top of her head two inches beneath my nose. I could smell her hair, though, and feel her body quivering against mine.

"What did you do with Nueve's gun?" she asked.

"Put it in my pocket."

"That's what I thought," she said. She sighed with relief. "Good."

I closed my eyes. I didn't feel so cold; in fact, I actually felt warm. The cold snow beneath me and against my back felt like a warm blanket, and I began to float off to sleep.

"Talk to me, Alfred," she said suddenly. "We c-c-can't fall asleep . . ."

"Okay," I said, and immediately my mind went blank.

"What's the plan?"

"Plan?"

"The plan you're working on."

"We can't hike out," I said. "So we're flying out."

"You saw a show about making a glider out of tree branches, deer droppings, and spit?"

"They've got one chopper here already and probably more on the way," I said. "And only one place to land and take off. Can you fly one?"

"What makes you think I can fly one?"

"It's a key part of my plan."

"I can't fly one."

"It's also a key flaw in my plan."

She laughed. It felt good to feel her laugh.

"I keep trying to decide if meeting you was the best thing that happened to me or the worst," she said.

"Maybe both. Why did you come back to help extract me, Ashley?"

"Because I knew what it felt like," she said after a pause. "To lose everything. I went into Field Operations right after college, Alfred, and a field operative can't have a past . . . family . . . friends . . . Medcon took care of it . . . OIPEP 'kills' all its field operatives, fakes their deaths . . . Ashley isn't even my real name. And when I left, I couldn't go back to my old life. Everybody from it thought I was dead . . . They gave me a new identity after I resigned, a new place to live, but it was like I was nobody. I couldn't be who I was before and I couldn't be 'Ashley' either. I was totally alone. I was . . . no one."

"Ashley's not your name?"

"No."

"What is your real name?"

"Gertrude."

I thought about that.

"Can I still call you Ashley?"

I felt her smile against my neck.

"Sometimes I think of her as a different person," she said. "Gertrude. Someone I used to know a long time ago, like another person who really had died."

I nodded. "Me too—the old me before the Sword came along. I miss him sometimes. The old me. Like I was wondering if OIPEP has a time machine. Does it?"

"I don't think it does."

"Be great if it did."

"If it did, I would go back and be sixteen again."

"Really? Why?"

She sighed against my neck and we didn't say anything for a while.

"You're not talking," she said.

"Vampires," I said.

"Vampires? That's random."

"Well, this morning I was thinking about vampires," I said. "I never understood why people were so fascinated by them, girls especially—I guess because they're usually good-looking guys with all these superhuman powers, plus the fact that I guess they're sort of tragic and girls feel sorry for them. Maybe it's because they're blessed with immortality but cursed with death."

"Maybe it's the way they dress," she said. "You never see a vampire in dorky clothes."

"And they're always handsome and fit. You never see a fat, ugly vampire."

"Maybe it's just the fact that love is blind." Her voice got soft and lazy, as if she were drifting off to sleep. "You can't help it, you know? Who you fall in love with. Sometimes you want to help it. You would do anything not to be."

"Not to be what?"

"In love!"

She gave my shin a light tap with the toe of her boot, one of those girl kicks that isn't meant to be taken as a kick.

"What about you?" I asked. "Have you ever been?"

"I thought I was—once. We broke it off."

"How come?"

"I decided to leave the Company and he became the new Operative Nine."

"Nueve?" I was floored. "Nueve was your *boyfriend*?"

"My taste in guys has never been that good."

"Ashley, he was going to shoot you!"

"I know, can you believe it? The jerk. But being the Operative Nine means never having to say you're sorry."

"I am," I said. "For shooting you. For pulling you into this. And you don't believe me right now, but I'm going to pull you back out of it. We're getting off this mountain, I swear, Ashley, and we'll go somewhere they can't find us."

She didn't say anything for a long time.

"There is no such place," she finally said, pressing her lips against my neck, and I thought of vampires again and how their kisses brought life to you, through death's doorway.

01:17:58:54

We crawled from our cave at dawn, sore, stiff, and very cold. Thick clouds marched overhead; it looked like more snow was on the way.

We began the morning with an argument. I wanted to make for the landing pad to commandeer a helicopter.

"It'll be heavily guarded," Ashley said. "Exactly where they expect us to go. It's a zig, Alfred. We've got to zag."

"But zag where?"

"The château. There's food, shelter, clothing—"

"Right. Along with Nueve and Mingus."

"And a secure satellite hookup. If we can get to it, we can SOS Abby."

"And she says to him, 'Back off, buddy. Give them a cup of hot chocolate and a blanky,' and then Nueve puts an extra log on the fire."

"Okay. Then you tell me how we're going to get past fifty armed agents and an Operative Nine who's got no problem with putting a bullet through his girlfriend's head."

I opened my mouth to answer, closed it, opened it again, and said, "I'm working on that."

Behind us, from somewhere in the woods came the sound of barking.

"Well, you better work fast," Ashley said. "Because they've brought in the bloodhounds."

I listened to the braying of the hounds for a couple seconds. They were getting closer.

"You're working, right? Not just panicking?" she asked.

"A little of both. We could make a run for it."

"We're both dehydrated and weak from hunger. I don't think we'll get very far."

"Okay, then we wait for them to find us," I said. I offered her Nueve's gun. She didn't take it.

"Well," I said. "Those are the options, Ashley. Fight or flight."

"There's a third," she said. "Take off your clothes."

"Huh?"

"Strip."

"Right now?"

She began to unbutton my jumper. Her cheeks were red from the cold. Mine were red from being stripped.

Fifteen minutes later two men in heavy parkas with AK-47s slung over their shoulders came into the clearing, pulled along by two massive bloodhounds. The dogs didn't hesitate: they made straight for the figure in the OIPEP jumpsuit slumped against a tree at the far edge of the clearing. Once they passed our cave, Ashley and I burst from the snow and were on them in five steps, mine very exaggerated knees-up-to-the-chest steps, the kind of running you see in cartoons. Somehow that feels more natural when you're wearing just boxers and boots in subzero weather. I put Bullet-Foot's gun against one guy's head and Ashley put Nueve's against the other's.

"Hi, Pete," Ashley said to her guy, pulling the AK-47 from his hand. To mine, she said, "How's it going, Bob?"

"Hi, Ashley," Pete and Bob said.

"We'll take your parkas and walkie-talkies, too."

"And the gloves," I said.

"Right," she said. "And the gloves."

Ashley ordered them to sit on their bare hands while I shook the snow out of my jumpsuit and got dressed. Maybe I should have taken Pete or Bob's jumpsuit, too, since theirs were dry and mine was wet from stuffing it with snow. We slipped on the gloves and parkas. Ashley tied their hands behind their backs with the ends of the leashes and the blood-hounds watched us, tongues lolling from their blubbery mouths, with the happy attitude of all dogs. At that moment, I envied their obliviousness. I knelt beside one and he slobbered all over my face. His spit was warm and thick and under any other circumstances I would have been grossed out, but now my heart pounded with joy. It's hard to think of a single thing that can bring you more happiness than a good dog.

We hiked west, keeping the ravine on our left, so we wouldn't end up walking in circles. Occasionally we could hear the steady *thumpa-thumpa* of a helicopter over the trees to our right, louder, then fainter, then louder again. Ashley walked in front of me, the AK-47 slung over her back, the walkie-talkie pressed against her ear as she monitored the chatter.

It started to snow. Flinty little flakes at first, then fat wet balls the size my thumbnail. The ground began to rise and the trees thinned out.

Ashley stopped suddenly, one gloved finger pressed against her ear while she held the walkie-talkie against the other. Snow and ice clung to the fur of her parka, framing her round face in shimmering crystals. She wore no makeup and her cheeks were bright pink from the cold and her lips slightly blue, but I don't think she ever looked prettier.

"What is it?" I asked.

"Shh!" She listened for a few more seconds.

"They're talking about a package . . . on its way . . . This sounds like Nueve . . . All units to rendezvous at the helipad . . . Nueve's en route . . ."

"Package?"

She looked at her watch. "Thirty minutes."

"What package?"

She was walking again, quickly now, back into the trees and up the slope. Our boots crunched in the fresh snowfall.

"I'm guessing it's a replacement for the SD 1031 in your pocket," she said.

"He gets his hands on that and we're toast," I said. "What's the plan?"

"We have to stop him before he takes delivery."

"That's more of a goal than a plan," I pointed out.

"I'm open to suggestions."

I tried to come up with one. We were two against OIPEP's full force on the mountain. Ashley was a trained field operative and I wasn't exactly a novice by this point; still, there were only two of us and a lot of them, plus Nueve who wouldn't let niceties like keeping casualties low stand in his way. Even if we took a hostage, Nueve wouldn't care. A frontal assault was suicidal, but how could we sneak in? They knew Ashley and they sure as heck knew me.

"We have to create some kind of diversion," I said. "A fire or explosion—and while they're distracted . . ."

"And what are we going to blow up, Alfred? The only bomb we have is inside your head."

I stopped walking. She didn't notice at first, she was so focused on making it to the helipad before the chopper landed. When she did, she turned and stared at me.

"What's the matter?"

"I've got it," I said. "The one thing he wants that we have."

"I know, but he's getting another one." She had a concerned look on her face, like she was worried I had finally cracked.

"No," I said. "There might be a hundred little black boxes, but there's only one Alfred Kropp."

01:17:04:39

Twenty-five minutes and a hard hike through dense woods and heavy snow later . . .

A helicopter hovers over a landing pad nestled in a valley in the Canadian wilderness . . .

While forty heavily armed men encircle the perimeter . . .

. . . and a dark-haired man with a lean face and piercing black eyes waits, leaning on a black cane, thinking, maybe, that the kid should have killed him when he had the chance because it's done now, the game's over . . .

. . . as the kid lies on his belly a dozen yards away, hidden in the trees, sweating despite the bitter cold that's caused icicles to form on his eyebrows, praying he still has one move left in the game that the Operative Nine assumes is over . . .

Beside him, the girl whispers, "Now?"

"Not yet."

Must move before Nueve reaches the chopper. Timing was everything in this game and up to this point the kid's had none. Events have controlled him and the kid is now at the point where he either takes control of events or the events overwhelm him. Dr. Mingus waits at the château with his scalpel and his vials.

So when the skids of the chopper brush the icy concrete, the kid is up and running, straight for the pad, tossing his AK-47 to the ground, both hands over his head, one empty, the other holding the black box, his thumb resting on the blue button.

The foot soldiers don't get it. They swing their rifles toward the kid, fingers quivering on the triggers, centering his tall, lanky frame in their scopes.

The Operative Nine gets it though. He gets it immediately, because that's his job—to get it before anyone else does; in the time it takes for most people to realize a new move's being played, he's already absorbed the play and all its repercussions, and he's making his countermove.

He shouts for them to lower their weapons, but they can't hear him over the roar of the chopper, so he makes a slicing motion across his throat as the bird settles to the ground. The pilot cuts the engine.

The kid keeps walking, up to the line of the men standing between him and the chopper and the place inside the circle of guns where Nueve stands.

Hands high.

Thumb on the button.

If he's wrong about this, he's dead. The girl, too, probably. Nueve would kill her because alive she serves no purpose. And it doesn't matter that she loves him—or used to love him—and his feelings—if he has them—don't matter either. He is the Operative Nine, and nothing matters but the mission.

The kid prays there's a purpose to Mingus and the vials.

He doesn't know what that purpose is, but he prays he's still a Special Item in OIPEP's eyes.

"Lower your weapons," Nueve said in a calm voice. "Let him through."

I walked through and their line closed around me. I held the box, Nueve held his cane, and the men behind us held their assault rifles.

"This is the moment when I say, 'Ah, Alfred Kropp, we meet again,' " Nueve said.

"We're checking out of Club OIPEP," I told him. "Me and Ashley."

"It's more akin to the Hotel California, Alfred," he said.

"What?"

"An obscure reference to a song well before your time. You intend to press the blue button. Proceed. Press it."

My thumb hovered over the button.

"He who hesitates," Nueve said softly.

I pressed the blue button. The red one next to it began to low.

"You truly are extraordinary, Alfred," he said. "In another life, you would have made a superb Superseding Protocol Agent. You are about to say you have no choice because we've given you no choice."

I nodded. "You've given me no choice."

"That the choice between spending the rest of your life here as our lobotomized guest and dying here, right now, is no choice at all. You would rather die."

"That's right. I'd rather end it now than spend the rest of my life as a vegetable."

"And you are gambling that your death would completely disrupt our plans for you."

"I knew you'd get it."

His dark eyes danced. "I get everything. What would you say, Alfred, if I told you that we have more than enough samples to render your continued existence irrelevant?"

"I would say you're bluffing," I answered.

His right eyebrow climbed toward his hairline. "Because?"

"Because if that were true you wouldn't have ordered them to hold their fire. You still need me. I'm not sure why exactly, but you need me, and if I push this button you won't have me. Bottom line: if you want me, Nueve, you're going to have to let me go."

"That much is true, yes," he said with a nod. "But not the issue. The issue is . . . will you do it? *Can* you do it? I must believe the answer to that question is yes for this to work. You understand that."

I turned to Ashley. "Get on the chopper."

She looked at me. She looked at Nueve. She didn't move. I said it again: "Get on the chopper."

She took a step toward it and Nueve's cane whipped in the air, the six-inch dagger protruding from its base. I raised the box over my head and yelled, "Do it and I hit the button, I swear to God I will, you Spanish bastard!" and the blade froze a centimeter from her throat.

Our eyes met . . . and Nueve blinked first. He slowly lowered the cane. His eyes met Ashley's and he gave the slightest of nods.

"Go," I said to Ashley.

Nobody said anything as she trotted to the chopper and disappeared into the hold.

I turned back to Nueve.

"Are you familiar, Alfred," he said, "with the law of diminishing returns?"

I backed away, keeping my eye on Nueve. The guys with the guns didn't matter. Only Nueve mattered. With a flick of his wrist, he could signal for them to open fire. But he wasn't going to do that. Halfway to the chopper, I realized he really *was* going to do it: he was going to let us go.

"There is no escape, you know," he called to me. "No place on earth where we cannot find you. You are merely delaying the inevitable, Alfred."

"You do what you have to do and I'll do what I have to do," I said.

I climbed into the hold and fell into the seat beside Ashley. I tossed the box into her lap and told her to hold it because knowing my luck I'd hit the red button by accident.

The pilot was staring at us. I twirled my index finger and the engine roared to life. A minute later we were off the ground and climbing above the treetops. I looked out the window and saw a solitary figure below, and he wasn't so far beneath me that I couldn't see the ironic smile playing on his lips.

HELENA REGIONAL AIRPORT

HELENA, MONTANA

01:12:49:55

I dialed the eight hundred number from a pay phone outside Captain Jack's Bistro & Bar, the airport's sole restaurant, while Ashley waited at a table inside. I was interrupted a couple of times by travelers asking directions. In my black jumper, I must have looked like a maintenance worker.

A lady with a foreign accent answered. "Office Directory Services, how may I direct your call?"

"Abigail Smith," I said.

There was a pause. "Dr. Smith is not available at the moment."

"I need to get a message to her. A very important message."

"I could direct you to her voice mail."

"I've already left her a voice mail."

There was another, longer pause.

"Dr. Smith is currently indisposed," the operator said.

"That's the problem," I said. "So am I."

I hung up and dialed Mr. Needlemier's number. I didn't have any money, so I made the call collect. On my first try, he refused to accept the charges. I called right back and the operator came on the line and relayed the message that my party didn't appreciate prank calls and if I persisted he would report me to the FCC. The third time was the charm. I told the operator my name was Samuel St. John and he accepted the call.

"Mr. Needlemier, it's me, Alfred Kropp. Don't hang up."

"Alfred Kropp is dead. I should know; I buried him myself. Well, not personally, but I was there."

"I can prove it's me." I bit my lower lip, trying to think of a way to prove it.

"The picture," I said finally. "You remember the picture you gave me at the hospital? You found it in the ashes after Jourdain Garmot burned my father's house down. It was me and my mom . . ."

He didn't say anything. The silence dragged out.

"Oh my dear Lord!" he whispered. "Alfred!" His voice climbed an octave, cracking on the last syllable. "Alfred, this is extraordinary!"

"OIPEP faked my death," I said. "I'm sorry. I thought you knew."

"They brought me your ashes in a can! A tin can!"

"Really? Look, Mr. Needlemier, I need to find—"

"I was in quite a quandary. Your mother is buried in Ohio and your father here in Knoxville, and we never discussed where you might prefer to be laid to rest."

"Right," I said. "Mr. Needlemier, here's the thing: I've extracted myself from the extraction and—"

"In the end I buried you in Ohio, next to your mother. You met Bernard only once as I recall and knew him only after his death—or *of* him, I should say—so burying you here would be a reunion of strangers or near strangers."

"That's good," I said. "You did the right thing. Here's why I called—"

"A lovely service, Alfred. Cold, but clear skies and not a bit of breeze . . ."

"Who came?" I asked. He had sucked me in.

"It was—an intimate gathering. Myself, the priest, of course, and a gentleman by the name of Vosch, who told me he had worked closely with you on a special project."

"That would be the attempted beheading," I said. Only three people at my funeral? One, the priest, had to be there, and the other guy was there for his job, which was to kill me. "Vosch works for Jourdain Garmot. Probably there to make sure I was really dead. What about Samuel? He was there, right?"

Mr. Needlemier didn't give me a direct answer. "The last time I saw Samuel was after his release from the hospital. He asked all sorts of questions about the arson and the suit involving the estate. Your death has complicated things a bit and nothing's been decided, but you see you have no heirs, no living relatives. Jourdain has a good chance now of seizing control of your father's business as well as the estate . . ."

"That doesn't matter," I said. "I don't care about that anymore. I need to find Samuel."

"Well, he did give me his cell phone number should I need it."

He gave me the number.

"Did he say where he was going?" I asked, although I was pretty sure I knew. He was going after Jourdain. He was going to kill him, if he hadn't already, or die trying.

"Not a hint, but between us, Alfred, I have the impression he doesn't like me very much."

"He gives everyone that impression," I said. "Does he know I died?"

"He left before I received the news . . . I don't know, Alfred."

"But Vosch was at my funeral. So Jourdain thinks I'm dead. He'll tell Sam and maybe that will save his life. I'm not sure. Samuel might kill him anyway, if he hasn't already."

But I hoped I was in time to stop it. I didn't think Jourdain was evil—just messed up by his father's murder and he had thought taking me out would bring him some peace. I knew better.

"Well," Mr. Needlemier said. "I hope you don't take this the wrong way, but it certainly would solve all your difficulties if Jourdain were, um, shall we say, in your current perceived condition—but in actuality."

I sighed. Lawyers. "Not all my difficulties, Mr. Needlemier. Not by a long shot. That reminds me. I need cash. There's a Western Union here at the airport. Can you wire me some?"

"Some what?"

"Cash, Mr. Needlemier. Money. We need clothes and plane tickets—and food. We haven't eaten in almost two days."

"We?"

"Me and Ashley."

"Ah, the lovely secret agent person. Of course, Alfred. I'll wire you as much as you need. Are you flying back to Knoxville?"

"I don't think so," I said. "It's the first place he'll look."

"Jourdain?"

"Nueve."

"Nueve!"

"Well, both. Jourdain and Nueve. The list keeps growing."

"Ah, so that's what you meant by difficulties. I thought perhaps you were referring to the Skull."

"The Skull?"

"The Thirteenth Skull. You asked me about it at the airport, remember? Well, it tweaked my curiosity, so I took it upon myself to find out a little more about it."

"And?"

"And I did."

"No, I meant what did you find out?"

"The Thirteenth Skull may be another name for the Skull of Doom."

"The Skull of Doom?"

"Or then again, perhaps not. The literature is quite contradictory and vague, like all such literature, but utterly fascinating . . ."

"Mr. Needlemier," I said. "I'm very tired and very hungry and I'm running out of time."

"Of course. In a nutshell, there are, or were, thirteen skulls, fashioned from solid crystal sometime in the late first century. By whom and for what purpose no one seems to agree, but one legend that I thought you might find interesting—or thought you would if you were alive, because of course at the time I thought you weren't—one legend has it that the Skulls were made by Merlin—"

"Merlin," I echoed, remembering my dream in cabin thirteen. The old man unzipping his head and ripping out his skull. "Touch."

"The magician. From Camelot . . ."

"I know who Merlin is, Mr. Needlemier."

"Of course you do! You would almost have to! Carved

from crystal by Merlin himself . . . including the Thirteenth, the last and most terrible of the Divining Skulls, as they were called. Merlin was so horrified by what he had fashioned that he divided the first twelve between Arthur's bravest knights, ordering them to scatter the Skulls to the ends of the earth and to tell no one where they had hidden them. The Thirteenth, called the Skull of Doom, Merlin himself hid away—or more precisely *threw* away."

"Threw away? Where did he throw it away?"

"Not where, Alfred. *When*. The legend says he hurled the Skull of Doom into a time warp or vortex, casting it far into the future, so far that the wizard was certain no man would still be alive to use it."

"Why? What could it do?"

"By itself, hardly anything. It could be used much like a crystal ball—like the others, it was cut from the purest crystal—to see into the future. But the Skull's real power came when aligned with the first twelve. You see, if the twelve were arranged in a circle, with the thirteenth in the middle, all time and space could—or most definitely *would*, according to some—be literally ripped apart."

I thought about that. "The end of the world."

"No, of *everything*. The entire universe."

"No wonder Merlin ordered them scattered."

"Yes. And no wonder that Jourdain might know of them. His father was, after all, a Knight of the Sacred Order."

"He went to Suedberg," I said.

"Suedberg?"

"This little town in Pennsylvania where one of the knights lived—or used to live before Mogart's men killed him. But his mother is still there—and she's a soothsayer. She can see the future."

"Perhaps with the help of a special crystalline object designed for that purpose?"

"Maybe," I said. It was hard to think it through. I was hungry and tired and still chilled to the bone. "I stayed in that house and never saw any crystal skull, but it wasn't like I searched the place."

"No doubt Jourdain has, though."

"But it still doesn't add up. Unless Jourdain thinks I knew where the Thirteenth Skull was—which I don't—and besides he didn't even give me a chance to tell him one way or another. Nueve swooped in right before he was going to chop off my head."

"He didn't ask you where it was?"

"He just said he was on the 'last knightly quest,'" I said. "That must be why Sam's so bent on finding him. If anyone would know about some magical crystal skull, it would be the Operative Nine for OIPEP."

I made him repeat Samuel's cell number one last time before hanging up. I dialed the number and got a very stern recorded message from the phone company that I needed to deposit three dollars before making my call.

In the restaurant, Ashley was working on a sloppy hamburger about the size of my head, a plateful of fries buried under globs of ketchup, and a big bowl of baked beans.

"I ordered," she said unnecessarily. "I couldn't wait any longer. Lemme guess: the director is 'indisposed.'"

"I've got a feeling something bad has happened."

She laughed. "I wonder why."

"I'm thinking the board said 'no.'"

"Well, my guess would be it's not going too well."

"I don't get it," I said. "All this time I thought the director was in charge of OIPEP."

"We call OIPEP the 'Company' for a reason, Alfred. It's set up like a multinational corporation. Countries who've signed the Charter send representatives to sit on the board. The board sets the policies and selects a director to implement them and run the day-to-day operations. But any decision the director makes can be overturned by a simple majority vote of the board."

"Do you think she can convince them to leave me alone?"

"She hasn't been able to so far."

The server came by to take my order. I ordered a grilled chicken salad and a glass of ice water.

Ashley took a big pull on her chocolate shake and said, "Salad?"

"My tummy feels funny."

"Did you just use the word 'tummy'?"

I looked around the room. A man was sitting by himself, talking on a cell phone in a loud voice. Something about the meeting in Denver and what a slam dunk the presentation was. A frazzled-looking woman sat in a booth wrangling two toddlers fighting over a red crayon, their faces smeared with what looked like mashed potatoes. Another man sat at the bar wearing blue jeans and a buckskin shirt with the leather danglies on the sleeves.

"Why did he let us go?" I wondered aloud.

"He thought you were serious about hitting the button."

"Maybe. But maybe he wasn't bluffing when he said they already had what they wanted. But if they already had what they wanted, why didn't they just let me go after I shot you? Why chase us into the mountains? Why fly in another black box?"

"He's just protecting the Company's investment."

"Investment in what? OIPEP used my blood to fight

demons before, but only because it didn't have the Seal. It has the Seal now, so why does it still need my blood?"

She thought about it. I guessed she was thinking about it. She might have been thinking about her fries as she swirled the end of one in a dollop of ketchup. I remembered when I first met her in Knoxville, when she was posing as a transfer student, the big burger and milk shake she scarfed down without taking a breath. She tapped the fry on the edge of her plate like she had to get the ratio of potato to tomato just right.

"The Company was created to investigate extraordinary phenomenon and preserve items of peculiar and special significance. I guess your blood fits into both categories. Nueve doesn't want it falling into the wrong hands."

"He's protecting the world from Alfred Kropp."

"From what Alfred Kropp can do."

"Right. We wouldn't want some kid with the power to heal the world running amok, healing the world."

My food came. I picked at it. She grabbed the bread stick off my plate and ate it.

"How do you do that?" I asked. "Eat so much and stay so thin."

"I'm like a lioness," she said. "I gorge, but only once a week."

"If it's true the SD 1031 has a range of only about a mile, then he has no way of finding me," I said, looking at the guy hunched over at the bar. He was watching a basketball game on the TV mounted on the ceiling. "He's not that stupid."

"He knows where you are," she said.

"How?"

"A Company plane dropped us here."

"And took off again. Do you think we're being watched?"

She shook her head. "Maybe. Maybe not. I don't know. We should have killed the pilot."

She said it so nonchalantly that for a second I couldn't think of anything to say.

Finally, I said, "So say we aren't being watched. How will he know where I'm going next?"

"Where *we're* going next."

"Well," I said. "That's something we need to talk about."

Her big blue eyes got even bigger. "Oh?"

"Look, Ashley, the last thing I want to be is alone, but facts are facts and everybody who gets close to me or tries to help me ends up hurt, very hurt or dead. My uncle. Bennacio. Samuel. And you've already been stabbed—"

"And shot."

"Yeah, but I wasn't counting that."

"You weren't counting my being shot?"

"Because I did that."

"Still counts."

"To save you."

"You shot me for my own good?"

"It was a zagging thing; I thought I explained that."

"You're cutting me loose."

"I don't want you to get hurt."

"I've already been hurt."

"Hurt worse."

"Maybe I'm a grown-up and don't need a teenager to make that decision for me."

"Nueve gets this. You used to be a field operative, so I know you get this. It's why Mingus used you to test me. It's why Nueve threatened to kill you to get me to give up. I can't do that anymore, Ashley. Not to anybody, but especially not to you."

She angrily slurped the dregs of her milk shake through her straw, if it's possible to slurp angrily.

"And where am I supposed to go, Alfred? I can't go back to the Company—what do you think they'd do to me after I helped you escape? I can't go back to my old life. They took my old life away. God, I wish I knew you were going to do this back at the château; I would have told you to let me bleed to death after Mingus sliced me open. You can't do this to me. I won't let you do this to me. I'm coming with you, wherever you go, until I'm dead or you are or we both are."

"That's what I'm telling you," I said. "That's what I'm trying to say. I don't know what's going to happen to me, but if the past proves anything, I'm pretty sure I know what's going to happen to you, and I don't want that to happen to you, Ashley. I'd rather be cut open myself than see something happen to you."

She tossed her napkin on her plate, leaned over the table, grabbed my face with both hands, and kissed me full on the lips. I tasted chocolate.

"You don't get it," she said, touching my cheek. "I've been *assigned* to you, Alfred Kropp. You *own* me."

01:11:57:02

I left Ashley in the restaurant so they wouldn't think we were running out on the check and went to the Western Union office where the money from Mr. Needlemier was waiting for me. I cashed a twenty and used the change to call Samuel's cell phone.

On the third ring someone with a vaguely familiar voice came on the line.

It wasn't Samuel's voice.

"I believe I know who this is," the man said in a French accent.

"Where's Samuel?" I asked.

"Mr. St. John is indisposed," Vosch said, echoing the OIPEP operator. "But if you'd like to leave a message, Alfred, I'd be happy to pass it along."

I fell back against the wall and closed my eyes. I could taste the dressing from my salad and wondered if I was going to be sick.

"Is he alive?" I asked.

"He is, but of course you are not. You should have been at your funeral, Alfred. Quite touching, if ill attended."

"You didn't buy it."

"It was a poor sell. Why would St. John need to protect a corpse?"

"I want to talk to him."

"He's indisposed. I thought we covered this."

"How do I know you're telling the truth? Maybe you've already killed him."

"That would make me stupid *and* a liar, like a person who would fake his own death."

"What do you want?" I asked.

"You know what we want."

"I don't have it."

"Excuse-moi?"

"I said I don't have it. I never had it and I don't know where it is."

"Where what is?"

"The Skull. The Skull, Vosch. The Thirteenth Skull."

He didn't say anything at first. Then he laughed. "Ah, Alfred Kropp, you are a witty one. Tell me where you are and I shall help you locate it."

The airport was crowded; a plane had just landed, and people were hurrying to make their connecting flights, vacationers mostly, judging by the way they were dressed. Couples and families rushing past with that flushed excitement of travel, chattering and laughing, pulling tired kids along. Where they were going, I could never come. Where they were now, I could never be. *Tell me where you are.*

"Outside," I said.

"Pardon?"

"I said outside Helena, Montana. At the airport. And bring him with you, understand?"

"I'll make the arrangements. Why don't we break with tradition, Alfred? Stay where you are and don't do anything stupid."

"I'm not going anywhere," I said. "Can't promise about the stupid part."

I went back to the restaurant and paid our check. Ashley's eyes were red, and I wondered if she'd had herself a cry while I was gone.

"What took so long?"

"The wire hadn't come in yet," I lied. "I had to wait."

We ducked into a store and bought some jeans and sweatshirts with BIG SKY printed on the fronts. I went into the men's room to change.

Ashley gave me the eye when I came out.

"Where are the guns?" she asked.

"Tossed them in the trash," I said. "Guns and planes don't mix."

"Plane to where?"

"We're flying to Knoxville," I lied. That was two lies in about thirty minutes. Lying in general is a bad idea, but sometimes you're shoved between the evil of lying and the thing-that-must-be-done. I pushed that thought away; it was Op Nine thinking. *In another life, you would have made a superb Superseding Protocol Agent.*

"A little obvious, isn't it?" she asked.

"That's what I'm counting on. So obvious its obviousness makes it unobvious."

"Nueve will have an operative at every gate, in every restaurant, probably in every public restroom. We won't last thirty seconds in Knoxville."

"I don't have a choice," I said. "I've got a bomb in my head and there's only one guy who can help me get it out—the guy who ordered it put there."

"There're neurosurgeons in every major city in America, Alfred," she said.

"Right, and what do I tell them? 'Excuse me, Doc, but would you mind pulling this top-secret explosive device from between my hemispheres? It's been bugging me.'"

"He's a lot of things, but I don't think Samuel is a brain surgeon."

"Well, I have to start somewhere, Ashley."

There were no direct flights to Knoxville, so we booked a connecting flight through Chicago, where we would have a two-hour layover. Since landing in Helena, I had the weird sensation of a ticker or clock inside my head, winding down like a timer to some apocalyptic event. I was familiar with apocalyptic events. This time was a little different, though. I wasn't trying to save the world, just two people in it . . . three, if you counted Samuel. But then, as we settled into our seats at the gate, I thought no, it was just me. Not the world this time around, just Alfred.

I looked down at the top of Ashley's head against my shoulder. She was sleeping off her burger and fries. What about Ashley? She had nowhere to go either, nowhere she would be safe from Nueve. The longer she stayed with me, the greater the danger. It wasn't a pleasant fact, but this wasn't the time to dwell on the pleasant ones, like the way she had looked at me in the restaurant and the way the chocolate on her lips tasted slightly salty from my bread stick. This was the time for necessities. This was the time for doing the thing-that-must-be-done.

Taking care not to jostle her too much, I eased a few

twenties into her pocket. She murmured something in her sleep, smacked her lips a couple times (what was she dreaming about . . . chocolate sundaes, big happy slobbery dogs, vampires?), and nuzzled my neck.

Sometimes, when I got down, I would remind myself I had saved the world—twice—and that I was a hero, like the firefighter who rushes into a burning building to rescue a trapped kid. But I was no firefighter. I was no hero. Even when I faced Mogart and Paimon, the demon king, it was about me, not the world. The only reason I got stabbed by the Sword was I gave the Sword to Mogart. And I took on Paimon because he was killing me, from the inside out, filling my body with maggots and slowly driving me insane.

It was never for the sake of the world. It was always for the sake of Kropp, and that the world got saved too was a kind of happy by-product.

I leaned my head against Ashley's and after a minute I fell asleep. I was flying again. I came to a towering cliff, and on that cliff rose a castle of sparkling white stone with flags flying from its ramparts and a man in shining armor sitting on a horse before its gates. He drew a black sword from the scabbard at his side and raised it over his head in a salute.

Then I started to fall. I dropped like a stone toward the sea. A monster reared its head above the crashing surf, its mouth stretching open to reveal fangs as tall and glittering as the walls of the castle.

I woke up before I fell into the dragon's mouth.

"Alfred," Ashley was saying. "Alfred, we're boarding."

On the plane, I sat down beside her—she took the window seat—and waited, my knee popping up and down, counting off the seconds in my head. This was goodbye, but it was a goodbye without a farewell.

I gave her hand a squeeze and said, "I think I got hold of some bad lettuce—have to go to the bathroom," the third lie, and then I worked my way toward the front of the cabin with a lot of "excuse me's" and "I'm sorries" as I slid sideways past passengers filling the overhead compartments. At the front of the plane, I risked a glance toward our seats. All I could see was the top of her blond head and for some reason that broke my heart: the last I would see of her would be the top of her head.

I told the lady attendant I'd left my carry-on at the gate. She was distracted, trying to find room in a little compartment for a first-class passenger's coat. She waved me through the hatch but told me I'd better hurry.

I hurried all right, bumping into people on my way to the gate, counting the seconds in my head. Once they close a hatch on an airplane, they can't open it again. Hopefully by the time she realized I was missing, it would be too late.

I sank into a chair just outside the double doors of the gate and waited for her to come rushing out. When she didn't, I stood up and walked to the big window facing the tarmac. The plane was already backing away from the terminal. I wondered if she was going berserk, demanding they let her off. If she pitched a big enough fit, they might. I stood and watched until the plane was out of sight, heading for the runway. Then I stood a few more minutes until it took off, and I watched it until it dwindled to nothing in the blue.

Goodbye, Ashley.

01:07:54:12

I hoofed it back to the men's room, praying no one had made a garbage run while we sat at the gate. The guns were still at the bottom of the bin where I had stashed them, buried beneath three feet of discarded paper towels. I tucked one gun in the front of my jeans and one in the back and examined my sweatshirt in the mirror for any unsightly bulges.

For the next three hours, I wandered the Helena airport. Besides algebra class and anyplace where you have to wait in line, airports are the most boring places on earth. This was my opportunity to come up with a really brilliant plan, like creating a disabling device out of a shampoo bottle and my pee. But I was a little panicky and tired and already regretting not keeping Ashley with me. Having a seasoned field operative by my side might come in handy when Vosch and company touched down.

When you have time before a life-threatening situation, you feel the need to clear the air, to settle any dangling loose ends, so I called Alphonso Needlemier to unstick the thing stuck in my craw.

"You lied to me," I said.

"Alfred, I would never—"

"You knew they had Samuel the whole time. Hell, I bet you *gave* them Samuel."

"Alfred . . . Alfred," he sputtered. "I hardly know what to say."

"Vosch and Jourdain must have contacted you after Nueve pulled me from the warehouse."

Pushed into a corner, he went all stiff and formal on me. "That is an outrageous assumption on your part."

"And you were scared out of your mind. I understand that. But I also know how these things work. They'll lean on anyone who knew me—anybody close I might have confided in. So they leaned on you—they *must* have leaned on you. Was that the deal, Mr. Needlemier—did you offer them Samuel if they let you go?"

My answer was the soft hiss of the long-distance connection.

"When did you tell them my death was faked? At my funeral? Or did Vosch go with you so you wouldn't try to give them the slip in Ohio?"

"Alfred, may I say, this is completely . . . Alfred, from the beginning I have always done all I could . . ."

"Stop lying to me!" I yelled into the phone.

"I have a wife!" he yelled back. "A family! I never had any business in this business! You don't understand what it's like to face losing everything, Alfred."

Oh boy, I thought. Oh, boy.

"They said they'd kill them if I didn't cooperate!" he went on.

"Did you set him up, Mr. Needlemier? *Did you give them Samuel?*"

"I would pay any price to protect my family. I am not ashamed of that. I will not apologize for that."

"That's it," I said. "I knew it. It didn't make sense. Even at half speed, Samuel could have taken Vosch. You lured him somewhere and they ambushed him."

"I saved his life," Mr. Needlemier said. "Say what you want, judge me if you wish, but I saved his life."

"They're going to kill him anyway."

"Alfred, truly, I never meant to harm anyone. I was put in an untenable position. I can't . . . there must be . . . please, Alfred, tell me what to do. Is there anything I can do to help you?"

I remembered this fifteen-year-old kid, scared out of his mind, chasing a tall, lion-haired man down a hallway, crying after him as he marched to his doom, *There's gotta be something I can do. Take me with you; I could help.*

And I remembered the tall man's answer.

"Yes," I said. "Pray."

01:06:38:29

I was sitting in Captain Jack's drinking a Diet Coke and listening to an old Billy Joel song ("Saturday night and you're still hangin' around . . ."), when a voice came over the intercom instructing Alfred Kropp to meet his party at baggage claim. *Baggage claim,* I thought. *Perfect.* I dropped a five on the table and said goodbye to Captain Jack's. I felt like a regular.

Two men wearing trench coats were standing by the conveyer belt, hands jammed into their pockets, hats pulled low over their faces. Between them stood a third man, tall and pale, with a hound-dog face and very bushy, very black eyebrows. His face showed no expression as I approached; if he was happy to see me, he wasn't going to show it. I figured he wasn't happy to see me. I was right.

"You shouldn't have done this, Alfred," Samuel said.

Vosch was standing on his right, the slit-eyed, flat-face brute I first met driving the Town Car on his left. I ignored Samuel and turned to Vosch.

"Where's Jourdain?" I asked.

"At the end of the circle," Vosch said.

"A circle doesn't have an end," I pointed out.

"Or a beginning," Vosch said.

He smiled a humorless smile and gestured toward the terminal doors.

"Shall we? We have a private jet with all the amenities."

I looked at Samuel. He looked back at me.

"Which one do you want?" I asked him.

He cut his eyes toward Vosch. "That one."

"Take the big one. Vosch is mine."

Samuel's chin dipped toward his chest. Mr. Flat-Face's mouth came open and he said, "What?" Samuel punched him in the throat. Flat-Face fell to his knees, spitting and choking. Vosch's right hand rose from his pocket. I reached behind my back. Vosch raised his gun toward Samuel.

I didn't fumble. I didn't hesitate. I didn't weigh the odds. Nueve would have been proud.

I shot Vosch point-blank in the chest.

He fell straight back, landing hard on his butt, his shot going wild and puncturing the ceiling tile. Flat-Face reached inside his coat. "Sam," I called softly, tossing the gun from my waistband at him as I rushed toward Vosch. Samuel caught the gun and swung the muzzle against Flat-Face's flat face.

I straddled Vosch's chest and put the end of my gun against the end of his nose.

"Get his gun," I called to Samuel.

Behind me, I heard someone yell, "Call security!"

I pulled the gun from Vosch's hand and shouted, "Somebody call the paramedics! This guy's been shot!"

I bumped Samuel in the shoulder as I pushed off Vosch's

chest. Sam was holding a gun in each hand just like me, the one I threw him and the one he took from Flat-Face.

"We go," I said.

He took it in quickly: the terrified onlookers, the red emergency light pulsing, the alarm howling in the distance. He didn't need me to explain it to him: Vosch was down and Flat-Face was in no shape to chase us. Time to haul it, not kick it.

We burst through the doors into the biting cold. A taxi was parked next to the curb, engine idling so the driver could run the heater. The only other vehicle nearby was one of those big tour buses. Samuel dived into the front seat of the taxi; I took the back. He put one of the guns against the startled driver's temple and told him to get out. No big surprise when he did. Samuel slid over, slammed the door the cabbie left open in his haste, yanked the gearshift into drive, and floored the gas. He merged without looking into the driveway leading to the exit, scraping the side of a minivan that had slammed on its brakes to avoid running over the terrified cabdriver.

I twisted around to look out the back window. Vosch and Flat-Face came out of the building. Flat-Face pointed at our cab and Vosch didn't hesitate—he made straight for the bus.

"What is he, Superman?" I wondered. "I shot him point-blank."

"They're wearing Kevlar vests," Samuel said in his trademark deadpan.

"You could have told me."

"I didn't know you were armed."

We roared past a sign for the I-15 ramp.

"Get on the interstate," I said. "They've hijacked the bus." The taxi was old—it smelled like stale cigarettes and coffee and the seats were torn—but I figured even this old rattletrap could bury a big bus at high speed. He grunted something at me in appreciation for my grasp of the obvious and ran the red light for the southbound lanes, barely missing a pickup truck. The bus behind us didn't—and didn't let the truck concern it: the Vosch Express slammed head-on into its side, sending the truck into a spin, tires screaming in protest as they slid sideways across the asphalt.

I rolled down the window as Samuel accelerated onto the lane.

"Don't waste bullets!" he shouted over the whipping wind.

The bus lost some ground making the grade up the ramp, but once it hit the highway it began to make it up. I heaved myself through the open window, planted my butt on the doorframe, and twisted to my right toward the bus. I could see Vosch at the wheel as it barreled straight toward me. I tried for the tires first. I didn't want to fire at Vosch. Not that I had deep feelings for him, but if I did take him out, the bus would wreck and might hurt some innocent person. Then I saw the door on the side of the bus slide open and Flat-Face leaning halfway out, taking aim at me with what looked like a rifle.

I dove back into the cab and yelled at Samuel, "He's got a rifle! Where the hell did he get *that*?"

"Under his coat!" he yelled back.

"I told you to take his gun!"

"I did!"

"But you left the rifle!"

"My hands were full!"

The window behind me exploded. Glass rained down, dusting my head and shoulders.

"Thanks, Mr. slitty-eyed flat-faced big hulking fatso palooka man," I muttered. I kneeled on the seat, pressed my chest against the back and, holding the gun with both hands, leaned out the busted window, resting my elbows on the trunk to steady my aim.

"Alfred!" Samuel shouted. "Get down!"

I ignored him. Maybe Vosch was out of season, but Flat-Face was fair game. I fired at him; he fired at me; and neither one of us scored a hit.

We were slowing down. Flipping around, I peeked over the back of the front seat. We were coming up on a bottleneck: a car in the left lane was trying to pass a flatbed semi in the right, so both lanes were blocked.

"Take the emergency lane!" I shouted in Samuel's ear.

Too late. When we slowed down, Vosch floored the gas, sending the front of the bus into the back of the taxi at seventy miles per hour. Samuel's chest smacked into the steering wheel, mine into the front seat, and the cab's rear bumper crumpled like tinfoil. The passenger headrest, about three inches from my head, exploded into a mass of cheap vinyl and yellow foam cushioning: Flat-Face had scored a hit.

Samuel yelled at me to get down again and this time I didn't ignore him. I threw myself onto the floorboards as he whipped the cab into the emergency lane.

Suddenly the back of the car slung hard to the right, as if punched by a gigantic hand. Samuel fought the wheel as the cab filled with the acrid smell of burning rubber. He eased off the gas.

"Got the tire!" he shouted.

I peeked out the right window. Showers of sparks danced in the billowing smoke rising from our back bumper. I looked up, saw the big flatbed cruising in the lane beside us, then reached over the seat and tapped Samuel on the shoulder. He was hunched over the wheel, knuckles white as he fought to keep us from running off the road.

"Speed up!" I called.

"Can't!"

"To your left!" I screamed. "Get us close!"

He glanced that way and nodded with a quick snap of his head. He used to be an Operative Nine; he got it right away. The steering wheel was jerking in his hands as if it might pop off the column any second. He eased us to the left, within a couple feet of the truck. I put my mouth close to his left ear and yelled, "Me first, then you!"

"Impossible!" he shouted back.

"Necessary!"

I forced the door slowly open—it's hard to open a car door into a sixty-mile-per-hour headwind—looking straight ahead toward the truck because looking back was scary and looking down was terrifying. The flatbed was hauling a load of timber, a stack of twelve-foot two-by-fours held down by canvas straps. Holding the door open with my right, I reached out with my left hand and grabbed one of the straps. Now I was hanging halfway out of the car as Samuel fought to keep us more or less even with the truck, but the blown-out tire was giving him problems and the car bounced up and down violently—if the rim tore apart before we could bail, we were roadkill.

There was no going back now. If I let go, gravity would take me and the wheels on that bus going round and round would finish me.

I pulled—quick and hard—and flew out of the backseat. The toes of my boots hit the pavement, bounced, then collided with the spinning tire of the flatbed. I knew I couldn't hang here long; my biceps and shoulder muscles were already cramping, plus you couldn't be in a more exposed position, plus I had to help Samuel get out of the taxi before one of

Flat-Face's rounds tore into the gas tank—or into my explosive-filled head.

I roared at the top of my lungs (I don't know why something like that helps in this type of situation, but it does) and heaved myself up, flinging my right hand past the strap into the pile of wood. My fingertips slipped between two stacks and that allowed me to let go of the strap with my left hand. About a foot was all I needed to gain a toehold on the edge of the truck bed, and then I was on.

No time to congratulate myself and no time to catch my breath. Vosch was a car length behind me, straddling the right and emergency lanes to give Flat-Face the best shot at the taxi. I scrambled over the top of the wood as Samuel, who must have seen me in the side-view mirror, eased off the gas, bringing his door roughly even to my position on the stack of lumber.

I flopped onto my belly at the edge and stretched my right hand toward him. He was shouting something at me, but the roar of the wind tore the sound apart. This would be tricky. We'd have one shot at it with no margin for error and then there was no predicting what the runaway cab might do. But Sam was a former Operative Nine. He already had the next move figured out. He had probably already rehearsed it in his head, *seeing* it happen in his mind's eye, and had completed the maneuver a dozen times.

With his right hand on the wheel, he opened his door with his left, struggling to push it open just as I did against the wind. What came next happened very fast.

In the instant before he jumped, Sam whipped the steering wheel hard to the right, put his left foot on the footboard and pushed off, flinging himself in my general direction, trusting me to catch him in the one and only chance I'd have to catch him.

I caught him.

Then I rolled, fingers locked around his wrist, pulling him up.

One of Flat-Face's bullets found its target, the rear of the taxi jumped, and with a loud *whumph!* the gas tank exploded.

The flatbed swerved left as the driver reacted to the blast. Sam and I lay on our backs on top of the wood, too winded to speak, contemplating the cloudless sky above.

"You okay?" I asked.

"I'm thinking . . ." he gasped, "that we should have killed them at the airport."

"He's slowing down," I said, meaning the trucker. I didn't know if he knew he had a couple of stowaways onboard, but he knew a taxicab had just blown up in the emergency lane and maybe was he going to check it out. "He's pulling over."

"That would be counterproductive."

"Still have the guns?"

"Yes."

"You take the driver; I'll take Vosch."

Samuel rolled over and crawled slowly toward the front of the truck. I looked behind us: Vosch had seen it all, apparently, because he was in our lane and coming up fast. When I rose, he eased the bus over the center line and I saw Flat-Face leaning out the door with his rifle. I glanced over my shoulder in time to see Samuel swing into the cab of the truck. We whipped back and forth, as the driver reacted to the dude with the gun appearing out of nowhere, and then Samuel must have told him to floor it, because with a belch of black smoke the truck began to accelerate.

Commandeer truck—check. Time for Vosch.

Canvas straps were spaced four feet apart along the span

of the stacked two-by-fours. I scuttled across the top as Flat-Face commenced firing, but the angle was bad: I was too high and partly shielded by the stack.

The first clasp gave me some trouble, but by the third I had the hang of it. I left the last two straps closest to the cab connected to give the stack some stability; otherwise it might collapse completely and send me cascading over the edge with it.

If Vosch understood what I was up to, he didn't let on. He kept within half a car length of our bumper, jockeying first left, then right, trying to give Flat-Face a decent shot.

My target was a little easier to hit.

The first board was an experimental toss, just to test the force needed to hurl it off the stack. It flipped straight up coming off the back, the far end impacting off the pavement, which flipped it again, the opposite end hitting the front of the bus with a satisfying smack. It startled Vosch. His hands jerked on the wheel, which almost tossed Flat-Face onto the road.

I shoved boards off the stack as fast as I could. Vosch pulled into the left lane and began to accelerate.

Smart: I couldn't just push the boards off the side of the truck, not with the ends still strapped down, and from that side Flat-Face would have a better shot. Or maybe the idea was to take out the driver and send us barreling off the road.

And I had left both guns in the taxi.

No time to undo the two straps. I fell onto my stomach as the bus came beside the truck bed. One of the loosened straps was flapping beside me. I grabbed it. I waited. I knew he'd come. If it had been me, I'd come.

He came. Vosch brought the bus within two feet of the bed, and all Flat-Face had to do was jump onboard. I crouched in the center, like a running back waiting for the snap, left fist knuckle down on the wood for balance, the strap wrapped twice around my right—for Flat-Face.

He came at me like a crab shuffling across the seabed. He had ditched the rifle; I guessed because he needed both hands for the jump. But now, as he came at me, I saw a black dagger in his right hand.

Saint Michael . . . Prince of Light . . . hear my prayer . . .

I didn't feel the wind. Or the wood beneath me.

Pardon my sins . . . forgive my trespasses . . .

I didn't see the bus, the truck, the sky, the road.

Prince of the heavenly host, be my protection against all evil spirits . . .

I was in the still place that had no center. And all I had to do was wait for Flat-Face to join me there.

. . . who wander through the world for the ruin of souls.

Three feet away, he paused, his big head cocked to one side, expecting me to run or try to, I guess, but I didn't budge; I froze, he froze, and then I raised my free hand and crooked my finger at him.

He came into my centerless space, dagger raised. I punched his upraised wrist and pushed off hard, driving my shoulder into his chest. Off balance, he fell back onto his wide butt. I slung the four-inch-wide canvas strap around his big bull neck, whipped it three times around his head, then yanked it tight. Slipping on the loose boards, I hauled him to his feet and drove him toward the opposite side of the truck.

He sailed over the edge; the canvas line played out until it hit the clasp holding it to the truck; and then the strap went taut. Over the rush of wheels and howl of the wind, I could hear Flat-Face's strangled corpse popping up and down in a series of rhythmic, sickening thuds.

I scrambled away, scooping up the fallen dagger as I went. Vosch's turn.

Only Vosch was gone. I looked behind, I looked ahead, I looked over at the northbound lanes—maybe he had crossed the median strip—but the bus was nowhere in sight. I scooted to the front of the bed, dislodging boards as I went, sending them over the side, where they fell with a loud clatter onto the road, until I reached the cab. I pounded on the top to let Samuel know that I had made it, that Vosch was gone, that at least for now we were safe.

Then I looked over the cab and saw the bus, about a hundred yards ahead, not speeding away, not coming back at us the *wrong* way, but turned sideways, blocking both lanes.

The trucker must have seen it too, because the wheels locked as he slammed on the brakes. He whipped the wheel hard to the right, which sent me hard to the left. I lost my balance and fell onto the jumbled stack of wood, flailing for a handhold in the slipping two-by-fours, while the truck, its wheels still locked tight, slid sideways toward the bus, then completely around, creating a slingshot effect: I flew off the back of the truck on a rollicking raft of lumber heading straight toward the bus.

At the last second I tucked my chin into my chest and flattened my body onto the bucking and bouncing wood that carried me under the bus and out the other side. I saw a flash of muffler and tailpipe before coming to a stop twenty feet later.

I pushed myself up and stumbled around on the lumber like a drunk. I heard sirens wailing in the distance, but I hardly paid attention to them. A man was standing between me and the bus, and that man was pointing a pistol at my head.

"Hands where I can see them, please," Vosch said.

I dropped the black dagger and raised my hands over my head.

"There's something you should know before you shoot me," I said.

"A cliché," Vosch said. "But better than begging."

"Samuel St. John is standing behind you."

"Drop your weapon, Vosch!" shouted Sam.

Vosch didn't flinch. "Perhaps I'll kill you first," he said to me.

But he dropped the gun. Sam rushed forward and twisted Vosch's arm behind his back and forced him to his knees. He put his gun against the side of Vosch's head.

"No!" I said sharply. "Don't kill him."

"It is the only way to stop him, Alfred."

I picked up the dagger.

"If you shoot him, I'll cut myself open and heal him, understand?"

"Actually, I would prefer that you kill me," Vosch said.

"I bet. Jourdain's not going to be happy that this went hinky. You might lose your job."

"And I love my work."

I looked over his shoulder into Sam's dark, deep-set, black-ringed, hound-dog eyes. "Let him up."

"You shot him at the airport," Sam reminded me.

"Only because I didn't have a choice."

"What if I just wound him grievously?"

His right eye was twitching. The hand gripping the gun was shaking.

"What's the matter with you?" I asked him.

He showed no sign of emotion, other than the twitching of his eye and the quivering of his hand. For the first time since our reunion at the airport, I noticed something odd about his hand: he was missing his pinky finger. I looked at his other hand. The little finger on that hand was missing too.

"You did that?" I asked Vosch. "You *tortured* him?"

"We considered it a no-brainer."

That sent Sam over the edge. He twisted his fingers into Vosch's hair and yanked his head straight back. He commenced to whisper something that sounded like Latin into his ear.

". . . *Per sacrosancta humanea reparationis mysteria*—By the sacred mysteries of man's redemption—*remittat tibi omnipotens Deus omnes praesentis et futurae vitae paenas*—may almighty God remit to you all penalties of the present life and of the life to come. *Paradisi portas aperiat, et ad gaudia sempiterna perducat*—May He open to you the gates of paradise and lead you to joys everlasting . . ."

"You're wasting your time, priest," Vosch said. "I'm not Catholic."

"And I'm not a priest."

Vosch acted like he didn't hear him. "You're supposed to forgive."

"God's business, not mine," Sam answered.

He started to squeeze the trigger. I brought my hand down hard on his wrist and the gun clattered to the pavement.

"Please let me, Alfred," he said. He had never begged me for anything before.

"Yes," Vosch said. "Please let him."

I picked up the gun and tucked it into my waistband. "We're getting out of here."

Sam held on to Vosch's hair for a second longer. His eyes darted wildly back and forth, from me to Vosch and back again. Sometimes the bloodiest battles happen inside our own hearts.

He drove his knee into Vosch's back, sending him sprawling onto the pavement. Then he spat on him, took a deep breath, and looked away, finally, from Vosch, toward me.

"It's good to see you again, Alfred," he said.

Then he did something he rarely did.

He smiled.

MOTEL 6

HELENA, MONTANA

01:00:06:14

I walked around the building a couple of times to make sure the coast was clear, then knocked on the door to room 101. The chain lock rattled, the dead bolt slid back, and Samuel opened the door. He tossed the gun onto the bed and took the plastic sack from my hand.

"I was about to come after you," he said.

He threw the lock and fell into the chair by the little table. I sat in the other chair across from him. He fished a deli sandwich from the bag and dug in, eating with his nose about three inches from the table. I took out my meal and slowly unwrapped the yellow paper.

"Corn dogs," he said.

"I'm superstitious."

The TV was tuned to a cable news channel. A car bomb had killed some people overseas. Somebody important was going to speak at the UN tomorrow. A car maker was set to announce record losses for the third quarter.

"Anything?" I asked.

He shook his head. "Not yet."

"You know that trucker gave a description."

He shrugged.

"And the taxi driver."

He shrugged again.

"Those people at the airport."

He shrugged a third time. What was it with Op Nines and the shrugging?

A pickle slice had fallen from his sandwich and he picked it up and carefully tucked it back in.

I went on. "I'm so popular. Wanted by OIPEP, Jourdain Garmot, and now the feds."

He shook his head. "The feds won't get involved until we cross state lines."

"Oh, okay. What a relief. I was about to panic."

I scraped the skewer of my dog clean with my front teeth and started on the second one. Deli mustard is best, but the gas station only had packets of regular yellow.

I had brought up the two-ton elephant in the room, but he refused to acknowledge it. So I moved on, reminding myself not to forget to move back.

"It was Needlemier, wasn't it?" I asked. "How they got you."

He nodded. "He said he had a meeting scheduled with Jourdain regarding the status of your father's estate. I should have considered the possibility they were using him—perhaps I would have, but I was eager to remove the threat, driven by emotion . . ."

"Gets you every time," I said. "Emotion."

His eyes cut away. "Jourdain Garmot is mad," he said. Then he started to eat again. "And like all madmen, he fails to see the world as something outside himself. He truly believes that killing you will bring him peace."

"Like you with Vosch," I said.

He looked at me hard. "With Vosch gone, there is one less pursuer."

"But one more gallon of blood on my hands."

"There is no sin in self-preservation," he said.

"I don't care about all the ins and outs of it, Samuel. All the pie-in-the-sky philosophy won't change the facts. For every Vosch we kill, Jourdain will send five more Vosches to take his place."

That reminded me. I laid my half-eaten corn dog on the table and went to the telephone by the bed. Samuel shifted in his chair so he could watch me. I got the same recording I got the first time I tried, right after we checked in. I hung up without leaving a message. Samuel shifted again when I sat back down and picked up my corn dog.

"Perhaps Mr. Needlemier doesn't need us to point out the prudent course," he said.

"I hope it's that," I said. "I hope he's taken off, gone someplace safe, but what if he hasn't? What if Jourdain already has him?"

"Then may God have mercy on him."

I looked at his hands. He saw me looking at his hands. I looked away.

"He doesn't know where I am," I said. "Maybe Jourdain will believe him and let him go."

"He didn't believe me," he pointed out.

"Well, one life at a time. One thing I can't figure out—well, there's a lot of things—but the biggest thing is how killing me gets Jourdain the Skull."

He frowned. " 'Jourdain the Skull'?"

I nodded. "The Skull of Doom."

He didn't say anything. He just stared at me.

"You've never heard about the Skull of Doom?" I asked.

"Of course I have. I was an Operative Nine."

"Well, he told me he was on 'the last knightly quest for the Thirteenth Skull,' which everybody knows is the Skull of Doom."

"That is one of its names, yes. And if that is his ultimate goal, he is doomed to failure."

"Why?"

"Because the Skull of Doom is a myth. It doesn't exist."

"How do you know?"

"I was an Operative Nine."

"And that means what? You're all-knowing like God?"

"Far from it."

"Then how are you so sure it doesn't exist?"

"Because we could find no evidence of its existence."

"That doesn't mean it's a myth."

He shook his head and waved one four-fingered hand.

"It doesn't matter. Jourdain believes it exists, apparently, and that's all that matters."

"Which is the point I was trying to make! He somehow thinks killing me is going to help him get it."

"It may be something far simpler than that."

"Like what?"

"Like revenge."

I thought about that. He was right, as usual. The *why* really didn't matter. It didn't even matter if killing me had anything to do with getting the Skull. The only thing that mattered was he wasn't going to stop until I was dead.

"Right. On one side, a madman chasing a myth and on the other a sociopath on a crusade to lobotomize me. So we slip between them and head straight for headquarters."

He said, "Headquarters." His eyes cut away. The elephant was back.

"Only I'm not sure exactly where headquarters is, but you know and that's where Abby Smith is."

"Who may or may not be in a position to help us," he said.

"We don't have a choice."

"No choice," he said. He wadded up the wrapping from his sandwich and dropped it into the bag. Then he took his napkin and carefully wiped off the table.

"Why did you do it, Sam?"

He didn't need to ask what I was talking about. He knew. "I was the Operative Nine."

"And putting a bomb in my head was the thing-that-must-be-done?"

"Yes."

"Why?"

"The reason was classified."

"Declassify it. Now."

He nodded. Swallowed. "I wish I had a drink," he said softly, as if to himself.

I slid my Big Gulp toward him.

"Not that kind of drink," he said.

"You're not the Operative Nine anymore," I said. "You're my guardian. You owe me the truth."

"The price for that is very high, Alfred."

"Whatever it is, I'll pay it."

"It won't be you who pays."

"Tell me why you did it, Sam."

He sighed and his voice now barely rose above a whisper.

"Sofia . . . Alfred. Because of Sofia."

"Sofia. I've heard that name before."

He didn't say anything.

"I heard you saying it in your sleep at the hospital," I reminded him. " 'Ghost from the past,' you told me. Then I overheard Nueve and you arguing about her before we left, and Nueve said you were talking about the goddess of wisdom, but somehow I don't think you were."

"Hardly," he said.

"When Mingus had me in his lab, I saw some vials of my blood labeled 'sofa.' And I thought that was really weird. What did my blood have to do with sofas? It doesn't have a damn thing to do with sofas, does it, Sam?"

"No."

"So no more hints and half answers and riddles. Tell me who Sofia is and tell me now."

He nodded. "Sofia isn't a person, Alfred. Sofia is a thing. An acronym. Special Operational Force: Immortal Army. SOFIA."

The room was quiet except for the humming of the heater by the window. Suddenly the room seemed very dark. I got up from the table and turned on the floor lamp by the bed.

"Catchy name," I said. "Who came up with that?"

"The Operative Nine." He didn't turn to watch me this time. He sat very still, his back to me.

"The idea being my blood could be used to create some kind of supersoldier . . . ?"

"It was conceivable."

". . . An army whose soldiers are instantly healed on the battlefield, whose troops are immune to disease and injuries . . ." I saw it then—the only real use somebody like Nueve would have for my blood. I remembered what I said to Ashley at the airport, *We wouldn't want some kid with the power to heal the world running amok, healing the world,* and felt sick to my stomach. "The possibilities are endless, aren't they, Sam?"

"That it *was* a possibility made SOFIA necessary."

"And SOFIA made the SD 1031 necessary."

He nodded. "Necessary, yes."

"Because the Operative Nine couldn't risk the Item of Special Interest falling into the wrong hands."

"The results could be catastrophic."

"So he needed a way to keep a thumb on the Special Item—and a way to . . . terminate the experiment if that became—"

"Necessary," he said.

"Necessary. Right. The Operative Nine didn't have a choice."

"No choice," he echoed.

"Because he's the Operative Nine. He has to consider the inconsiderable. Think the unthinkable."

"The unthinkable."

"Not just the zigs—the zags too."

"Alfred, I—" He turned around to face me.

"And it didn't matter this Item of Special Interest was a fifteen-year-old kid."

He went stiff on me; I was touching a raw nerve. "Your . . . gift was crucial in recovering the Seals—indispensable, in fact. If we had had access to it in previous missions, lives would have been saved, needless suffering avoided . . ."

"Previous missions? What missions? Missions like Abkhazia? Those kinds of missions, Sam?"

"Of course, yes. Of course, missions like Abkhazia." He cleared his throat. "You have said it yourself, Alfred. An Operative Nine must think the unthinkable, consider *every possible* application of a Special Item, particularly those scenarios in which it might fall into unfriendly hands."

"Why didn't you tell me?" I asked.

"You know the answer to that."

"No, Sam, why didn't you tell me *after* you left OIPEP? Why didn't you tell me when I decided to go with Nueve?"

"Because I thought SOFIA was dead. Dr. Smith told me she killed the project when she took office as director, and I believed her."

"I guess Nueve overruled her."

"With the backing of the board," he said with a nod.

"You still should have told me."

"Yes. You're right. I should have."

"Well," I said. "Well, okay. All right. Abby's working on that. Or maybe she isn't. Can we trust her? *Should* we trust her?"

"I trust her," he said. "I always have."

"Okay. So she's gonna work on getting the board on our side and we're gonna work on getting this thing out of my head."

I slid into the empty chair across from him. He refused to look me in the eye. I should have guessed the reason. I should have figured there was something else he wasn't telling me, but I still wanted to believe the best. I still wanted everything to be okay. Because after everything I'd been through, I was still a kid. I didn't know then that my childhood was about to come to a crashing end. *That* was the *ticktock* inside my head. Not a bomb, but a clock: the clock of my childhood winding down.

"Alfred, the SD 1031 cannot be removed."

"What are you talking about? Of course it can. You put it in; you can take it out."

He slowly shook his head.

"Any attempt to extract it will cause the device to detonate."

His head was bowed, his shoulders rounded, his hands pressed together in his lap, palm to palm, as if in prayer.

"It can't be removed," I said.

"No."

"Or disabled."

"No."

"Or the signal jammed somehow."

"Alfred . . ."

"And OIPEP will always know where I am."

"It isn't a matter of . . . yes. Yes, Alfred. Always."

"And anytime it feels like it, it can hit the red button, and I'm dead."

"Yes."

"And there's not a damn thing you or Abby Smith or any other of the six billion people on the planet can do about it."

"Yes."

I stood up. I shoved the table out of the way. I grabbed him by the shoulders and hurled him onto the bed. He fell next to the gun. I picked it up and rammed it against his temple.

"You were my *guardian*. You swore you would protect me. 'I will never abandon you or betray you.' That's what you said. That's what you said!"

He didn't say anything at first. Then he whispered, "Forgive."

"God's business," I said. "Not mine."

"Your business too," he whispered. "Especially yours."

I ignored him. "You've done it now, haven't you? Just like

Mogart, just like Paimon, only you've aced them, you've done 'em one better. You think you can save me? You were supposed to, you promised to, but instead you've killed me, Samuel. You've killed me."

00:23:39:07

We were interrupted by a soft, insistent rapping on the door. Samuel heard it before I did.

"Alfred," he said.

"Shut up."

"Alfred, there's someone at the door."

"Good. Maybe it's the maid and she can clean up the mess after I blow your ugly hound-dog head off."

But I rolled off the bed and took a position a few steps from the door, gun raised, as Samuel got up and peeped through the peephole. Then he glanced back at me.

"Extraordinary," he said. He opened the door and there was Ashley standing in the doorway. She looked at him; she looked at me; and then out came the sunny Southern California prom queen smile.

"Hi!" she said.

Samuel grabbed her arm, made a quick survey of the parking lot, and pulled her into the room.

"Are you going to shoot me again?" she asked me.

I lowered the gun. "How did you find us?" I asked.

"You gave me this, remember?" She was holding the black box. "If you're going to give someone the slip, Alfred, you should take the tracking device with you."

Samuel pulled it out of her hands.

"Why are you here?" he demanded.

"The same reason you are," she shot back, looking at me. "Some things matter and some things don't."

"Alfred," Samuel said. "Give me the gun."

"He's going to shoot me, Alfred," Ashley said calmly. "You can take the Op Nine out of the job, but you can't take the job out of the Op Nine."

"You may have been followed. Alfred."

I handed him the gun and he disappeared into the night. I sank onto the end of the bed. All of a sudden I was very tired, the most tired I'd been in a long time. She sat beside me.

"I thought—I was sure—you were dead," she said. She took my hand.

"I'm not."

"I'm glad."

Then she hauled off and slapped me across the cheek.

"Don't ever do that again, understand?" she said. She punched me as hard as she could in the chest. "You're my *assignment*."

She burst into tears. I held her while she cried. Then she pushed away and angrily brushed the tears from her perfectly formed, perfectly tanned cheeks.

"You shouldn't have come back, Ashley."

"You shouldn't have dumped me."

"You know why."

"Doesn't make it right."

" 'Right.' Does it still matter, Ashley? Not what's necessary, but what's right?"

"Of course it still matters."

I nodded. "So if it still matters, if right isn't wrong, then there's just one thing left to do."

"What?"

"Complete the circle."

Samuel came back in. He locked the door. He looked at Ashley for a long, uncomfortable moment. She looked right back at him, her chin raised in defiance.

"I wasn't followed," she said.

He ignored her. "Alfred, I've been thinking, and perhaps your instinct was correct. Our hope lies in Director Smith. She still might be able to persuade the board to abandon SOFIA and reinstitute the Phoenix Protocol."

Ashley agreed. "It might be possible for our engineers to find a way to disable the SD 1031 without killing you."

"So we make for headquarters in the morning and pray we stay one step ahead of our enemies," Sam said.

I started to say no, I couldn't go, not yet, and then it hit me if I said no I would have to say why: I had to save Mr. Needlemier from Vosch. But if I told them that, Sam would do anything it took to stop me. My thing-that-must-be-done wasn't his thing-that-must-be-done, and if I told him my thing, he was going to do his thing, and that would mean Vosch would do *his* thing, and that was torturing Mr. Needlemier like he did Sam, maybe even killing him and his family, all because he had the misfortune of knowing Alfred Kropp. I wasn't going to let that happen.

00:20:56:31

Sam tried reaching Abby Smith twice before we turned in for the night. He had the top-secret number for the cell phone she kept with her at all times, but even that call wouldn't go through.

"She's dead," I told him. "Or been fired. Or captured by Nueve. We're walking right into a trap."

"Simply because something is possible does not make it probable, Alfred," he said.

"Oh. Thanks, Sensei, I feel better now."

Ashley took the first watch. She pulled a chair in front of the door and sat there with the gun in her lap. I waited until Samuel was asleep, then eased out of bed and sat in the empty chair across from her.

"Why did you come back?" I asked.

"Because I'm an idiot," she said.

"You're not an idiot," I said. "Which is why I asked in the first place."

"I'm in love with someone I shouldn't be in love with," she said. "It's wrong and I know it's wrong and still I can't help myself."

I was shocked. It wasn't the answer I was expecting. Ashley began to cry. She slumped in the chair and I came out of mine to catch her. The gun fell to the carpet. She pushed her face into the nook between my neck and shoulder and sobbed.

"Whatever happens, Alfred, I want you to understand something."

"Sure."

"I meant what I said about that time machine."

"And I meant what I said," I said, though I couldn't remember what exactly I said or when, exactly, I said it.

I pressed my lips into her hair.

00:19:48:05

After she calmed down and told me she was going to be okay, I dragged myself back to the bed and had another dream.

I was walking across a familiar field of tall grass and in front of me was a yew tree, and under the tree sat a beautiful woman in flowing white robes. It was the Lady in White. I hadn't seen her since Mogart killed me with Excalibur. I was crying with joy as I ran toward her.

She turned to me and her beauty took my breath away, the absolute perfection of her.

"You never told me who you are," I said. "Who are you?"

"You know, Alfred. You have always known."

A radiant light shone around her face.

"Who am I, Alfred son of Lancelot?"

She smiled and the light around her face began to sear her flesh, burning it away until her skull gleamed white in front of me, wearing the leering, knowing smile of all skulls. Her voice thundered inside my head.

"I AM THE DRAGON AND MY NAME IS SOFIA!"

I woke up. The room was silent except for the humming of the air unit beneath the window. I looked toward the door. Ashley was still sitting there. In the bluish half-light eking through the window, she looked as if she too was part of a dream. I watched her for a couple of minutes, glad and not glad at the same time that she had found me.

If you're going to give someone the slip, Alfred, you should take the tracking device with you.

I slipped out of bed and padded to the table in my sock feet. Mom always said you should never go barefoot in a hotel room because carpet was a breeding ground for all kinds of nasty germs and contagious diseases. Mom had a thing about stuff like that. Every week she went through about twelve cans of Lysol.

Ashley watched me slide into the empty chair across from her. I thought she looked tired, especially around the eyes.

"Let me take the watch," I said. "I can't sleep."

"Why can't you sleep?"

"Bad dreams."

The black box sat on the table between us. I touched it. She watched me touch it. Her eyes flicked from my hand on the box to my face then back to the box again. She didn't say anything. Box. My face. Box.

"This huge flat-faced dude tried very hard to kill me today," I told her. "Big. Six five, six six maybe, at least three hundred pounds, with a dagger about the size of my forearm. Came right at me."

"What happened?" she whispered.

"I took him out." I drew in a deep breath. "I killed him."

She ran her hand through her golden hair.

"I'd rather have a hundred Flat-Faces coming at me than

this," I said, stroking the edge of the box. "Nueve said it was no bigger than a pencil lead. It's the little things that kill us faster—sometimes better. Like germs. Or cancer cells. The spot on my mom's temple was the size of a pea when she found it, and six months later she was dead. It's those things you can't see. Like that old story of the blind men and the elephant."

"I don't know that story," she said. Her eyes shone in the ambient light coming from the parking lot.

"These guys blind from birth are taken to this elephant and each one touches a different part. One guy feels the trunk, another the tail, another a leg and so on, and someone asks them, 'What is an elephant?' The one who felt the trunk says an elephant is like a plow; the one who felt the tusk said it was like a tree; the one who felt the leg said it was like column to a temple. All of them got it wrong because they couldn't see it whole, but that didn't change what it was. It was still an elephant."

"Okay . . ." she said. She was waiting for the punch line.

"See, sometimes it's right there in front of you, only you're too close to see it."

I pressed the blue button. The red light came on. She jerked forward, her free hand instinctively going for the box. I pulled it away and cradled it in my lap.

"Alfred, what are you doing?"

"Seeing if what I felt was a tree or an elephant."

If you're going to give someone the slip, Alfred, you should take the tracking device with you.

"At Camp Echo I asked you about the range of the tracking device," I said. "You said maybe a mile or two."

"It's a GPS, Alfred," she said slowly, carefully. "I didn't know that until I tested it in Knoxville. I really didn't know the range when you asked me."

"GPS, gotcha." I ran my fingertip over the glowing red

button. "So it doesn't matter how far I run, Nueve and company will always know where to find me."

She swallowed. "I guess so."

"You guess so? Don't you know so?"

"Alfred, you're making me very nervous. Why don't you put that down before you do something you shouldn't."

"I probably should," I agreed. "I'm not sure what happened next, whether the blind men were told what they really felt and if they got mad because they had it all wrong. Maybe it's better for everybody involved to call an elephant a tree and leave it at that."

"Give me the box, Alfred." She was leaning over the table, her left hand extended toward me, her right gripping the butt of the semiautomatic.

I'm in love with someone I shouldn't be in love with. It's wrong and I know it's wrong and still I can't help myself.

"Nueve let me run off into the woods even though he had no way to find me. I had the only box on the mountain. Then he let me fly off the mountain with both boxes, free to go wherever I wanted and he'd have no way to track me, at least until he could get another box and that would take time, time he really couldn't afford because anything could happen, right? There'd be a huge gap where he wouldn't know where I was and he'd have no way of protecting the Company's investment. That's what I am—the investment—and that's his job: protecting it. So why did he let me go?"

"Why?" Ashley echoed.

"The answer is the elephant, Ashley. The answer is *he didn't let me go.* I never escaped from the Company, except once, when I gave you the slip on the plane."

"That's crazy," she said. "Alfred, you're . . . you're being paranoid. That's understandable, but I told you—"

"Right. I *own* you. I'm your *assignment*."

"No, not like that. Not that way." She shook her golden hair and it swirled around her tanned face, which didn't look so tan right then.

"Who assigned you to me, Ashley? Was it Director Smith or the Operative Nine?"

I pressed the red button. Her whole body went rigid as the display sprang to life: *30 . . . 29 . . . 28 . . . 27 . . .*

"See, I'm pretty confident I know," I said. "So confident I'm willing to bet my life on it."

She lunged across the table at me. I sprang from the chair and it thumped onto the germy carpet.

19 . . . 18 . . . 17 . . . 16 . . .

"Who is it, Ashley? Me or Nueve? Who really owns you?"

I tossed the box at her. She dropped the gun and caught it in both hands. Her shoulders shook as her thin fingers danced over the keypad.

The red light went black.

I picked up the fallen chair and sat down. She slumped into hers in front of the door, the gun lying forgotten at her feet as she cradled the box like a newborn baby in against her chest.

"Now tell me some bull crap about that being a lucky guess," I said. "In love with someone you shouldn't be. I guess so. Guessed wrong the first time, guessed right this time."

"It isn't what you think," she whispered. She wouldn't look at me.

"You don't have to explain anything, Ashley."

I got up, went into the bathroom, and came back out with a few sheets of toilet paper, which I tried to hand to her. She said, "I won't wipe my face with toilet paper, Alfred."

I pushed the paper into my pocket. "Okay."

"I really do want to protect you," she said. "And I really do—I really do have feelings for you. That's the reason, Alfred. The *only* reason I agreed to any of this."

"Where is Nueve?" I asked.

"I have no idea—" she started. Then she stopped herself and said, "On his way."

"How soon?"

"An hour, maybe two—"

"I want a head start."

"There's nowhere you can go where he can't find you."

"We," I said. "Say it. *We.*"

"We," she said.

"A friend of mine is in trouble. I've got to save him before some very bad people do a very bad thing to him or his family. So I'm leaving, and you're going to let me."

"I can't let you, Alfred."

I gently pried the box from her fingers.

"You're not going to wake up Sam. You're not going to come after me. You're going to sit here and wait for your boyfriend and when he gets here you're going to say I took the box and bopped you over the head with it. I'll bop you right now, if you think that'll make it more believable."

"Don't," she said. "Don't make me do something I don't want to do."

"That's what I'm counting on," I said. "That it's something you really don't want to do."

I stepped around her and unlatched the door. I heard a clicking sound behind me. Turning around, I saw the gun in her hands, and the gun was pointed at the center of my thick forehead.

"Were you lying?" I asked.

"You know I was."

"Not about Nueve," I said. "Not about your assignment. About the right thing still mattering. Were you lying? Does it still matter? I think it does. Sometimes I get confused about what the right thing is, but in all this, in everything that happened since I found Excalibur, I always tried to do the right thing. Like now *my* right thing is trying to save my friend. *Your* right thing is giving me the chance to save him. That's the right thing, Ashley. The thing-that-must-be-done. Sometimes the thing-that-must-be-done and the right thing are the same thing for both people. Sometimes they're not, like Samuel putting a bomb in my skull. Right for him. Wrong for me. But just because something like that happens doesn't mean you stop trying to do the right thing."

I was feeling a little dizzy and a lot tired. I needed to leave. I said, "So you do your thing and I'll do my thing and maybe in the end everything will turn out just fine."

I opened the door and cold air poured into the room. The hair on the back of my neck stood up. Maybe from the cold, maybe from the fact that Ashley was pointing a semiautomatic at my face.

"At least tell me where you're going," she said.

"Where it began," I said, and then I stepped into the night and the door swung closed behind me.

I walked across the parking lot, and the muscles between my shoulder blades twitched, expecting the bullet. I knew she had to be watching me through the window, but I didn't care. The only thing that mattered to me at that moment was Mr. Needlemier. The world wasn't in jeopardy this time, just one person in it, and that's just as important.

I walked a half mile down the road to the gas station where I bought the corn dogs. I asked the clerk if I could use her phone.

"Why?" she asked.

"My car broke down. I need to call my dad."

"You don't have a cell phone?"

"It's dead." So was my dad, but I didn't want to overload her with too much information.

She clearly didn't believe me. Maybe if I bought something she'd let me use the phone. I bought a Big Gulp and asked again if I could use the phone.

"There's a pay phone outside—or don't you have any money either?"

"I just bought a Big Gulp," I pointed out. I went back outside. I hadn't seen the pay phone: it was on the far side of the property, out of the bright lights of the station. I walked into the shadows and got the number from the operator. How many hours was England ahead of us? Or was it behind us? On the twelfth ring, a lady came on the line and thanked me for calling Tintagel International World Headquarters.

"Jourdain Garmot," I said.

The line popped with static.

"Hello?" I asked.

"Mr. Garmot is not in at the present. May I take a message or direct you to his voice mail?"

"Vosch, then."

"I'm sorry—who did you say?"

"Vosch," I said louder. "I don't know his first name."

"One moment please." Music began to play in my ear. I had snuck out of the room without a jacket—mostly because I didn't have a jacket. I shivered. The line popped and I heard her say, "Sir, I've checked the company directory and there's no listing for a—"

"Check again. This is Alfred Kropp."

"Kropp? Is that with a C or a K?"

"With a K."

"One P or PP?"

"PP."

The music came back on. I stamped my feet and shifted my weight from side to side and blew on a cupped hand, then switched the receiver to blow on the other.

"Mr. Krapp?"

"*Kropp.*"

"One moment please for Mr. Vosch."

A series of clicks and pops as she routed the call. I looked up. The sky was cloudless and brilliant with stars. I'd never seen so many stars.

"Kropp," Vosch said.

"Vosch. I'm ready."

"Where are you?"

I told him.

"Stay there. I'll make the arrangements."

"I'm going to wait inside the store," I said. "It's cold. And Vosch? Is it too late for Mr. Needlemier?"

"No, Alfred. You're just in time."

I waited inside the store, sipping my Big Gulp. The clerk was glaring at me, so I bought a Snickers. I thought about buying another corn dog, but two was the lucky number. I kept glancing at my watch. Every second that passed was a second where Ashley might change her mind or Nueve might arrive and change it for her. I wondered if Sam would kill Nueve or if Nueve would win that battle. They were both Op Nines at the top of their game; it would be a close match. I watched the deserted lot through the plate-glass windows.

"Get hold of your dad?" the clerk asked.

I nodded. "It won't be long now."

A black Lincoln Navigator pulled up next to the building. The front passenger door swung open and Vosch stepped out, snapping the collar of his fashionable tan duster. He did a slow turn, surveying the lot, right hand inside the pocket of the duster.

I told the clerk bye and she said, "Hey, let's do it again real soon," and then I was standing outside in the cold before Vosch.

"I'm alone," I said.

"You wouldn't lie to me, Alfred."

"I'm the son of a knight. Honesty's in our blood."

He laughed like I had gotten off a good joke, opened the door for me, and I slid into the second seat. I was sitting beside a small, weaselly looking guy with a sharp nose and narrow shoulders, who smelled like peanut butter. He said, "Don't move," and then he frisked me. Vosch rode shotgun next to a big, flat-faced, slitty-eyed goon who could have been a clone of the big, flat-faced, slitty-eyed goon I took out on the highway. Like pretty girls, I guess, big, flat-faced, slitty-eyed goons were a dime a dozen.

"He's clean," Weasel said.

We got on I-15 heading north toward the airport.

"I know where you're taking me," I said. "I know where the circle ends."

"Most apropos, yes?" Vosch asked.

"*Oui,*" I said.

00:11:03:21

When you look down at it from thirty-five thousand feet, the Atlantic is as featureless as a chalkboard and about as interesting to watch. But I watched it, hoping the gray monotony would make me drowsy. I needed sleep.

Vosch reclined in the leather seat across from me, wearing a white turtleneck and gray slacks. Flat-Face II sat directly behind me and Weasel beside him, both fast asleep, their snores bugging the heck out of me. Nothing is more annoying than a person sleeping when you can't.

I watched the ocean. Vosch watched me.

" 'Alone, alone, all, all alone,' " he said softly. " 'Alone on a wide wide sea!/And never a saint took pity on/My Soul in agony . . .' 'The Rime of the Ancient Mariner,' by Coleridge. Do you know it?"

I didn't answer. He didn't seem to care.

" 'Poetry is how the soul breathes . . .' I forget who said that. I suspect your exposure to it is limited to the lyrics of

P. Diddy and Jay-Z. You can listen to them if you like. We have satellite radio. And television. There's also a full library of DVDs onboard. We just added the complete six-volume Three Stooges collection. In high def! You might find the parallels comforting."

"No thanks," I said.

"And books," he said. "Classics and popular literature. No comics, I'm afraid. You strike me as an Archie fan. That Jughead! And will Arch ever choose between Veronica and Betty?"

"You're really a well-rounded guy," I said. "Poetry, books, music, comics, kidnapping, torture, assassination."

"Oh, I dabble. What is the American expression? Jack of all trades, master of none."

"There's one thing that's been bugging me," I said. "About the Thirteenth Skull."

He smiled, an eyebrow climbing toward his hairline.

"Yes?"

"Why does Jourdain need to kill me to get it?"

"Why does he—?" Vosch cracked up. He laughed until tears shone in his eyes.

"What?" I asked.

"Ah, Alfred," Vosch said as he dabbed his cheek with a white handkerchief. "I suppose for the same reason the chicken must cross the road."

"A friend told me Jourdain was chasing a myth."

"A friend told you this? You should exercise better judgment in your choice of friends, I would say!"

He reached forward suddenly and, before I could react, grabbed my head, his palm pressed against my nose, fingertips digging into my scalp.

"There is nothing mythical about our quest, Alfred

Kropp. Even now the Skull is within our possession and in a few hours it will find its place among the Twelve."

He started to go on and then stopped himself. I wondered if he was disobeying orders by telling me.

He changed the subject.

"I knew you would call, of course. Once you realized we would take Needlemier. He's the largest piece left on the board; you couldn't afford to lose him. And 'Greater love hath no man than this,' yes?"

"I know that one. It's from the Bible."

"Though Needlemier somewhat stretches the definition of 'friend.' He gave Samuel to us quicker than you can say Judas."

"Maybe he's just not cut out for this kind of chess."

"Not like we are, certainly."

"Don't lump me in with you, Vosch."

"Why shouldn't I? We're not so different, you and I. You grasped immediately my move against the lawyer, just as I discerned your countermove to contact me. Even our motives are similar, Alfred. You would do anything to protect your friends, just as I would do anything to protect my patron Jourdain Garmot. Now we near the end of the game: I bring you to him while you plot your response. What is it? An ambush at Tintagel? Your guardian and this mysterious yet beautiful blonde await our arrival? Or have you enlisted the aid of the saber-wielding Spaniard and his powerful Company?"

"Maybe it's simpler than that," I said.

The sun was setting over the Atlantic and the chalkboard-gray had changed to burnished gold. The shining patina hid a world teaming with life, fantastic creatures for whom our world above was deadly. Predators and prey, from the microscopic to the huge—the sea was empty and chokingly full. In my dreams lately, it was full of dragons.

"Like Lancelot upon the Plain," Vosch said, "he marches to the drumbeat of his sin, toward his certain doom."

"Who said that?" I asked.

He smiled. "I did."

TINTAGEL, CORNWALL, U.K.

THE CASTLE CAMELOT

00:06:35:10

The ruins clustered near the cliff's edge gleamed in the moonlight. You could hear the surf crashing into the rocks three hundred feet below. There was a storm far out at sea; you could see the dark line of clouds on the western horizon and the flicker of lightning, though it was so far away you couldn't hear the thunder.

The stones were white, worn down from a thousand years of sun and wind and rain. They stuck out from the ground like the huge, discarded teeth of a giant. Here great halls once stood, courtyards and chambers with vast, cathedral ceilings and, somewhere in the rubble, a great hall with a round table in the middle of it, and around that table sat a king and his knights, including the bravest in the kingdom, his best friend and my ancestor, whose disloyalty would lead to the crumbling of the white stones and the death of the king he loved.

It was midnight and Camelot was deserted.

"Where's Jourdain?" I asked.

"You know where he is," Vosch answered.

Of course I knew. Flat-Face II and Weasel stayed in the Land Rover while Vosch and I descended the steps cut into the cliff side. On the eastern shore of the inlet the mouth of a cave yawned toward the open ocean and the silent, raging storm.

We entered Merlin's Cave. Torches burned along one wall, throwing our shadows across the floor and against the opposite wall of the chamber, where a collection of human skulls sat grinning, grouped in a circle on a natural ledge about chest high.

"What are those?" I asked, horrified.

"Can you not guess by now?" Vosch asked.

Shadows danced in the empty eye sockets, creating the illusion that the skulls still had life—that they were looking back at me as I stood still, shivering, looking at them, while the wind whistled and howled through unseen cracks and fissures in the stone.

"They are the Knights of the Sacred Order, Alfred. There is Windimar of Suedberg. There is Bellot of St. Etienne. And that one is Cambon of Sicily. The ones closest to you are the remains of Lord Bennacio and of course, your father, the great Bernard Samson, heir to Lancelot."

So that's what Jourdain was doing in Pennsylvania: the same thing he did in Knoxville. Digging up the knights and taking their heads.

I counted the skulls. Twelve. I remember my father's words, spoken so long ago in Uncle Farrell's apartment. *Only twelve of us are left now . . .*

Behind me, Vosch said, "You'll note there is room for one more in the center, in the place of honor."

The last knightly quest . . . for the Thirteenth Skull.

"That would be my spot," I said. "I'm the Thirteenth Skull."

No wonder Vosch had laughed at me on the plane. I was a lot of things, but one thing I wasn't was a myth. Jourdain wasn't searching for a magical crystal skull carved by Merlin. That had nothing to do with this. Just like SOFIA was no goddess at the left hand of God, Alfred Kropp was no Skull of Doom.

Vosch put his arm around my shoulders, as if he wanted to comfort me. The gesture was so over the top and obscene that I felt my stomach do a slow roll.

I shrugged his arm away and said, "I wasn't part of the Order. I didn't even know he was my father until after he was dead. I don't belong with them."

Plus I was responsible: I took the Sword and gave it to Jourdain's father and that's why they died. Putting my skull inside the circle of skulls belonging to the last twelve knights on earth, knights who died trying to right my wrong—talk about obscene gestures!

Vosch faded into the shadows. After a minute he came back holding a long, thin object wrapped in white satin. He tugged on one corner and the fabric fell away.

"A parting gift," he said, offering me the black sword I had left in Knoxville. "From the faithful Alphonso Needlemier."

I took the sword. The torchlight skittered along the blade. The sword of the last knight, whose skull stared at me now from its stone perch.

"You know," I said. "It would have been a lot simpler to chop off my head in Montana."

"Simpler . . . but not nearly as poetic!"

He took me by the elbow and led me toward the back of

the cave. Our shadows stretched out in front of us and twisted up the back wall.

He didn't have to lead me; I knew the way. I had gone down this path before. We reached the fissure in the stone, the opening to the passageway that descended to the hidden chamber where I had first used Bennacio's sword in defense of the world.

Vosch stopped at the opening. "And now I must say good-bye, Alfred. You won't be seeing me again."

I looked over his shoulder at the skulls on the wall. I wouldn't be seeing him, but he would be seeing me.

He followed my gaze. "Can you think of a more fitting resting place, Alfred? Here, beneath the symbol of all they held dear, in the last refuge of the wizard who seduced a farm boy into believing he could create perfection on earth. And, tonight, the circle comes round: Lancelot brought down the walls there above and now his last son pays for their fall here below. Of course you belong here. Of course you do!"

I stepped into the passageway. Vosch called softly behind me, "*Adieu, adieu,* Alfred Kropp! 'An orphan's curse would drag to hell/A spirit from on high;/But oh! more horrible than that/ Is the curse in a dead man's eye!' "

Rock crunched beneath my feet. The way down was very narrow in places, forcing me to turn sideways and shuffle carefully between outcropping of razor-sharp stone. The walls wept with moisture and the wind whistling from the entrance chamber became a high-pitched wail: the cries of Merlin's ghost for the kingdom love had lost. I touched the sharp stones with my fingertips and thought of dragons' teeth. The opening behind me was the lips and I was in its mouth, heading for its gullet.

I reached the opening to the main chamber. A year ago I

had died in there, the belly of the dragon. But, like a year ago, I didn't see what choice I had. None of it was going to stop unless I did something to stop it. I didn't ask for it, but I had it and, like Nueve said, what I had was a gift, not a treasure. Treasures you hoard away. Gifts you don't.

I had gifts to give. A gift for Mr. Needlemier and a gift for Sam and, in a really weird way, a gift for Jourdain Garmot.

I stepped into the chamber.

THE WIZARD'S CAVE

00:05:25:19

There were no points of reference inside the belly of the dragon. The walls and ceiling were wrapped in shadow, and once you walked a little ways into it, you couldn't tell if you were in the middle or more toward one edge or the other. Wherever you stood, that was the middle.

And that's where Jourdain was standing, holding a black sword identical to mine, ghostlike in the ambient light streaming through hidden fissures in the ceiling.

I walked toward him. When I got within ten feet of him, he said, "Stop."

I stopped.

He said, "Do you know who I am?"

I didn't answer. Of course I knew who he was and of course he knew I knew who he was. I had the feeling he had been practicing for this moment, had rehearsed it over and over in his mind ever since our meeting in Knoxville. He was following a script he had written and rewritten until he knew every line by heart.

"I am the son of the man you murdered here."

"And I'm the son of the man he murdered in Játiva," I said.

"Yes, the last son of the house of Lancelot. Tell me something, Alfred Kropp, do you know from which house I descend?"

I didn't. No one had ever told me which knight Mogart had come from.

"From the house of Mordred," Jourdain said. "Mordred, the only son of Arthur. I am the true heir to the king, the true heir to the throne of Camelot. Do you understand now why my father sought to claim the Sword? It was rightfully his."

"Mordred killed Arthur," I pointed out.

"He took his mortal life. It was your ancestor who betrayed him, killed his spirit and sent him into the arms of Mordred's mother. If not for Lancelot, Camelot would not have fallen."

He raised his sword in both hands, bringing the blade against his chest.

"In a dream the Lady came to me," he said. "Your blood will bring an end to the curse upon Arthur's house, Camelot will rise again, and the Archangel shall return the Sword—to me, the last son of Arthur.

"Let us end, Alfred Kropp, what a thousand years ago our forebears began."

Jourdain Garmot rushed toward me. I brought my sword up just in time, as his came whistling down toward the top of my head. The black blades met with a ringing crash and my knees quivered with the impact. Little shards of glittering metal exploded from our blades, spinning away into the shadows.

He forced his sword downward. I reached between us

with my left hand and grabbed the wrist of his blade hand. I yanked his arm across his body, freeing my sword, and then plunged it into his side. The blade hit something hard: his rib, which turned it away from his chest and sent it down, toward his stomach. His eyes went wide.

He stepped back. I stayed put. He stood panting in front of me, his white shirt glimmering with blood.

"That's it, okay?" I asked. "We don't owe our fathers anything, Jourdain. They're dead. All the knights are dead. The castle is just a bunch of rocks and in another thousand years even those rocks will be gone. The Sword isn't coming back. Let it go."

He switched his sword to his left hand and came at me again. I slapped the blade away and slashed back to the right. The tip of my sword ripped through his shirt, opening up a two-inch-deep gash in his exposed stomach.

And I heard his father's voice echoing inside my head:

Did noble Bennacio tell you how your father met his fate? . . . I tortured him. I cut him a thousand times, until upon his knees he begged me to finish it, to end his miserable life . . .

Jourdain's mouth came open, as if he had something to say. He staggered backward, but I didn't follow.

"I don't want to kill you," I said. "I never wanted anyone to die—not even your dad, but I didn't have a choice. But I have one now and so do you, Jourdain. You can let it go. We can both let it go."

He still didn't say anything. We were off script. This wasn't the way he imagined it, the way it was supposed to go.

"Let me save you," I whispered to Jourdain Garmot.

He came at me a final time, right arm dangling uselessly by his bloody side, his left swinging the sword crazily back and forth. I sidestepped to his right, pivoted, slung my left arm around his neck, pulled his head back against my chest, and rammed my sword into him, all the way to the hilt.

His body went stiff against me. His fingers loosened on the black blade and it fell to the ground. After that all I could hear was his breath and my breath and the distant wailing of the wind.

I pulled the sword from his body and tossed it away. Then I gently lowered him to the floor, going down with him and then resting his head on my thigh. His eyes were open and his mouth moved soundlessly as he looked up into my face.

"Forgive," I told him.

"God's business!" he choked out.

I picked up his father's sword and sliced open the palm of my left hand.

"We'll see whose business it is, Jourdain," I said. "I know this will heal your body. But the real wound is a lot deeper."

I pressed my bleeding hand into his side. "In the name of the Archangel," I said. "Prince of Light."

His eyes rolled to the back of his head. I could feel my blood flowing into him.

"May he bring you peace."

00:04:47:19

He was too weak to walk, so I carried him up the narrow slope of the dragon's throat, cradling him like a baby, past the glittering teeth of its mouth, into the upper chamber, the cave of skulls, where Vosch was waiting. When he saw us emerge from the cleft in the rock, he pulled his gun and pointed it at my face.

"No," Jourdain gasped. "Put it away."

Vosch lowered his gun.

"He's going to be all right," I said. I didn't know if Vosch believed me: Jourdain was covered head to foot in blood. I lowered him to the floor and leaned him against the wall opposite the skulls. I sank to the floor on the other side of the chamber and rested against the rock shelf, the circle of grinning skulls over my head.

Vosch looked at me. He looked at Jourdain.

"Alfred has taught me mercy," Jourdain said. "Does that not beg mercy?" He smiled. "He has offered me forgiveness.

Does that not beg forgiveness?" The smile traveled from Vosch to me. Vosch smiled too. I was surrounded by grins. Jourdain's. Vosch's. The skulls'.

Jourdain said, "Put away the gun, Vosch . . ."

Grinning.

"It should not be quick."

Vosch got it right away. Too bad I didn't. He was on me in two long strides. I looked for the gun in his right hand. I should have looked at his left, because that's the hand that held the two-foot-long, dragon-headed black dagger.

He slammed it into the same spot I stabbed Jourdain, only my rib didn't deflect the blow. The blade slid straight into the center of my chest.

Vosch. Jourdain. The skulls.

Grinning.

00:04:34:19

Their faces swam in and out of focus in the torchlight, and their voices seemed far away beneath the wailing of the wind and the rattling of blood in my chest.

"He's dead already," Weasel said. "Look at his eyes. They don't blink."

"No, he's alive," Vosch said. "I hear him breathing."

"Hey, Kropp," Flat-Face II said, poking me in the ribs. "You alive?"

Light and shadow dueled across their faces. They reminded me of fun house masks or those carnival sideshow creatures leering at you through yellowed glass.

"Call him, Alfred," Vosch said. "Call down the Archangel! You are his beloved—surely he'll save you. He will bear you up in his hands lest you dash your foot against a stone."

"He won't come," Weasel predicted. "Kropp's pissed him off."

"No," Flat-Face II said. "He won't come because he don't care."

Weasel touched my side and squinted at his bloody finger-tips, turning them in the golden light.

"Gave him this, though," he said, and he stuck his fingers into his mouth, tasting my blood. Vosch told him to cut it out. "Can't hurt," Weasel said. "I got a bad ticker. You know, the kid's kinda like a vampire, only the opposite."

"You're both wrong," Vosch said. "He won't come because he doesn't exist."

"Well, I'm not saying whether he does or doesn't," Flat-Face II said. "But you can't just say there's nothing, Vosch."

"Why not?" Vosch asked. "If there was something that loves us, how do you explain that?" He pointed over my head at the skulls on the ledge.

"Who said anything about love?" Flat-Face II answered with a rumbling laugh. "I'm just saying you can't say for absolutely one-hundred percent there ain't anything. It can't be all random."

"Why not?" Vosch asked. "Randomness explains it just as well. Better, in fact."

"I told you," Weasel said crossly. "The kid killed off all the knights, and that pissed God off. It's what God does to people who piss him off. Like how he smote the Egyptians, all those plagues and such."

"What kind of God is that?" Vosch said.

"The kind you don't piss off," Weasel said.

"I think we should let Alfred settle this," Vosch said. "What do you think, Alfred? God is there, but you've upset him terribly and he's punishing you, letting you die a slow and painful death? Or God is there and he is as indifferent and bored as a teenager at a bad movie, texting his saints while he waits for the closing credits to roll? Or God is there not at all, and heaven is merely the empty space between the stars? What do you say? Do you say, 'Wherefore I abhor myself and repent in dust and ashes'? Or do you say, *'Eli, Eli, lama sabachthani'*? Or do you simply say, 'Water, water, everywhere, nor any drop to drink'? Speak up, Alfred. Settle our debate."

"He'll be here soon," I said. It hurt to talk.

"Right!" Vosch said sarcastically. He thought I was talking about the Archangel, but I wasn't. I pushed myself up, using the hard stone behind me for support, and stumbled toward the cave's mouth. They didn't come after me. They just kept arguing about God.

I fell to my knees on the shore of the little inlet. I coughed, and my mouth filled with blood. I began to crawl toward the steps. I could hear the rise and fall of their voices as they continued the argument. Was God there or not there? And if he was there, what was he doing there? Why wasn't he doing anything down here? Over my head, the stars seared through the blackness around them, and the stars were silent about it.

I began the slow climb up the stairs.

He would come. I *knew* he would come.

I wanted to be there when he did.

00:00:12:44

The helicopter that brought him came in from the east, sil-
houetted against a crimson sun.

I was waiting for him at the edge of the cliff. Three hundred feet below, the incoming tide smashed against the jagged
stones that rose from the sea like the teeth of the dragon from
my dreams.

The chopper landed. I stood. I wouldn't be able to stand
for long: I had lost too much blood.

Out hopped a tall, thin man dressed in an expensive suit
and carrying a gold-handled black cane. Next, a very tall,
gray-looking guy with a hound-dog face and enormous hands,
and finally a lithe blue-eyed blonde.

The three of them walked toward me, picking their way
between the white stones of Arthur's castle.

I raised my hand. They stopped.

"Alfred," Nueve said. "You are expecting us?"

"Nueve," I said, and the word caused a fiery stab of pain
deep within my chest. "You know you should avoid asking

questions you already know the answers to. People will think you're stupid."

I couldn't stay up any longer. I went down to my knees and Sam rushed forward. He caught me before I landed face-first on the rocky ground. He pulled my head into his lap. His hand touched my side. He felt the wetness there, and his long fingers explored my wound.

"Start the chopper!" he called to Nueve. "We've got to get him to a hospital immediately."

"No," I said.

He looked down into my face, puzzled. "We're taking you to headquarters, Alfred. Director Smith has arranged for you to plead your case personally before the board."

"No, Sam," I said. "I go to the board . . . beg them not to use me to create the perfect army . . . and maybe they say yes, but it can't change the fact that anytime they change their mind or some power-hungry jerk"—I looked at Nueve—"decides to change it for them, I can be snatched and lobotomized and drained to feed baby SOFIA. Or the day when they decide it's just too dangerous having me in the world and they hit the button . . ."

I choked up. I had had a lot of time by the ruins of Camelot, and sometimes that's a good thing and sometimes it isn't. I wasn't sure about this time, but I was pretty sure I knew the-thing-that-must-be-done.

"And if OIPEP doesn't decide to finish SOFIA, somebody else will."

"You don't know that, Alfred," Sam said.

"Sam, you gotta listen to me. Why do we have atomic bombs? Huh? Because it's possible. Because we can. Somewhere, sometime, sooner or later, someone will use me to make SOFIA. Because it's possible. Because they can."

He started to cry. I'd never seen him cry before. Most

people look uglier when they cry. Samuel was ugly to begin with, so now he looked *really* ugly.

"Alfred, remember the Devil's Door? Remember what you said to me when I told you there was no hope? You have to go on, Alfred. Just a little bit farther. Just a little bit . . ."

The helicopter came to life, but the sound of it was muffled, the roar of the engine coming as if from behind a screen or curtain. Sam's face looked fuzzy around the edges as I began to slip through the membrane into that space—the white, centerless space that wasn't home but felt like home, warm and comforting and totally me-less.

"Here's the thing," I told him. He had to bow his head close to my lips to hear me. "Here's the deal, Sam. With Mogart and the demons, I thought I was saving the world, but the main thing wasn't the world, it was me. This time . . ." I coughed. Blood filled my mouth and I forced myself to swallow it. "I thought it was all about saving me, but it was never me. It was the world. I'm going to save the world, Samuel. And there's nobody else who can save it but me."

I couldn't see Sam at all anymore. But I saw the castle, not a collection of fallen stones, spotted green with lichen and worn down to pitiful shadows of what they used to be. I saw them as they were supposed to be: brilliant white, walls and parapets that rose to heaven, and standing on the ramparts was a knight in shining armor, his sword raised toward me in salute.

On the other side of the white space, I heard Samuel's voice. "Well, don't just stand there! Help me get him to the chopper! *Help me . . . !*"

The knight upon the ramparts dipped his head.

00:00:00:13

I am scrambling up a mountain of fallen rock and razor-sharp crystal in the middle of the white, centerless space.

I confess to Almighty God . . .

Bloodied from my climb, I reach the summit. Here long grasses grow and caress my fingertips as I walk toward a yew tree, its branches bare.

. . . to blessed Michael the Archangel . . .

A man stands under the outstretched arms of the tree. He looks a little like Barney Fife from the old *Andy Griffith Show*.

"Al," my uncle Farrell says. "It's about time you got here."

. . . to all the saints, and to you, Father . . .

He gives me a big hug; he's only pretending to be mad. Over his shoulder, I see a tall, white-haired man standing in the long grass, and the grass is blushing bright spring green.

Before the last knight, I bow my head and sink to one knee.

I have sinned exceedingly, in thought, word, and deed . . .

"Oh, Alfred," Lord Bennacio says tenderly. "It is I who should kneel to you."

. . . through my fault—striking my chest with a fist after each *fault—through my fault . . . through my most grievous fault . . .*

He helps me to my feet, and now I see behind him a golden door and, beside that door, a large man with a flowing mane of hair.

Therefore I beseech you . . .

Smiling, my father raises his arm and a woman steps through the door. She takes his offered hand and together they stand, not moving, not coming to me, but waiting.

My mother takes me into her arms, and she is no ghost or dream. I can feel her. I can smell her hair.

I beseech you!

They gather around me. Bennacio laughs, pats my shoulder, and says, "Come, Alfred Kropp! You don't want to be late for the feast!"

Together we walk toward the golden door.

00:00:00:03

00:00:00:02

00:00:00:01

00:00:00:00

FINAL EXTRACTION INTERFACE REACHED

Epilogue:
OIPEP Emergency Safe House
(ESH: "Kingfisher")
Somewhere Outside London

That was my second death.

Which brought me to my third life: I didn't make it through the golden door. Just as I was about to step over the threshold, I heard a woman's voice calling me back. I didn't want to go back. I guess that isn't hard to understand. But the voice kept calling and the door began to recede into the white mist that also wrapped itself around the shapes of my mother and my father, then around me, until I couldn't feel them beside me anymore but felt something or someone else, hugging me, and then there was this sensation of falling and this being was falling with me. I didn't have to hear the voice calling me *beloved* to know who it was. I "pushed" against him. I was hungry and tired and I never wanted to leave my mom again, but I heard *Not yet, not yet, my beloved.*

I told him I hated him. I told him it wasn't fair, that some fine guardian angel he was, letting me steal his Sword and letting all the knights get killed and me too—twice now. I wanted to stay with my mom.

Someone kept calling me, though, and that someone wasn't the Archangel Michael.

That someone was Abigail Smith.

"Alfred . . . Alfred . . . ! Alfred, can you hear me?"

I opened my eyes. I was lying in a bed inside a room with whitewashed walls and a wooden floor, and beside me on a little table was a vase full of flowers. Daisies, I think.

"Oh, crap," I said. "Extracted again."

She was sitting beside the bed, smiling, and the white on the walls seemed yellow compared to her dazzling orthodontics.

"More lives than a cat," she said.

"Two down, seven to go," I said. "Where am I?"

"A safe house."

"Am I? Safe?"

"Of course you are."

"Where's Sam?"

"He's here. Would you like to see him?"

"Maybe not right now. Did he tell you what happened after you left Camp Echo?"

She nodded. She took my hand. "I should not have left you there, Alfred."

"Well, that's obvious," I snapped back. "Why did you?"

"I believed the only hope of saving you was a direct appeal to the board."

"And you didn't know what Nueve was planning?"

"Of course not. I left specific orders that nothing was to be done without my authorization."

I thought about that. "It's hard to find good help these days, isn't it?"

She gave one of her gentle English trilling-type laughs.

"Dr. Mingus has been terminated. You won't be seeing any more of him."

"That's good. He didn't have much of a bedside manner. What about Nueve?"

Her smile went away. "The Operative Nine has been

suspended pending a full review of his actions upon my leaving Camp Echo."

"Oh. What's that mean exactly?"

"It means he's in deep doo-doo."

"You got the board to change its mind?"

"I made the board's mind irrelevant. I've taken on emergency powers, Alfred, which I am allowed to do under certain unique circumstances. And this circumstance certainly qualifies as unique."

"What about Ashley? Is she in trouble too?"

"Don't you think she should be?"

"So you arrested her."

She studied my face for a long time before answering.

"What do you think I should do to her?"

I thought about it. "Nothing."

She seemed surprised. "Really? Nothing at all?"

"I don't think she ever wanted to hurt me. She was trying to protect me the best she could, but she was in a bad spot, because of Nueve. Because she . . . well, I guess she loves him. And you can't always choose who you fall in love with, like those girls in vampire stories or in real life when a girl falls for a doper. It's one of those things that just happen and then you're kind of trapped in a situation you want to control but can't. It's almost like being an Op Nine or a knight like my dad or even somebody really messed up like Jourdain."

She was looking at me like a mom with a babbling kid who was just learning how to talk.

"The thing-that-must-be-done," I said. "My father swore to protect the Sword no matter what, even if that *what* meant the Sword would kill him. When he was the Operative Nine, Samuel had to think the unthinkable, even if the unthinkable meant putting the SD 1031 in my head. See? Even Nueve and

Mingus—well, maybe not Mingus, that dude was seriously messed up with a capital *mess*—thought there was no choice, and Ashley was given one between just abandoning me to Nueve or trying to help me the best she could . . . though I wish she had told me when she had the chance.

"And Jourdain. I think he really believed his dream that the Sword would come back if he took revenge for what I did to his dad. What happened to Jourdain anyway?"

Just like with Ashley, she said, "What would you like to happen to him?"

"Nothing. Well, he probably should get some therapy. We both should. I used to hate going to therapy, but now I'm thinking we should maybe do a group thing. Me, Sam, Ashley, Jourdain."

She laughed like I was making a joke, but she didn't know it was only half a joke.

"Not Nueve?"

"I don't think therapy would do him any good. He'd probably just whip out his sword cane and chop off the therapist's head."

Thinking of heads reminded me. "We gotta get those skulls back," I said. "Put them back in the graves where they belong."

"The twelve are being taken care of even as we speak," she said.

"Good," I said. "Which leaves the thirteenth. What happens to me now?"

Again, just like with Ashley and Jourdain: "What would you like to happen?"

"What I'd like to happen, you can't give," I said.

"I can give anything now, Alfred."

"Oh, that's right. You've taken emergency powers. Queen Abigail. Well, when you say 'anything' . . . ?"

"We could still extract you, give you a new identity, take you anywhere you'd like to go."

"Give me a normal life."

"Yes."

"Insert me into a normal interface."

"Yes."

"And leave me alone."

"Yes."

"Forever."

No "yes" this time. "For as long as I am in charge."

"You won't be in charge forever."

"It's the most I can offer, Alfred."

"And if you lose your job . . . or when you retire . . . or maybe if somebody does something to you . . . then I'm fair game."

"What's done is done," she said carefully. "I can't go back and undo the past, Alfred."

"I guess that's been my biggest problem," I said. "Getting hung up on that—the undoable part."

"You have another choice. An alternative."

"Those are good to have. What is it?"

"Do you remember a year ago my telling you that we are always looking for fresh talent?"

"Yes. And I called you after I got home and you basically told me to grow up first."

She smiled and again for about the tenth time I reminded myself to ask her about her oral-hygiene regimen. Her smile had the power to blind you.

"A lot of that has happened, hasn't it?" She didn't wait for my take on it, but hurried on. "Alfred, I'd like to offer you a position with the Company."

She waited for it to sink in. It had a long way to sink, but

Abby Smith was a patient person. She didn't move a muscle while I stared at her.

"A couple of days ago you people are sharpening the knives to lobotomize me, and now you're offering me a job?"

"That wasn't us," she answered. "That wasn't *my* Company. We weren't created for it and we will not tolerate it. No, Alfred, you would be working directly for me. In return, I will see to it you receive the best of educations as well as the safest environment to pursue it. And, when you're eighteen, you can decide if you wish to stay with us."

"What's the catch?"

"It might prove a bit . . . dangerous at times. But you've proven more than once that you're more than capable of handling yourself."

"What about SOFIA? How do I know you're not just bringing me onboard to use me again?"

When I said the word "SOFIA," her smile evaporated. The room got dimmer, as if she had flipped off a light.

"SOFIA is dead. The data has been purged from our systems and all the samples destroyed."

"You could have told me about it. You had the chance. I asked in Knoxville about SOFIA and you said there was no such thing."

"I believe I said there was no such *person.*"

"Ho, well, at least you were being honest about it. How do I know you're being honest now? How do I know I can trust you?"

"You don't, Alfred," she said, and she sounded sad. "We've done very little to earn it. I can't give you a reason to say yes. To be perfectly honest, if the roles were reversed, I might very well say no."

"So why shouldn't I?"

"Because you're something very special, and I'm not."
She stroked my forearm as she talked. "Though I've studied it
all my life, I've never quite touched it, Alfred, not in the way
you have."

"Touched what?" I asked, though I knew what.

She put a hand on my shoulder. "I shall tell you a secret: I
envy you, Alfred Kropp. We long for the divine. We long to
touch it. We long for *it* to touch *us*. At every turn in this affair
you were met by betrayal and treachery—Samuel, Nueve,
Ashley, among God knows how many others—and yet at the
end, you were willing to sacrifice yourself for a world that
must seem cold and brutal and quite unforgiving."

"Well," I said. "It wouldn't be right to let your personal
hang-ups get in the way of the stuff that really matters. There
wouldn't even be a thing like OIPEP if the world wasn't
worth saving, right?"

"Then your answer is yes?"

"Can I think about it?"

"Of course. Take all the time you need. It will take a
while to decide Nueve's fate."

"What does Nueve's fate have to do with me saying yes?"

"The day is coming, Alfred, sooner rather than later,
when I must designate a new Operative Nine."

She waited patiently for that one to sink in. I let it sink till
it reached bottom, and then I said, "You're going to train me
to be an Operative Nine?"

"I can't think of anyone better suited for the job. Perhaps,
in the most ironic sense, you've been training for it for quite
some time."

I didn't say anything. She gave my hand a squeeze.

"Don't answer now. You'll have two years to think about
it. The Company needs people like you, Alfred. Sometimes we

lose sight of what really matters in our relentless pursuit of our goals—but through all this, you never lost sight of that. Of the things that really matter. It's a rare quality, and something without which our organization—well, the entire world, as a matter of fact—will perish."

"Sounds like you're asking me to save the world."

"Yet again," she said with a smile. "Do you think you're up for it?"

An orderly brought me a light meal after Abby left. Beef broth, hot tea, and some tasteless crackers. After I ate, a doctor came in and checked my vitals.

"Hey, I know you," I said. "You're Dr. Watson from the *Pandora.*"

"My name isn't Watson," he said.

"I know," I said. "That was just my name for you."

"Is that what you do?" he asked. "Give people names?"

"I was filling in the void," I said. "You remember, we talked about butts."

"I don't remember talking about your butt."

"It wasn't my butt in particular."

"Whose butt, then?"

"Nobody's really."

"It was a philosophical discussion about butts?"

"I didn't know why we had cracks."

"And did we resolve the issue?"

"When somebody laughs really hard, you say they 'cracked up.'"

"Few people know this, but we're born crackless, until our first hearty gale of laughter splits apart the glutes."

After he left, I closed my eyes and tried to sleep. I was a little afraid of what I might dream, but I was pretty tired.

I was just drifting off when I heard the door open and the heavy tread of boots on the wooden floor. I didn't need to open my eyes to know who it was.

"Hi, Sam," I said.

He hovered near the door.

"You can come in," I said.

He walked slowly to the chair beside the bed. Sat. Looked at me.

"I guess you got me on that chopper in the nick of time," I said.

"Thankfully, yes. The doctor expects a full recovery."

"Did you hear what Abigail Smith expects?"

He answered slowly, choosing his words carefully.

"Not what either of us expected, of course. But I think it's an intriguing proposition."

"I'd have to trust her."

He nodded. "Do you?"

I thought about it. "Oh, heck, Sam, I guess if I gave up on that I might as well stay dead."

"Nueve will fight for his position. And it's quite difficult to fire an Operative Nine. It's considered a lifetime appointment."

"It's weird," I said. "Until all this happened, I wasn't sure what I wanted to do with my life, but it sure wasn't being a Superseding Protocol Agent."

"Becoming one might be your only way to ensure SOFIA is never reborn."

"You gotta become a devil to fight him?"

He looked at me with those dark, hound-dog eyes, so homely and also so sad.

"Somehow I don't think that will ever happen with you, Alfred." He changed the subject. "She's asked to see you."

"Ashley."

"Yes."

"Should I?"

"It was the worst kind of blackmail, Alfred. Nueve used her to monitor you after your escape from Camp Echo, used her feelings for him. She never wished any harm to come to you."

"She should have told me the truth."

"We avoid truths that terrify us."

"Is that why you didn't tell me about SOFIA?"

He looked away. I looked at his hands, at the missing fingers.

"You never told Vosch anything, did you?" I asked. "Even when he chopped off your fingers, you didn't tell."

He cleared his throat. "When I left the Company, I abandoned the oath that bound me to insert the SD 1031. I took a new vow, a vow to protect and guard you against all enemies. I will never break that promise, Alfred. But now we are back to trust, aren't we?"

I didn't give him a direct answer. That's an Op Nine quality. I said, "I'll need a trainer."

He nodded. "Most definitely."

"Someone who knows the ropes. Someone who's been there. Someone who can show me the way between doing the-thing-that-must-be-done and doing the right thing."

"A narrow path full of pitfalls and hazards."

"Because the right thing still matters."

"The right thing will always matter."

I thought about it. I thought about what he said and what I said and what had happened and what might happen. I thought about the golden door and the smell of my mother's hair and the empty sockets where my father's eyes had been and even ol' Mr. Weasel, licking my blood from his fingertips.

Life shouldn't be what happens while you're running from your own shadow. Maybe that's why the angel pulled me back: I didn't want to die because I loved the world so bad my death was the only way to save it. I wanted to die for the same reason I struck the deal with Nueve in Knoxville: I thought it was the only way to hide from the shadow with my name on it. The problem was you can't run from it and you can't hide from it, so what are you supposed to do about it?

I didn't know, but I thought I knew how to start. I patted his knee with the hand I cut open to heal Jourdain, to heal Ashley, to heal him.

"I forgive you, Sam," I said.

"And that matters most of all," he said.